Dark ages
Assamite
™

Dark Ages and Vampire Fiction from White Wolf

The Dark Ages Clan Novel Series
Dark Ages: Nosferatu by Gherbod Fleming

The Grails Covenant Trilogy
To Sift Through Bitter Ashes by David Niall Wilson
To Speak in Lifeless Tongues by David Niall Wilson
To Dream of Dreamers Lost by David Niall Wilson

Other Dark Ages Fiction
Dark Tyrants by Justin Achilli & Robert Hatch (editors)
The Erciyes Fragments by C. S. Friedman

The Clan Novel Series
Clan Novel: Toreador by Stewart Wieck
Clan Novel: Tzimisce by Eric Griffin
Clan Novel: Gangrel by Gherbod Fleming
Clan Novel: Setite by Kathleen Ryan
Clan Novel: Ventrue by Gherbod Fleming
Clan Novel: Lasombra by Richard E. Dansky
Clan Novel: Assamite by Gherbod Fleming
Clan Novel: Ravnos by Kathleen Ryan
Clan Novel: Malkavian by Stewart Wieck
Clan Novel: Giovanni by Justin Achilli
Clan Novel: Brujah by Gherbod Fleming
Clan Novel: Tremere by Eric Griffin
Clan Novel: Nosferatu by Gherbod Fleming

For all these titles and more, visit **www.white-wolf.com/fiction**

Dark ages ASSAMITE ™

Stefan Petrucha

AD 1204

Second of the Dark Ages Clan Novels

Author: Stefan Petrucha
Cover Artist: John Bolton
Series Editor: Philippe Boulle
Copyeditor: Anna Branscome
Graphic Designer: Aaron Voss & Mike Chaney
Cartograpy: Eric Hotz
Art Director: Richard Thomas

ISBN 1-58846-818-6
First Edition: September 2002
Printed in Canada

White Wolf Publishing
1554 Litton Drive
Stone Mountain, GA 30083
www.white-wolf.com/fiction

What Has Come Before

It is the year 1204 and the Fourth Crusade, diverted from its goal of striking Muslim Egypt and recapturing Jerusalem, has come instead to Constantinople. Over three days and nights in April, the so-called Army of Christ sacks and pillages the greatest of Christian cities, claiming boundless treasure for themselves and making the Byzantine Empire their own. For the Greeks of the city, it is a time of defeat, outrage and despair.

Away from the eyes of men, vampires lurk on both sides of the conflict. The predators of the Byzantine night have found their city torn open and Michael, the ancient vampire who led them, destroyed. Disheartened and displaced, they gather in a makeshift refugee camp near the city of Adrianople, awaiting word from the Nosferatu Malachite, who has left for the East in search of answers.

European vampires followed the crusade, come to settle old scores and feed from the carcass of the Queen of Cities. Monsters dressed as traders, Templars and soldiers claim new domains and drain their enemies dry. And some even speak of carrying the crusade forward into the Holy Land.

For Clan Assamite—which claims the lands of Islam as its own—that is simply not acceptable.

BULGARIAN
EMPIRE

SERBIA

ANDRIANOPLE

CONSTANIN

THESSALONIA

LATIN

DESPOTE OF EPIRUS

KINGDOM OF THESSALONIA DUCHY OF ATHENS

EMPIRE

NI

EMP
OF NI

SMYRNA

ATHENS

DESPOTE OF ACHAIA

N

DUCHY
OF NAXOS

CRETE

BYZANTINE

CK SEA

SINAPE

TREBIZOND

A

A

ULTANATE
F ICONIUM

CYPRUS

MPIRE

Prologue

The Present

Ruya Hazan, a dark beauty in her mid-twenties, in modern though relatively conservative dress, waited dutifully in the second-to-last row, fourth seat from the right. Her attention settled naturally on the proscenium, where the aged historian, Professor Rufus Abaz, ruffled his notes. She had to chuckle. The lectern lighting and the professor's neatly trimmed white beard conspired to make him look like an odd doll of Sigmund Freud, capable only of limited positions.

Strange, she thought, that he should resemble the very man who'd put the West's understanding of female sexuality back a thousand years, whose theory of the vaginal orgasm was still used to rationalize the ritual mutilation of women's genitalia. Bira, her mother-in-law to be, often quoted Freud when speaking of her own clitoridectomy. Though annoyed Ruya had not experienced the same "liberation," the gnarled tree of a woman fell short of suggesting she do something about it. Even so, Ruya was careful to pour her own drinks in Bira's presence, lest she awaken with a particularly well-liked part of her anatomy missing.

A loud cough came from the front of the room, and Ruya's smile vanished. Abaz too stopped his shuffling to stare at its source: a tiny woman, seated mere feet from him in the first row. She coughed a second time, as if it were some sort of signal, then slipped her small hand into the darkness of a carry-bag.

Ruya's eyes narrowed.

A gun? Is this why I was summoned here? To witness some sort of attack?

By now, the entire audience was focused on the woman. A demure smile showed the attention pleased her. With all eyes on her, she slipped a light pastel-colored cloth out and wrapped it about her head. Though not the feared weapon, Ruya and the rest of the students remained tense. Rather than acknowledge the covered woman with eye contact, Abaz stiffened and turned away.

With the grace of grungy, ill-maintained machines, two oafish security guards shuffled toward the petite offender. In their best impersonation of silence, they brought her to her feet and, each clasping a sweater-covered elbow, steered her toward the flat rectangular darkness of an exit door.

Ruya followed with wide eyes, uncertain how to feel. The offender was barely twenty, possessed of a foolish certainty in some countries considered a privilege of youth. Wearing the head scarf in a classroom taught by a man was a symbol of faith. Here in metropolitan Turkey, it was also tantamount to sedition. Under current law in the one successful modern Muslim democracy, she could be charged with "obstructing the education of others" and given six months in prison. Thousands of Turkish women had been barred from campuses for the offense.

Shrugging inwardly, Ruya told herself she didn't make the rules. She also told herself she didn't necessarily disagree with them. She knew well that blocks away, in the Grand Bazaar, fans of Smashmouth rubbed elbows with believers in a fanatical version of *shaheed*, which told them dying as a martyr was the greatest service they could perform for the creator of the Universe. In exchange, they would receive a bevy of virgins. *With or without clitorises?* Ruya wondered. In any event, it was as though all the world's history had decided to coexist, and the inhabitants of a dozen dissonant millennia were crammed into too small a living space, forever tumbling together, forever falling apart.

She glanced at the young woman as she passed—only to find her staring back. Gazes locked, something passed between them. The woman-child smiled, bringing slight crinkles to the corners of her full lips and a shiver to Ruya's spine. Concern for her civil rights faded utterly. She had seen that same inky blackness in Bira's eyes. Turning away, she found herself emulating Abaz, resolutely facing the room's tall walls and their covering of burnt-orange soundproofing, which looked more like cheap carpeting.

The woman gone, Abaz shifted his gaze to the sole window and nodded at the smoky gray stones of Beyazit Tower poking above the tree line. "That tower is over a hundred years old," he said. "But to this city, it's an infant. Istanbul was founded more than 2600 years ago, by Byzas the Greek. As Constantinople, it became capital of the Roman Empire, ultimately outlasting its European sister by centuries. Let me state for the record, however, that I did not witness any of that personally."

Titters meandered through the audience of students. A whisper made its way to Ruya's ears: "I did."

The voice was as strong and even as a Black Sea wind flying low over the waters of the Bosporus. It came from the seat directly behind her.

"So you're here, my dark angel," Ruya whispered back. She forced herself to stare ahead, as previously instructed.

"The only question was whether you would be," Fatima al-Faqadi answered. "Does this mean you've decided to accept my offer, or do you still aspire to mere political power through your fiancé?"

The portrayal of Ruya's betrothal was cold, but accurate. When she had agreed to marry Deren, Ruya was certain she would be able to influence public policy, to further women's rights, and move to destroy those she deemed enemies to her cause.

Then she'd met Bira.

closer to Allah. Though the other clans grew corrupt and rejected his judgment, the Children of Haqim did not."

A pause in Fatima's speech left Abaz's lecture the only sound.

"Imagine what it was like eight hundred years ago," he said. "The rising tide of Islam had swallowed much of Asia Minor, and the Byzantine Empire was left a shell of its former glory. Still, it took the Byzantines' fellow Christians, led by the powerful Frankish nobles Boniface and Baldwin, to bring about the end of what was truly left of Rome. For three days, the greatest city in Christendom was sacked by Christian crusaders. Women and children were slaughtered indiscriminately. Art and artifacts hundreds of years old were melted for precious metals. Libraries were burned. Churches desecrated. Why? Because the supposedly holy Crusade to free Jerusalem had run out of money. The banks, in this case the Venetians, aggravated when the Byzantines denied them a more favorable trading status, called in their due. The crusaders were thus diverted to Constantinople, and they expected payment for returning the deposed Emperor Isaac to the throne. They also expected he would live up to his agreement to bring the Byzantine Church back under the rule of their Pope. Instead they found Isaac lacked the support of the people. Worse, perhaps, he lacked money."

Before Abaz could begin his next sentence, Fatima's whisper rose again: "Just as there were mortal kings and sultans in those days, many cities also had Cainite princes lording over the night. Constantinople was ruled by Michael, an ancient member of Clan Toreador. Michael was a particularly gifted leader, and offered a spiritual vision that helped many Cainites keep their dread hungers in check. He and his two lovers ruled the Byzantine night for centuries in a self-proclaimed golden age, what they called the Dream.

"But in the fullness of time his triumvirate fell to internal division. Losing his two lovers, Michael melted into madness, believing himself on the road to becoming a god. He was slain, willingly perhaps, during the crusaders's sack of his city. For the Greek Cainites who had called Constantinople home, it was a rude awakening. They were shocked that Michael could desert his Dream and that a swell of mortals could dictate events. For the dozen petty kingdoms of the European Cainite clans, it was the opening of a world of opportunity. For myself and the other Children of Haqim, it meant that a less predictable, more barbaric enemy now controlled that much more of the border with Islamic territory.

"There was no telling what these fool Latins might do next."

Chapter One

August 3, 1204

The moon, its dappled shading wiped clean by an even haze in the sky, recalled its daytime counterpart the sun, which some in the crowd had not gazed upon for centuries. Directly below, wearing ceremonial armor that covered him from head to toe, Hugh of Clairvaux, standing on a balcony, framed by a tower-room door, recalled a god.

My sire has become a vision, Sir Gondemar thought as he watched from below. *His being sways between mere sensation and perfect idea, flooding the moment's happenstance with meaning.*

"An urgent message," a freckle-faced boy anxiously chirped. Gondemar, transfixed, didn't hear.

It's an orrery, he went on in his mind, *a model of the cosmos, with light and order emanating from the heavenly disc, reflected through Sir Hugh, then downward, imposing a righteous order on all, just as God imposed his Word upon chaos and so created the world.*

"A message, sir?" the boy tried again. Still, no answer.

Vaguely aware someone had spoken to him, Gondemar muttered, "Look at that, would you? In a short time, Sir Hugh will raise his hand to show his communion with the divine Virgin Mary is at an end. Then, our first group will begin its journey to the docks. Watch, but remember as you do that it is the Lord's will, not the hunger of any man, you see enacted this night."

Gondemar meant no rudeness. Though the circles under his eyes, coupled with heavy eyelids, gave his face an overall sleepy and unintelligent look, this was in fact natural camouflage for a keen Frankish mind that had proven deadly in battle. Most recently, he'd helped mastermind the destruction of an Assamite stronghold, something most Cainites considered impossible. Tonight, he was simply transfixed.

To the tower's right, a break in the trees afforded a distant view of the merchant ships in the harbors of Galata, with their rounded planked hulls and raised bows and sterns. Some were already loaded with supplies, waiting with skeleton crews of ghouls, who even now raised ladders from the yards and masts of the vessels, so high that they were a marvel to behold.

"Sir, my message? It is of great import."

Gondemar wondered if ever in the world's history had the desire for power and wealth blinded so many to so much. Here, under the noses of the very souls who had abandoned the noble goal of Pope Innocent to recapture the Holy City, a true crusade had actually been mounted. They were so busy with their new empire, with their cataloging, with their intrigues, they had no idea a very real army would soon take to the seas using their plundered harbors. Those sundry officials who might have cared had been bribed, coerced or otherwise rendered harmless to the effort at hand.

Once we reach our first goal, even those fools will be forced to look up from the husk of Byzantium that so distracts them. They will see what is happening and join us!

All around, on the grounds of this estate, hundreds of armed men, of varying power and ability, but of single mind, waited for their leader to signal the beginning of their holy war.

What could possibly stop us now?

"Sir Gondemar!" the youth finally shrieked, so loudly Gondemar was forced to face him. "Lady Gabriella's scouts believe that Assamites have penetrated the area to slay Sir Hugh!"

Chapter Two

April 14, 1204

Sir Hugh of Clairvaux, Poor Knight of the Temple, smiled for the first time in weeks, enchanted, despite the carnage outside, at the small marvel before his eyes. As it had for hundreds of years, the diminutive figure of St. Andrew bent forward at the waist in a warm gesture somewhere between a devout bow and a humble greeting. Curious to see the saint perform anew, Sir Hugh put another coin into the slot at the figure's base, setting the intricate series of weights and pulleys into motion.

The modest joy was short-lived. Before the device could pull back to standing, the flat of a broadsword slammed into it, sending its broken pieces hurtling into the cool marble-covered walls of the Church of the Holy Apostles. For a moment, little echoes of the blow muted the horrible sounds coming from outside. But then the nightmare crush of battle cries, shrill pleas for mercy and the deep cracking of great wooden beams giving way to fire returned.

"Was that necessary?" Sir Hugh barked, aghast.

"Always hated those things," the crusader, Sir Nudd, muttered back in a coarse voice. Boyishly pleased by the destruction, the man's piggish eyes narrowed beneath thick, red eyebrows. Broader and taller, Hugh glared, unable to conceal his disdain and fighting valiantly to contain an even stronger response. Oblivious, Nudd straightened from his swing with a wheeze, staggered back a bit and accidentally bumped into the already terrified donkey that carried their plundered items.

As it trembled, Hugh tried to soothe the rough beast, succeeding only in making it more afraid. He was surprised the smell alone hadn't already driven it mad. Even thick stone and marble couldn't stem the stench that wafted in through the high porticoes, designed by master craftsmen to help circulate the air.

As Nudd turned his back, Hugh gently prodded the broken statue's pieces with the tip of his sword, poking at tiny hands carved so carefully each fingernail could be seen. He knew the automaton's history. There was none other like it in the world. Now it existed only in the mind. Kneeling, he rolled the statue's broken head gingerly beneath his gloved index finger.

Am I so different from this?

The saint's head left a little trail of white powder on the stone floor, then balanced, nose up. There was a living mind present once, Hugh knew, that had grasped the results of such pieces fitted together. Where was that designing mind now? In some skull buried beneath the earth, or had it instead escaped that fate, only to die instead with the little broken system that once accepted coin and bowed in thanks and greeting?

And where, in this spiraling madness that was once a great city, is God?

"Oh, cheer up, good Sir Hugh! After all, this is hardly a proper church!" Nudd explained, as if the knight were ignorant. "The Pope excommunicated these Greek devils and their cursed emperor signed a treaty against us with Saladin himself not more than twenty years past! Everything here is a sacrilege! Which means everything here is ours… to reclaim for Christ's glory!"

His generous explanation greeted with stony silence, Nudd turned away and scooped twin goblets from a hollow in the wall, then dumped them into a sack by his side. After a moment, he hummed a little tune, as though shopping for trinkets at an open-air bazaar.

Hugh hissed at him, "You gather gold and smash works of art for His glory? His glory requires no finery and certainly no wanton destruction."

Nudd whirled, the rare and delicate metals jammed in his sack scratching and bending as he shifted his bulk. His recent days full of their own extremes, he gestured furiously at the knight.

"And *you've* spent so much time among the bloody Saracens you don't know who your fellows are anymore! What if I *do* desire some finery? I spent months in Venice, weeks on ship, and nearly a year here while Boniface and Baldwin dallied with that fool of an emperor! Then came days in the siege, and more in battle risking my neck! I was there when we breached the outer defenses, and when we stormed the walls! I still haven't regained all the feeling in my left arm from where a falling boulder hit it! Now our blessed monks are out there taking what they can, in His name and by your leave! Unlike you, I have lands to support back home, so why *not* me? And I couldn't help but notice the golden statues *you've* been piling on our poor donkey!"

The rebuke hit yet another sore spot. The Knights Templar were already misunderstood, some seeing their very sophistication as evidence of betrayal. Had Nudd been wise enough to remain silent, Hugh might have held his own tongue, but he was not.

"*I* was sent here to preserve holy relics and sacred items for the Poor Knights of the Temple of Solomon! *I* do not have, nor do *I* require, any property of my own," Hugh growled through gritted teeth.

At a strange new sound in the Poor Knight's voice, the donkey took two steps back. Seeing this, Hugh realized he was no longer quite in control of himself, but there was little he could do about it now.

One look at Hugh's ashen face made Nudd realize he'd gone too far. He quickly put his hands up in supplica-

Stefan Petrucha   19

tion. "Now, now. Peace in His name. There's plenty to share!" Nudd said.

Snarling, Hugh stepped forward.

No one would miss a single fool crusader.

Nudd reached for the hilt of his blade. The donkey brayed.

Hugh raised his arm, as if to slay Nudd with his hands, but instead of striking, the knight's great form suddenly crumpled in agony. His body shivered, his blue eyes filled with deep panic and despair. Barely standing, Hugh removed one of his gloves to wipe the copious red sweat that had suddenly appeared on his brow.

Thank you for stopping me, my Lord.

"Stigmata...?" Nudd gasped, leaning forward. "Hmph! No. Some phantom caused by the smoke in here. But, ack—see? You're as uncomfortable within these walls as I. That's because you're a good man, a good Christian. Not like these Greeks," Nudd said. Smiling, he patted Hugh on the shoulder and looked him in the eye. "It's a beastly business, Sir Hugh, no matter how you dress it up."

Hugh nodded mechanically.

"Was the little doll a treasure your masters coveted? If so, my apologies! I'd thought you were after bigger prizes, like the Holy Shroud they say carries the very image of our Lord as He lay in His tomb."

"The Mandylion was secreted away hours ago. You needn't concern yourself with it. We are here to find the crypt that contains the body of Constantine. If your sack is full, let's concentrate on that," Hugh answered weakly.

The mention of the pillaged relic proved too much for their third, unwilling companion and a stifled weeping came to the two Latins' ears.

"Good sirs, good sirs, praise His name," the Greek priest said in a shaking voice as he stepped from the safety of the shadows. "My children, my Aura..."

A mix of tears and gasps, brought on by smoke as much as feelings, choked off the rest of his sentence. The sad desperation evinced by this man of God brought Hugh fully back to himself.

"Don't fear," Hugh said reassuringly. "You'll go back to them. I gave you and the Lord my word on it, and in times such as these my word and the Lord are all I have."

In fact, Hugh's word was in many ways all he ever had. His honor, his commitment to the codes of chivalry, were the iron grate that kept him from the hell he carried inside. But he didn't think it wise to share that with the Greek or the crusader.

"And all you should ever need, good sir. But, my youngest, remember him? Biton, the little one with curls? His bad foot makes it hard for him to walk, let alone run. And Aura tires so easily even in the best of times. It's all the same to me and my poor old bones. I know the Lord will keep me in His bosom in the beyond, but I also know my family waits for me out there," he said, pleading. "The things they're doing, to women, to children…"

Imagining the priest could not plead so to a foreign invader without a loss of dignity and pride, Hugh found the fact that the Greek met his eyes all the more impressive, especially compared to Nudd's narrow, shifting glance.

The crusader stepped up and chucked the man under the chin as if he were the donkey. "Now, now, little priest, where's your faith? You'll be quite free as soon as you show us the entrance. And don't think to fool us with that pretty shrine outside meant for the visitors to gawk at."

"Yes, sir. Yes, sir. This way. Praised be His name."

The priest led the donkey down the main bay's center, in a clear effort to keep some distance between himself and his captors. As their guide moved ahead, Nudd bowed, imitating the broken automaton, bidding Hugh to follow.

Ignoring him, the Templar tried to find some comfort in the church's great design.

The ancient building was of the Greek-cross plan, with five great domes, one above each arm of the cross and the fifth shielding the huge central bay. A row of columns along the interior walls formed an upper gallery, reached by spiral stairs. Below, at the central nave, stood the Lord's Table, a vast silver altar. Hugh noticed at once that the famous marble pyramidal ciborium, the cup that held the Eucharist here, had already been taken in the sack.

Hurrying now, the priest led them past twelve stone sarcophagi, one for each Apostle, until they reached the western arm, that ended in an atrium. Beyond, Emperor Justinian had built a second mausoleum, where most believed he and his family were buried, but Sir Hugh knew that this too, was mere façade.

True to his word, the priest paused in the center of the western hall and tugged at an iron ring set in the center of a marble carving. Upon seeing the carving, Hugh shook his head. The priest, he realized, probably knew the smooth strong face as that of an archangel, but in it, Hugh recognized the visage of the fallen Toreador, Michael. With the heavy scraping of stone on stone, the wall opened, revealing another set of spiral stairs. This one, rather than up to a domed heaven, twisted down into darkness.

The priest motioned at the steps: "There is no light. You'll need a torch." Then, by way of what he hoped would be farewell, he crossed himself, and muttered, "May the Lord watch over… you both."

He turned, prepared to walk, or even run, hurriedly away. Hugh imagined him finding his family and making it safely away from this horrid patch of misery that had opened in the world's navel. But a single word stopped the priest in his tracks.

"Wait," Nudd said.

The priest turned to face the crusader. In two quick steps, Nudd came within a foot of him, then moved his right arm to his side as if to take some coins from his purse.

"Something for your troubles."

The priest looked to Hugh for reassurance. Hugh nodded.

Even Nudd wouldn't dare harm him.

At the Templar's nod, the priest relaxed, just a bit. Before Hugh realized what was happening, Nudd had driven a long dagger into the man's abdomen and pushed it up through his entrails. Hugh watched, horrified, as the priest's eyes wavered.

At the slicing sound of Hugh's sword sliding free, Nudd turned to look at the Templar, genuinely perplexed.

"He might have brought others, and then we'd have to share!" Nudd explained, as if his reasons should be perfectly obvious.

"I gave that man my word!" Hugh growled. "Do you know what my word means to me?"

Can't you see it's the only thing between me and madness?

The donkey, too thick with treasure to turn around quickly, tried to step backwards down the hall.

"Then thank me for helping you keep it! A woman with four children on these streets? One child lame as well? They were lost the moment I grabbed the father to fulfill your mission! The only thing to hope is that their deaths were as quick and merciful as his. And now," he said, letting the corpse slip to the ground, "they're together again. As promised! Besides, tell me what proper priest would have a family at all?"

Hugh was no longer able to explain that the Byzantine Church did not require celibacy of their priests, and, in fact, encouraged them to marry that they might better understand the needs of their flock. He was barely able to speak at all.

Nudd, however, again spoke too much. As he stepped over the bent-over body he glanced down at it and said, "Looks a bit like that bowing statue, now, doesn't he?"

A bestial rage drove Hugh's conscience deep and far away. A remaining devout kernel, no longer in control but forced to watch the scene as if from afar, quickly prayed:

Holy Mother give me the strength to wait until this man can raise his blade and defend himself.

"Draw your sword," Hugh said, half-spitting. "And make it quick or, Templar or no, I'll gut you while it's still in its scabbard."

A playful grin blossomed on Nudd's weathered features. He dropped his dagger and pulled his sword free. It was covered in dried blood and dull from over-use.

"All right, then," Nudd said, moving his feet apart until he found a comfortable balance. Holding the heavy blade in one hand, he beckoned to the Templar. Hugh leaned forward, but all at once, beads of red again burst from the pores on his smooth white skin, rolling along the side of his face in small rivulets. As Hugh swooned, a few drops fell from his chin to the ground. Seeing this, Nudd chuckled. He waved the tip of his blade in front of the Poor Knight's face.

"Sure you're up for it?" Nudd chided.

Nudd jutted the tip of his blade toward that handsome face, but, before it could make contact, it flew across the room and crashed into the center of the wall. It remained in mid-wall for a moment, then hit the floor, the hilt making a loud *thunk* against the stone.

Hugh smiled as Nudd looked around for an explanation. As far as the beefy Frank could tell, Hugh hadn't moved. Whatever he was thinking, Nudd soon looked forward and saw the Templar's blade was inches from his throat.

"Yes, I think I am up for it," Hugh said. "Now ask your Lord for forgiveness."

"Forgive me, milord," Nudd said, dumbfounded, locking eyes with Hugh.

"Not *me*, you idiot!" Hugh hissed.

Nudd managed two words before Hugh ripped off the crusader's chain-mail cowl, taking bits of flesh with it: "What are—?"

Hugh, still sweating blood, pushed Nudd's bare head to the side and buried his sharp canines into the man's thick, hairy neck. The teeth pierced and tore both skin and muscle until they found the jugular. Rending the vein, Hugh sucked in the steaming communion as though drawing in much-needed air. The vitae filled and warmed him, and all but drove down the Beast the fool crusader had helped conjure.

Having had his fill, Hugh grabbed Nudd's hairy jaw in his hand and regarded the fading light in his eyes. Spitting blood, the crusader, condemned to say the wrong thing to the last, spoke. "So I die, eh? Just as good here as anywhere. But remember this, Templar monster, you slay me, your fellow Christian, because of a doll. The dead man was just an excuse. So which of us is further from the Lord, demon?"

Though the monster that drove his feeding was quiet and satisfied, Hugh closed his hand and crushed Nudd's jaw. The crusader continued to speak, but the stream of gurgling sounds was utterly incomprehensible. The Templar shoved the man back, and severed Nudd's neck with a single swipe of his sword. Hugh spat on the severed head, then kicked it out of the hall. With a hollow clunk, it landed at the feet of the backward-striding donkey, which stared into the lifeless eyes and brayed.

Having given the cretin a chance to arm himself, Hugh's duty to law and the Order were done, but the surrender to animalism disturbed him. While Satan tempted the mortal, the Adversary *lived* within the Cainite's body, and sometimes he yet triumphed. Still, how better to test the soul's resolve? Did not Jesus traffic with thieves, beggars and whores? Why did the sun burn Hugh, forcing him to miss required temple prayer? So that his greatness would not compete in his own mind with the Lord's light. Why did it pain him so to walk the halls of this church? So that even those comforts would be denied him. Why did the Mandylion burn his fingers when he touched it? So the desire to seek a mere image of the Lord would be denied him. His sire, Sir Geoffrey, who also walked the Path of Chivalry, would doubtless understand and approve.

Turning his back on the gory scene, Hugh realized he missed the comfort of the cautious Gondemar, his second-in-command, and his other fellows, but again recognized the rightness of his decision to enter the city alone. He'd heard of others of the Order partaking in the carnage and he would not subject his own brother knights to temptation. Bad enough Templar monies had been partly used in funding this Fourth Crusade; he could not let this mad sacking reflect any further on the Order.

The stairs were small, the bottom not yet visible, but Hugh made his way until he was so deep below the earth that even the dying city's muted cries receded into watery whispers. Finally, there was only the sound of his heavy feet moving against old, dust-laden stone.

Before reaching the bottom, he lit a torch. As the flame licked upward, he noticed a few thin air vents in the ceiling, leading high up to the surface. A few stars poked out between passing clouds of smoke. Hugh wondered if they were the eyes of God.

The hidden crypts were a labyrinthine series of small square rooms, each equally sized. If the priest were to be believed, here lay the true remains of each emperor who had ever sat on the Byzantine throne. Hugh stepped from one room to another, reading the inscriptions on the single sarcophagus in each, moving further and further into the empire's past. Finally, he came upon a larger, rectangular central room, which an inscription in both Latin and Greek identified as the tomb of Constantine the Great, the emperor who had made Rome Christian. Excited, he placed his torch in a holder on the wall, and prepared to push aside the heavy stone lid. Catching himself at the last minute, Hugh stopped.

What a fool! I'm about to defile the resting place of a great Christian leader!

Instead of simply opening the lid, he went to his knees and lowered his head. Then, clearing heart and his head, he called to the Virgin Mary:

Oh Queen of Heaven,
pray to God for us always,
that He may pardon us and give us grace,
pray to God for us always,
that He may grant us peace in this life
pray to God for us always,
that He may reward us with paradise at our death.

With that, Hugh stood and pushed aside the stone cover. At once he noticed something odd about the shriveled body. The leathery, mummified skin was too smooth for something natural, the bones that poked through at the knees and elbows too square. In any event, the trip had been for nothing. The corpse's head was bare. Constantine's jeweled crown, the item his sire Geoffrey had requested, was gone.

Heavy of heart, he sank once more to his knees and wept a few ruby tears at having come so far just to fail. Nudd's last words drifted back. Had the automaton meant more than the man? There were so many people, after all, so many "kine," as the Cainites derisively called them. The automaton was one of a kind. But no, Hugh decided. It was neither doll nor man, but the forced breaking of a vow before God that had led him to blind rage. Even before

Stefan Petrucha

he became a Templar, or a Cainite, he'd never felt whole without some structure to give his spirit form.

An odd feeling of being watched snapped him out of self-reflection. Scanning the area and straining to hear in the silence, he concluded it was only shadows, conspiring with his mind to form strange creatures. Here in the crypts, the horrid feeling he had experienced in the church had seemingly abated, and he was confident his senses were keen enough to detect most anything. Recalling that sensation, he dreaded having to return, and dreaded even more taking again to the burning streets. Still, peaceful though it was, he could not stay here forever.

Wait. Something was here. A wall nearby, gray and ashen, flat mere moments ago, now held a rising shape. No, it wasn't the wall. Something was on the wall.

Long and lithe, pushed by naked heels, pulled by long, thin-fingered hands, the thing propelled itself across the stone as if weightless. Even Hugh's inhumanly quick mind barely apprehended the fact there was movement at all. As it made contact with him, he took a half-step backward, surprised at the leaden weight of a form which seconds ago had seemed as light as the whirlpools of dust it left in its wake. Bones hollow as a bird's, coupled with steely muscle and ligament, forced the Templar back and down. His sword clattered to the side, the mesh of chain-mail beneath his mantle folded over against his back.

Before he could raise an arm, the thing, a female, straddled him. She forced their crotches together and gyrated her hips in a wicked mockery of sex. Curling her back as a mountain cat would while stretching, she pressed again and further pushed the chain-mail mesh into his groin as she moaned.

"Hrgggg… What do *you* know of the Queen of Heaven?" she asked, having heard his prayer. "Your Mary is a lying whore!"

"How dare you speak that way of the Blessed Virgin—" Hugh began, but the creature grabbed his arms and

Assamite

pressed them down on either side of him.

"Virgin? The dark mother is more giving than *that*, little knight!" She leaned forward and pressed her parched lips close to his ear. He could feel the frayed, dried skin that curled from her lips in anchored flakes. Stagnant breath pulsed against his ear, numbing his cheek and neck.

"Do you know," she whispered, "why the dark mother was thrust from the garden of Eden? Because she wanted to be on top during copulation. Like you and I, right now. And Adam, in his stupid, bullheaded ignorance, refused her."

Clenching a small shard of gray stone in her right hand, she pressed it into her face lovingly, rolling it along her cheek, down to her neck. It scraped and cut the skin as it rolled, but no blood issued from the wounds.

"I know. I have a piece of her right here, and she has shown me so very much. She makes me so strong, so powerful. I must find the rest of her, but even I need help," she said.

Pressing it into her breast, she moved an index finger down from her exposed nipple to Hugh's nose and tapped him twice. "And *you* won't refuse me. You can't. It is forbidden. And as for Adam, don't worry, one day Lilith will take his very name away."

Hearing the name of Adam's legendary first wife, Hugh recognized the lineage of the creature atop him.

"Lamia," Hugh whispered. Cainites who worship Lilith, and through her, death, he recalled. But how had this one become so strong, so utterly vile?

She rose, seemingly grateful at the recognition, grasping her breasts with her hands as she pressed her pelvis even harder into him, threatening to break his hip bones.

"Yes, Lamia. And everything you've ever heard, every joy that's made you laugh, every sorrow that's made you cry, is a lie, Cainite, an utter lie. Creation was the crime of a misguided demon, born from the Truth's discarded afterbirth. But Lorah will fix that for you. I will peel back every layer. I will take your flesh, I will take your bone, I will take your language. And when you are so naked, there is barely anything left of you at all, then I will fill you again. You will be my vessel, my little mechanical man. I will animate you with truth and you will help me find the rest of this blessed rock," she said, slipping the stone shard into the folds of her tattered clothes.

"I am your Mary. I am your Lilith. I am Lorah. You prayed for mother. Now she's here. So, now, my little forever knight, come give her a kiss," she said.

As Hugh writhed in an increasingly feeble effort to free himself, the creature kept talking. Her voice, speaking a language Hugh did not comprehend, but which his very body understood, wafted in through his ears, down his chest and into his heart, where it began reconstructing his dreams. Already, the vast madness outside was fading from his consciousness, while a new one was being born within.

Chapter Three

May 4, 1204

The woman who called herself Amala watched amazed as, with an uncanny obedience, Sihr Haddad's black Arab charger responded to his unspoken command and halted inches from the massive blockade. Her own dark brown yearling, though well trained, stopped only when she tugged on the reins.

An advantage, she thought, *of having your mount bonded to you by the blood*. She was used to ghouls, those mortals made to serve vampires with a periodic taste of their master's blood, and to lesser thralls kept in control through a vampire's will, but the Bedouins were known to feed their blood to their horses—and now she was beginning to understand why.

But even that strange bond couldn't overcome the impossible. Though both steeds could manage steppes, slopes, sandy dunes, wide frozen rivers and all manner of severe weather, here, on the northern road that led to Adrianople, they had met their match. To the left was a ravine, one hundred feet down to a rushing river, and to the right a rocky hillside at an angle too steep for a goat, let alone a horse.

A crossbow bolt whizzed by her head. A second caught her in the shoulder.

Two armored men, positioned atop the wall of timber and branches that blocked the road moved to reload. One paused to shout in Greek, "Back to your barbaric holes, you damned Bulgars!"

Amala cursed herself for a *fida'i*, a novice, and winced a bit from the pain. She saw Sihr was about to draw his blade, but gave him a sharp glance and gestured that they should retreat. The tall, black-skinned man was obviously surprised, but he turned and rode away obediently, his worn burgundy robe twirling in the air behind him. Two more bolts whistled into the ground nearby. Amala pivoted her yearling to follow Sihr.

Once safely around a bend, she pulled the offending bolt from her shoulder. It had failed to pierce any bone, and the wound was already closing thanks to Amala's potent blood. She leapt from her mount and landed silently on the dirt and rock. Sihr let out an audible, contemptuous, "Tch."

"If you must make sounds," she said in a low, level voice, "at least speak."

Sihr was abashed, as if he'd been asked to dance naked during Ramadan.

"I should not question you," he blurted in a voice so deep it made her chest shake a little. "It is not permitted."

"Yet you constantly do," she answered, glaring as she tossed the bloody bolt away. "With shifts, rustles and facial tics. You're like an old woman, too tired to bother standing when her bladder is full of piss and needs to be emptied."

Goading the powerful sorcerer was dangerous, but better to discover the limits of his self-control now. As it was, an angry spark glowed briefly in his eyes, then faded.

"I realize having spent so much time alone, communication must be difficult, but it is essential. This is not Alamut. I am neither Haqim himself nor an elder in our clan. As long as you obey my commands, there will be no penalty for speaking your mind," she said.

For Amala's part, to traffic only with a horse and the pitiless stars would have been preferable to journeying with this inscrutable, brooding figure, but there were reasons the clan elders had paired them. Though also a Child of Haqim, Sihr had spent centuries alone in desert wildernesses, following a moral path—or *tariq*—that necessitated a nomad's existence. As a lone predator answerable only to his honor, he had honed his sorcery in communion with Allah only knew what. According to his tale, he'd heeded mystic visions and sought to reconnect to the Assamite leadership several months ago. But many of those leaders, who dwelled in the hidden mountain stronghold of Alamut, did not trust him.

To live by instinct as a vampiric Bedouin like Sihr did was suspiciously close to domination by the Beast. So Amala, though much younger and of the warrior caste, was put in charge of this mission and in direct command of the sorcerer. Obeying her would be a test of his loyalty and discipline.

"Why did we not attack?" he said at last, as if speaking each word were an unpleasant task.

"In the darkness, the fools mistake us for Bulgars," she answered. "Let them be mistaken until we learn how many there are. If one survived, they could alert others to our presence. Besides, they're not the issue so much as the wall."

Seeing her dark companion's expression had not changed, she added, "Something else?"

Suddenly concise and determined, as if his hesitation to speak had been a ruse, Sihr nodded sharply toward the bend and the pile of debris beyond it, which blocked their way.

"A mile ago we spotted that. I told you there was no sorcery I possessed that could clear it and suggested we double back. You refused, but didn't explain why. Now we've lost time. In a few hours, it will be dawn. We'll have to skip prayer for want of shelter from the sun," Sihr said.

A small smile played across her face.

"Good," she said, nodding. "Now, perhaps I can teach you something."

Sihr raised a single black eyebrow in response. It was the only part of his body, or of the horse for that matter, that moved.

Amala crept to the bend and peered around it. She turned her head right, and left, scanning the blockage's full surface and trying to count the guards that lay hidden in the darkness atop it. Sihr watched her closely.

"It will take two nights to clear," he warned. "And we still haven't dealt with the guards."

"I'll answer your question of a mile back, then. Doubling back would costs us a week. Going ahead without the horses, something I doubt you would approve of, would do the same," she said. "Already we've had word of the Latins passing through as town after town surrenders to them. In Constantinople, the mortals will crown that merchant's whore Boniface as their emperor soon. The Frankish clans of Cainites will possibly act in tandem in choosing a new prince. Events move quickly and if our mission is to have any meaning, we should be part of them."

Allowing herself a small smile, she silently moved forward along the road. She positioned herself as close to the wall as possible without resorting to any powers of her blood. She knew the ways to fade into near-invisibility or become as quiet as the tomb, blessings of Haqim upon his warrior caste, but she wanted Sihr to watch and hear. The Blood is a weapon—it is the wielder's skill that matters most. Satisfied she had her companion's attention, Amala folded her tall, slender body, covered with leather leggings and a vest for warmth and protection, into a cross-legged position. Despite the Damascene scimitar dangling from her belt, not a pebble was disturbed. Even the veil she wore as a Muslim woman, which covered the lower half of her face, did not so much as flutter.

To help her focus, she whispered a passage from the Qur'an: "No vision can grasp Him. But His grasp is over all vision: He is above all comprehension, yet is acquainted with all things."

Then she fell silent, meditating on the tangle of dead substances that blocked the road. As a cold wind blew thick clouds across the sky, the dead wood, trunks, sticks and stones that had been piled to render the mountainous road useless, danced in faded color between light and dark.

34   Assamite

Each piece was insignificant, but taken together they were as formidable as the high protective walls of Adrianople, the city that was to be the touchstone of this mission into Christian lands.

Amala stared.

Suddenly, she stood and sprinted down the road towards a spot on the irregular blockade's right side.

"Back for some more?" the guard shouted. Two more bolts zipped through the cool air. Both missed by yards. She'd been expecting them.

Sihr turned his mount back toward the wall just in time to see Amala spin, leap two feet in the air and execute a sharp kick. Her snapping heel found the center of a great log hanging catercorner in the pile, its far end vanishing into the browns, grays and blacks of the labyrinthine mass.

There was a loud crack. The great timber split down the center. The two guards, precariously balanced at the top, recklessly moved to reload. As the first was ready to fire again, the pile lazily shifted. With a rush of falling, splintering wood, the wall gave way.

The guards clung to each other. For a moment it looked as if they might catch their balance in the shifting pile, but Sihr pushed his arms out at the air and, in response, the two fell as if shoved. In seconds, the two screaming guards and most of the wall's fragments tumbled into the ravine.

Sihr and his charger trotted up, leading Amala's horse by the reins.

"They were alone?" he asked.

"Yes," Amala said, looking up at him. "Thank you for your help."

Sihr nodded and said, "They probably would have fallen on their own shortly."

Together, they cleared what remained in minutes. Sihr was silent for the duration of their brief work, but when their horses' heads were turned once more toward Adrianople, he spoke again.

"Your patience humbles me," he admitted.

"Tch." Now it was Amala's turn to use the deprecating sound. "Impatience is my greatest flaw. But I know that one person, in abject submission, doing the right thing at the right time, *insha'allah*, can move mountains."

Sihr nodded. But did he believe her?

After they located a suitable cave, some distance from the road, they made camp for the day. At the proper time, they started the dawn *salat* with the first of two *rakas*, or prayer cycles. Bowing southeast toward Mecca, they chanted:

Alaahu-Akbar
Subhanaka Allahumma Wa Bi-Hamdika
Wa Yabaraka-Ismuka Was
Ta'Ala Jadduk Wa-La Illaha Ghairuk

Pacing the prayers with due solemnity, they finished just in time. The mountains' ridged back had turned ruby, as if life's blood were pooling to the surface of the world. The glow was also a reminder of the Final Death that exposure to the sun would entail.

During the day, though the shadowy cave shielded them with darkness, the urge to slumber was great. Even to become aware at all during the day, much less move about, was an arduous task for Cainites. However, with great physical effort, Amala woke herself twice, for the noon and afternoon prayers. She was pleased to find Sihr awake and ready. It was rare to find one willing to suffer so for the ritual. Amala thought that, in their faith, at least, they had found a strong commonality.

Still, for much of the next evening's journey, Sihr returned to his stoic silence, riding tall and stiff, the appearance of his lanky, weathered body made fuller by

36   Assamite

his shifting robes. She wondered if she would ever understand him, or if he could ever be understood. Sometime after the road leveled from rough, hilly forests of thick, old growth into more verdant plains rife with poplar trees, Amala watched with some concern as Sihr halted his horse and pricked up his ears.

"Shouting," he said. "Rushing feet, less than half a mile due west."

"I hear it," she responded. Her face twisted in light surprise as she made out a few words, "Is that *Arabic?*"

Chapter Four

Far off the road, in the shadowed patches of wood, a running Arab man, white-bearded and with many wrinkles in his dark skin, cradled a sack as though it were his very heart and narrowly ducked a crossbow bolt.

"Elif air ab tizak!" he shrieked back at his three armored pursuers.

Though on foot, he moved fast as a wolf, ducking through the narrow spaces between trunks, sliding along fallen leaves, picking up a momentum that would leave any man, much less one of his apparent age, tumbling. Unfortunately, the dark figures pursuing him, only slightly slowed by their chain mail, were equally unnatural. While the largest paused to reload his crossbow, the other two fanned out in an effort to surround their quarry.

"There he is!"

"I have him!"

"Where, you jabbering idiots?" the larger one said, reloading. Then, with a terse "Ah," he let fly another bolt. The lucky shot perforated the old Arab's right elbow, immobilizing the joint. His arm suddenly rigid, the precious sack it cradled tumbled to the ground. A few leather-bound books and scientific instruments spilled out. Though clearly expensive and well cared for, these things were not his greatest concern. Rather than flee without the precious item that yet remained covered, he threw himself down on it, prepared to die in its defense.

As the crusaders tromped nearer, the Arab yanked at the bolt in his elbow using his good hand. With a sucking sound, it loosened. He was able to slide it half out before the tip stuck on bone. Normally he could heal the wound quickly enough, but he had not fed in quite a while. Worse, there was not much time. No war-hardened fighter, he hoped only that he might take a few of the Franks with him.

A heavy boot slammed down on his back, shredding the humble peasant robes he wore, but stopping short of breaking skin.

Their pace leisurely now that the chase was over, the two others sheathed their broadswords and wrested the sack from his good arm. As they did, they said odd things like, "That's a good fellow!" as if such words might be of comfort.

He hoped for a moment they would fight over the prize, but a grunt from the man whose foot held him in place made them hand the sack over. As the Latin invader moved to open it, the Arab put up a frantic effort to squirm free, the Beast in him welling as he struggled.

Stay in control or the prize is forfeit! he thought.

"Don't," he finally managed to say in clear Latin. "You mustn't!"

"Stop struggling," the crusader said, digging his heel deeper into the old man's back. "You'll see your precious Allah soon enough, and you can tell Him your worries. Still, it's lucky we found you and not the Greeks. After all, *we're* true Christians."

His companions smiled in agreement, showing white, pointed teeth. The Arab closed his eyes and waited for an opening. After rummaging about in the sack, the crusader, puzzled and annoyed, withdrew a crumbling scroll. The Arab gasped at the sight.

"All the gold of Constantinople litters the wilderness, but you stopped running for this old paper, Saracen?" The crusader turned the sack upside down and emptied it onto the dirt. As each clump of aged scroll hit the ground, the pinned Arab grunted and growled.

Not yet! Not yet! There may be some pieces still left!

Finally, he decided to speak, in the hopes that if they knew what they held, they might not destroy it completely. "That may well be the last extant copy of Aristotle's *Commedia*. I rescued it from the fires at Constantinople, nearly dying in the process. I would have seen it protected, guarded, copied by practiced hands for posterity," he shrieked.

"Muslim hands, you mean."

"Civilized hands," the Arab said.

He was considering telling them how much gold it was worth when the crusader who held him fast moved his other foot down toward the pile, as if to rub the scrolls into dust. It was the opening he'd been waiting for.

Now! something in him screamed.

With his captor's weight slightly shifted, the Arab thrust his good arm toward a hole in the man's leggings and smeared the naked skin with a dark liquid that flowed like black water from the center of his palm.

The crusader was confused at first, disquieted by the warm, wet sensation. He stumbled backwards, his feet ripping and tearing the precious scrolls as he went. As he fell to his knees, grabbing his throat, his two fellows once more drew their weapons.

"Poison!"

"Must be one of those Assamite devils!"

"Yes," the Arab said, hissing as he stood. "An Assamite devil. That's exactly what I am."

Rattled by the moans of their leader, one of the crusaders took a fearful step back, as if preparing to run. Trying to press his faux advantage, the Arab yanked the bolt fully free from his elbow, tossed it on the ground and forced his body into what he hoped looked like a battle stance. Promising his baser instincts a fine meal in exchange for a few more precious moments of control, he inched forward, snarling, hissing theatrically, trying to position himself between the Latins and what remained of the scrolls. But the second crusader didn't scare quite so easily. His eyes narrowed and he raised the tip of his sword toward the Arab's face.

"Hold on. Do you *really* think this scrawny scholar is one of those Saracen killers?" he sneered. "I mean if he *really* was, shouldn't we all be dead by now?"

Assamite

At that moment, though the night had been relatively clear, a cool fog started rolling in, obscuring the darkened view even further. Delighted, the Arab waved his hands about exaggeratedly, as though he had conjured the sudden change in weather.

"You would have been, had I not been so concerned with saving that book!" he intoned melodramatically.

Unimpressed, the crusader spat, "Now, you don't expect me to believe you control the weather, now, do you?"

"No, I expect you to die!" With a dreadful scream, the Arab lunged, palm out. The crusader stabbed with his sword, but the Arab shifted out of the way, then tried to smear his body's venom on the man's face. The crusader stepped to the side and quickly knocked the slight Arab down.

The Arab's chilling scream was enough for the frightened one, though. He whirled and ran into the denser patches of fog. After two quick steps, he collapsed to the ground in a fluid motion, his severed head rolling off to the side. Seeing the fate of his companion, but clueless as to its cause, the remaining attacker rapidly turned his own head this way and that, sword first, searching the misty darkness. Seeing nothing, and remembering the Arab with his strange poisons, he turned back to him, and prepared to strike.

Another blow from the unseen source freed this last crusader's head from his body as well. His body shriveled as it fell, first into leather, then into simple dust, leaving behind only worn chain mail and a tunic with a faded cross.

"*Salaam aleikum,*" Amala said, wiping the blood from her scimitar as she faded into view.

Wordless, the old Arab sprang upon the remaining decapitated corpse and fed. As the heady Cainite vitae quenched the Beast, and most of his anger, the Arab recalled his manners and turned back toward his savior.

"And peace be with you, as well, in the name of Ar-Rahman," the Arab replied. "And my apologies for... for... this," he added, indicating the blood on his face.

Amala shook her head. "There is no shame in feeding on them. These Latin dogs are clearly unworthy. Their blood is our right. I am Amala, Child of Haqim."

"Oh," the Arab smiled, wiping his lips. "I don't apologize for that, Amala, but for my rudeness in feeding ahead of you who killed them."

Feeling her own hunger surge at the sight of fresh blood, Amala quickly leaned down to the body and collected its remaining juices in a small ceremonial bowl.

The Arab watched, recognizing the ritual of an Assamite warrior.

"I saw them off the road, took them for kine and thought to pick through their holdings," he explained. "You never know what the mortals will be carrying these days. Oh my..."

Reminded of the scrolls, he turned toward what remained of them. A sharp wind tugged the vestiges along the ground, where they mingled with the fog, twigs and black night.

"*Masha'allah*," Amala said, and meant it to be of comfort.

"Yes, His will, no doubt. On better nights, I walk the Tariq el-Umma, pledged to protect both Cainite and mortal, but I'm embarrassed to say, I'd have sacrificed any number of lives for those words."

"Including your own?" Sihr said. His ebon charger cantered towards them, with Amala's yearling in tow.

"That is Sihr Haddad," Amala said. "You can thank him for the fog."

"A blood sorcerer, then. To answer your question then, friend, yes," the old Arab answered. Eyes narrowing, he peered curiously into the darkness past the lanky newcomer, to see if there were more visitors that as yet remained unseen.

"Such thoughts form the edifices of the soul," he endeavored to explain, "paving the roads we walk, providing shelter and home."

"Like a city?" Sihr asked, dismounting.

"Yes, like a city," the old Arab answered wistfully.

The sorcerer pulled a dagger from his side, opened a small cut in his palm and cupped the wound against the horse's mouth.

"I have no use for such fools' temples," he said, not bothering to look at the other man.

"Fools?" the Arab said, aghast. "I know your names, but who are you to say such things? How many of you are there? Do you journey from the north? Not from Constantinople, surely…?"

"How many of *you*?" Amala said politely, having finished half of the bowl. Though her hunger begged for more, she fought to keep it at bay, as part of her discipline. She offered the bowl to Sihr, who took it and drank quickly.

"Of me, there is only what you see. One of a school of viziers from Constantinople, where we lived peacefully among the Greeks for years, in Michael's 'glorious' shadow. Until, of course, someone foolishly pointed out to the Latins that there was yet a piece of earth they'd left unsullied." The vizier furrowed his brow. "If you're not fleeing, why are you here?"

Finished, Sihr handed the bowl back. Despite her control of a mere moment ago, Amala couldn't resist licking the dregs. Suddenly aware of her weakness, she let the warm liquid rest in her mouth as a test of her endurance. A sudden, bestial surge sent a powerful tingling through her limbs. She shivered visibly to contain it, but finally gave in and swallowed.

"Now I know some of your history, but not your name," Amala said.

"Fajr," he said simply. "And I thank you for your efforts on my behalf."

"Fajr?" Sihr repeated. Amala was surprised to see the grin on the Bedouin's usually expressionless face.

"Yes. Fajr," Fajr said. It meant "dawn."

"You were following the road from Adrianople. How fares that city?" Amala asked.

"Still Greek, barely. Still fearful of Bulgar attacks. I headed north before I reached the city to avoid a large refugee camp. Cainites and their followers, all fleeing Constantinople, gather there. It is said they do so at the behest of Michael's ally, the Nosferatu Malachite. I hear he is, most wisely, not present himself. There is no law, only despair, nightmare and the Beast's rule. For some, I suppose, this is better than remaining in the shell of Constantinople."

"Will you take us to this refugee camp, Fajr?" Amala asked.

He shook his head violently. "No. Didn't you hear? It is the Blazing Fire and Boiling Water! That which breaks to pieces, or any other description of Hell you prefer! What in Allah's name do you think would possess me to go there?"

"Are you still of the Mountain?" she asked.

After some hesitation, he answered, "Yes."

"The Vizier at Alamut gave me something," Amala said. She reached into a pouch at her waist and slipped out a small parchment. Fajr, fearing he already knew what it said, took it and read it quickly. Just as quickly, he handed it back.

"It would be a boon have someone with us who has lived in this land for so long, but I do not want a halfhearted vizier. You're free to part from our company," Amala said, rising to leave.

Fajr stopped her at once. "Do not embarrass me so. I will honor my commitment to my blood. In this quest I am your humble servant, " he said.

"Good," was all Amala said in response.

"Since we are all thus joined, uh… what might our quest be?" Fajr asked.

"We are here, among others of our clan, to ensure the Latins have no immediate plans to move forward into Islamic territory," Amala said. She turned to the sorcerer and added, "Sihr, help Fajr gather his belongings."

Practicing his humility, the sorcerer obeyed. He even, to Amala's surprise, offered to share his mount with the newcomer. Fajr, for his part, adjusted the dials on his astrolabe, checked it against the position of the stars, then directed them slightly farther off the road, promising he would take them on the most direct route.

For the rest of that night and the whole of the following one, they rode. Sihr had reason to regret his gracious offer, since their once relatively silent travels were now marked by an unending series of questions from Fajr. Sihr noted with equal disdain that, whenever they rested, the vizier spent a great deal of time scribbling down notes in handwriting he was at pains to make as small as possible, his store of paper being small. His annoyance with the vizier, however, forced him to speak more often to Amala.

"There is something about him I do not care for," Sihr confided to her in a moment when they were alone. "He has the wasteful mind of a city-dweller, collecting bits of information as if they were things, indiscriminately. How can such a mind ever travel lightly in the world?"

"It can't, I suppose," Amala said. "But in a complicated society, it is difficult to tell what will prove useful."

"That," Sihr explained, "is why I chose the desert."

The sorcerer's distrust grew, until, on the third dusk, his worst suspicions were confirmed. He opened his eyes to see Fajr's hand inching towards the leather backpack that contained Sihr's scant worldly goods.

The sorcerer rubbed his fingers together in a fluid motion. At once, his dagger slipped, of its own accord, out of the scabbard beneath his robe. Untouched by human hand, it sliced into the air, stabbing down to imbed itself in the dirt, in the small space between two of Fajr's fingers.

Fajr gasped, then snapped his gaze towards Sihr, to see the sorcerer glaring at him.

"Please, friend Sihr, you have to understand my curiosity," Fajr offered abjectly. "It's not something I can really control. There are things I just *need* to know. I mean no harm, and what I learn is often quite useful and…"

The sorcerer stared at the sheepishly grinning vizier with pitiless eyes. He let him go on with his babble, until his voice finally trailed off, as if melted into air by Sihr's dark eyes.

"Would it have been worth the loss of your finger?" Sihr asked.

"That depends," Fajr answered truthfully, shrugging, "on what was inside your sack."

Sihr's eyes narrowed in rage. His arm moved as if to complete the slice.

"Sihr!" Amala shouted, now awake as well.

She nodded toward the dagger. Begrudgingly, the tall sorcerer withdrew it by hand, never once losing eye contact with Fajr.

"Thank you," Fajr said, turning to Amala. "He does not understand, he does not realize how totally harmless…"

Amala cut him off. "If you try to take or examine anything of his or mine again, I will not hold him back. In fact, I will join him."

Sihr smiled at that and Fajr made no further incursions into property that was not his. But the Bedouin sorcerer's resentment only grew.

Later that night, a strange stench reached them, and grew steadily stronger as they progressed. When the high walls of Adrianople peeked through the spaces between poplars, Sihr insisted it was the smell of the city, but Amala and Fajr knew it was something far worse. Amala had them stop a half mile away from where Fajr indicated the refugees

46   Assamite

could be found. Leaving the horses and much of their supplies in a small grove, they marched the remaining distance on foot.

Their ears soon filled with barely human howls—fevered prayer, mixed with dying screams and a cackling laughter that verged on tears. There were no defenses to speak of. A mere fifty yards from the perimeter, Amala scaled a tall oak and took in the sorry view.

To call it a camp seemed wrong, since the word implied order. This place was less planned than the helter-skelter wall that had blocked the mountain road. Horses and livestock wandered freely, a few mortal prisoners, hands and ankles tied, stumbled about, hoping to find an edge to the camp from which to flee. Members of the clans that had once thrived in Constantinople were all present, but even these distinctions were muddied by ubiquitous despair. The mass of canvases and cloths insulted into shelters by badly cut branches looked more like refuse. It was a wonder any had survived the daylight, and from the few piles of charred bone and ash that lay beneath fallen shelters, it was clear that some had not.

The carnage did not surprise Amala. *With foes such as this*, she wondered, *why hasn't Islam already conquered the world?*

Chapter Five

May 10, 1204

It was, at best, a world of near-voices; cries and whispers, curses and shouts. Some still used words, but others simply forced air through their vocal chords in a more animal expression of despondency.

"My eyes! My eyes! If I am awake, why do I still see this place?

"Michael comes! He comes! He has not forsaken us!"

"Where is my home, my bed, my pretty statues? Why are my feet so dirty?"

"This hand, is it *mine?*"

"Quiet! All of you! Out of my head or I shall eat you!"

A man in monk's robes whipped himself steadily with a leather strap ending in a small bit of razor-sharp metal. A long-legged woman sat on a rotted log, and, in an effort to blot out her surroundings completely, tried to fold her body in upon itself.

Kosmas Pangalos, who'd never considered himself smart, handsome, or particularly deserving of any more than he had, looked on the scene in sadness from his little half-hidden spot in the hollow of a rotten tree. For the nobles, he thought, it was probably worse, but everyone here was a city creature, used to the statues, gardens, clean lines and magnificent domes of their beloved Constantinople. The wilderness was bewildering, the loss of Michael unbelievable, the lack of prey and comfort nearly intolerable. True, back in the city streets Byzantine Cainites were being slaughtered by the invading Latins, but here, many fell nightly into the deep despondency known as torpor, only, in some instances, to be used as food for the hungry.

In a way, Kosmas thought it all a mere continuation of a downward spiral that had started with his birth. Back in Constantinople, in his days as a kine, Kosmas had been a maker of kettles and other kitchen wares—but even these simple items were of bad construct. So much so, a large part of his day was spent fleeing dissatisfied customers and ducking the bits of cracked iron they hurled. His dark tedium was relieved only by his love of thick-necked women, a penchant that had often proven more trouble than it was worth. That was, until two years prior, when a visiting member of the proud Brujah clan Embraced him, seemingly out of boredom, then left him to learn of his new life on his own.

At first, he'd hoped being a Cainite would change at least the drudgery, but in truth, other than shying from the sun and living on the blood of man rather than the flesh of animals, he'd found little change in his existence. He did recall with some fondness the first time he'd heeded the call of his own Beast and was able to turn the tables on one of those serving wenches who chased him, gleefully plunging his open mouth onto the fat folds of her neck, sucking her nigh unto dry.

When the crusaders came, Kosmas fled because he had no other choice. Now he wondered if he should have stayed closer to the streets he knew so well, rather than take what now seemed another step down.

His ruminations were distracted by an odd sound. An insistent, patterned stamping increased in volume, making itself heard above the camp's din. The sound was followed by the sight of a wagon, drawn by a team of horses, driving into the dissonant landscape of tents and despair.

Kosmas stumbled to his feet for a closer look, only to find himself crowded by curious others. He forced his way past a few ghouls. Kosmas had never seen much use for the human servants, but some kept dozens. At any rate, he had earned a proper view. The wagon was small, its wheels wood slats, banded into circles by iron straps.

Whatever it carried was hidden by an old canvas stiffly folded over the back. The muscular driver, so nervous to be among this group he could barely keep his eyes forward, steered his team toward his best guess at the gathering's center. There, he wheeled the wagon about, carving out a small space in the swelling crowd. The horses, though uneasy, came to a halt.

A tall, languid man, so thin he practically vanished in the folds of his black cape and satin tunic, rose from the passenger seat and achieved an awkward standing position. As he did, he kept one hand wrapped tightly on the canvas that covered the wagon. He tried in vain to raise his voice loud enough to get the attention of all.

Someone used to being obeyed, Kosmas thought. *His dress isn't cheap, either.*

"Who is elder here? Who is prince, or seneschal?" the tall man's whiny voice shouted.

Kosmas smiled. Laughter burst from those near him.

Eyes rolling with annoyance, the newcomer held up a tightly wrapped collection of sticks and twine. After a flurry of activity by his long flat hands, a spark appeared in the torch's center. No mere flame, it soon grew to the size of a baby's head. With a flourish, the newcomer held it above his head.

Ah! A street magician! Kosmas joked with himself. *Perhaps he's come to entertain!*

The light, bright enough to cause discomfort, but cool to the touch, had its intended effect. The shouts and moans quieted to wincing stares. Kosmas noticed that those further off, who'd perhaps originally planned to ignore the newcomer, now moved closer and asked what he had said.

"What do you want?" Kosmas finally shouted at him.

"Who is elder here?" he said again. "Who is your leader?"

"Michael is dead and Malachite gone," someone wailed.

"Who speaks for them in their absence?"

Assamite

Silence. The tall figure nodded grimly.

"Very well. Heed my words and be sure they are repeated so that each and every one of you understands. You are in the territory of Prince Marcus Licinius of Adrianople. I am Cassius, his seneschal, and for these purposes, my word is his. At the moment, *for* the moment, he is willing to consider you guests," he said. "He appreciates the gravity of your situation and asks that you appreciate his. The Latin armies that destroyed Constantinople will soon be here. The mortals of this city are prepared to surrender to them, so that all this will be Latin land."

A pained howl went up from the crowd, as though a single arrow pierced them. Even Kosmas, who'd never had need for politics, felt a pang of fallen pride.

Cassius took to speaking quickly, for fear the pain would morph into anger.

"This is not our doing! That much the mortals have decided. With the Bulgars to our north, the remains of the Byzantine army and Emperor Alexius on the run, it would be suicide to do otherwise. But the sooner order is restored, the sooner we will all be able to move about more freely. For this reason, at this time, the prince is sorely limited in the assistance he can offer. Understand that the longer you remain here, the greater the chance you will be driven from this land, by ignorant kine or some other, less foolish faction. As for the prince, he says that so long as you do not journey within the city, there will be no difficulty between us."

A woman shoved passed Kosmas and screamed the question on everyone's mind: "How then will we feed?"

As if a court magician unveiling a rabbit, Cassius pulled back the canvas that covered the wagon, revealing a cowering woman and her four children. Kosmas's eyes grew wide at the sight, the savage in him stirring, thirsty for blood. He was not alone in this. All who saw the precious cargo shuffled forward, suddenly tugged away from their despair and into the bondage of Cainite hunger.

Kosmas watched, as if outside his own body, as the mother did her best to shield her children. Her worn body was too small to cover them all. Instead, lying in the cart, she executed a sad, writhing dance, first protecting this one, then that. One, a small boy with curly hair and sparkling eyes, had a swollen club foot.

Kosmas was shoved back as the crowd swelled toward the wagon. Unable to keep his balance, he landed on his broad butt in the mud. Others stepped on him as they pressed closer to see. With a roar that came out more like a whine, he struggled back to his feet.

Still visible to all from his perch on the wagon, the prince's representative shouted and waved his arms, trying to hold the hungry refugees' attention, but his premature revelation of the prince's gift made further conversation hopeless. Nevertheless, he dutifully iterated the remainder of his prepared speech. Kosmas, stifled by the crush of more powerful bodies, strained to listen, but caught only a few words: "In exchange for your understanding, recognizing your great need, the prince offers this small repast as a token of his good will."

Before he finished, the crowd was nearly upon the wagon. Kosmas, making some progress forward, heard the children cry. He again caught a glimpse of the wagon, but found himself caught in the middle of a fight between two Cainites on how they were to be divided. As they scuffled, unseen by Kosmas, the seneschal or his driver, others pried off the wagon's rear wheels. The back of the wooden base fell to the floor. The frightened family struggled as gravity rolled their frail forms toward the ground. Kosmas heard the mother bid her young to shut their eyes and pray.

Her plea brought Kosmas up short, and he froze, remembering something of what it meant not to fear the day. Briefly in control of his hunger, and, at any rate, hopelessly outnumbered by his betters, he decided only to watch the dread scene unfold.

Though the wagon's confines offered no real protection, the smallest child could not hold on and soon sprawled at the feet of a stout female from a merchant family. Only months before she'd spent her nights trying to perfect her skills at painting. Now, not believing her good fortune, she was about to throw herself atop the child when a deep, commanding voice burst through the din.

"Stop!"

The euphonious tone was so clear, so unique against the chaotic, clattering backdrop, it left many hearers dazed and spellbound.

"Who dares?" Cassius shouted, but no one was watching him anymore. Kosmas, indeed all, including the women and her children, had turned in the direction of the command's source. Between the patches of dirty browns, grays and blacks that made up the camp's world, mercurial flashes of white cloth and steel floated through the gloom. With the crowd silent, the sound of heavy horses tramping in unison made its way to Kosmas's ears.

The kettle-maker watched the crowd part like water splitting before the prow of a warship. A knight in mail, tall in the saddle, led the group. The crowd continued to make way, in part because of his size, in part because of his majestic bearing, but also, no less, because of the entourage of ten armed knights and forty men-at-arms he led.

Latins? Is that the Templar mantle they wear? Not Cainites then, not in that Order, Kosmas thought as they approached. *This may prove quick, and a bit of a feast.*

Further details supported his conclusion. The knights all wore identical chain mail, carried identical swords with curved hilts and bore identical triangular shields. They also wore white and red mantles, while the men-at-arms wore black with a red eight-pointed cross on the back. Their leader was distinguished from his fellow knights only by his greater size and charismatic demeanor. Clean and disciplined in their movement to the point of appearing ghostly, they stood out like diamonds in the midst of sewage.

The knights quickly encircled the frightened family, forcing the Greek Cainites back as they came. The men-at-arms widened the circle. Their leader, ignoring the increasingly enraged entreaties from Cassius, leapt from his horse. Kosmas caught a glimpse of sharp blue eyes and a square jaw. His wide shoulders and thick arms meant he might well put up a fight even against a Cainite.

But there are so many of us, Kosmas thought with a smile.

Revealing a sudden gentleness, the knight knelt before the smallest child, the one with curly hair and a twisted right foot. It was quiet now, other than the occasional warning from the seneschal, so Kosmas could hear every word.

"Biton?" the knight asked gently, in accented Greek.

Surprised in the deepest possible way, the boy simply stared for a moment then said, "Yes, sir?"

"I am Sir Hugh of Clairvaux. Do you believe in Jesus and his mother, the Queen of Heaven?"

"Yes sir, with all my heart."

"Good. Now I have a very important question for you. Think carefully before you answer. Look around you at these creatures. Whether they know it or not, many have a great gift from the Lord—but it is not a gift that just anyone can handle, or even the only gift God can give. I have that gift as well. We live mostly at night, but we are very strong, can do amazing things and seldom do we grow sick or die. Do you wish for you and your family to become like us or our servants?"

We? Kosmas thought. *Could he be one of us?*

The mother moved to silence the boy, but a sharp glance from Sir Hugh kept her still. The boy made a terrific effort to appear as if he were genuinely debating the offer, but, having been at the refugee camp for over ten minutes now, the answer was simple.

"No, sir," he answered, shaking his head.

"Very well," the knight said softly. Sir Hugh stood and turned to one of the mounted knights, a man with black oily locks, nearly as tall and slightly wider than he.

"Gondemar, see them back to our camp. Give them food, water, whatever else they request and whatever else they might desire. They are now our guests and will enjoy both our protection and our good will," he said. He spoke loudly, so that even those farther back in the crowd could hear.

Which means we shouldn't touch them, Kosmas thought. *Who does he think he is?* Though he found himself, in spite of his need, a bit pleased that the family had been saved.

Gondemar lifted a thick hand and held up four fingers. Three knights immediately slipped off their horses. Gondemar glared, a fearful fire suddenly rising in his sleepy eyes. Reluctantly, the fourth knight dismounted as well and helped the others gingerly lift the frightened family up onto their steeds.

Whatever the disagreement, as Gondemar trotted slowly out of the circle, all four followed. Though the crowd did not quite part as it had for Hugh, no one moved to stop them. Kosmas was beginning to feel as if he were somehow privileged to be present, watching something special unfold.

The whiny voice of the seneschal, Cassius, reminded the crowd of his presence. "Who dares?"

The seneschal made a slight move toward the receding group of horses, as if he might order that they be stopped, but Sir Hugh quickly stepped up to him.

Gritting his teeth, Cassius hissed again, leaving a wide space between each accented word: "I said, who dares?"

"I am Brother Hugh of Clairvaux," he answered, "of the Temple. In exchange for his service, I swore to their father his family would be protected. He performed his part of the agreement, now I perform mine. Or has the lack of law now spread even to Adrianople?"

"Sir, it has not," the seneschal said with a sharp nod. "At least not yet. But, as you may have noticed, the good people here are terribly hungry and disturbed to have even this slight meal taken from them. What is it you propose they eat, Hugh of Clairvaux?"

A good question! You tell this Latin bastard! Kosmas cheered inwardly. He heard grunts of agreement from the crowd.

Sir Hugh held up the index finger of his gloved right hand. His eyes scanned the crowd. Kosmas followed his gaze. Everyone, as far as could be seen, was either listening, or repeating the conversation in whispers to those at the crowd's fringes. The young family, already near the ill-defined edges of the camp, were now ignored by all save Hugh's men. Kosmas turned back to the knight in time to see him raise his hand high in the air and snap it into a fist.

There was another rush of activity. A tightly formed group of men-at-arms came tramping down a nearby hill, leading twenty barefoot male prisoners, tied waist to waist, toward the circle Hugh's remaining knights still formed. The hooded prisoners were exhausted, but not so tired that they missed the smell of their own impending death. Afraid, struggling against their bonds, but held in check by the Templar sergeants' spears, they required more than a little prodding to enter the circle.

"I give you the rapists, robbers and highwaymen we encountered on our way here. Some are Greeks like yourselves, others Latins like myself. In any case, I assure you they have turned their back on the Lord Jesus, and so bid you do with them as you will," Hugh said.

Not needing to hear more, Kosmas leapt, and found himself carried aloft by the crowd as it tumbled forward, a pent-up ocean enjoying sudden release. Without even an audible command from their master, Hugh's men returned to a marching order, abandoning the prisoners. As Kosmas's teeth found the calf of a hairy leg and its salty juice flooded his mouth, he caught a few whispers from the others, a sound not unlike the rustling of dead, dry leaves in the wind.

"Michael! Michael!" they said, in tones both aghast and bedazzled.

The only one unimpressed was Cassius, the thwarted seneschal, who eyed Sir Hugh with great disdain.

***

Amala and her companions, motionless as the rough-barked trunks of the gangly older trees that surrounded them as they faded back into view, had also taken in with rapt attention every detail of what had transpired. Fajr immediately began furiously scribbling notes in tiny letters. They'd spent a few days in the camp with little to show for it and were about to move on when Sir Hugh had arrived.

As the refugees shuffled back to their sad makeshift hovels to discuss at length the evening's events, and Sir Hugh vanished beyond a hill, the trio became convinced they were once more alone and it was safe to speak.

"He played the crowd. He seeks an audience. What could that Latin Ventrue want with these Greeks?" Fajr said.

"Your appraisal, sorcerer?" Amala asked Sihr. While his experience was written in the deep lines of his black face, his thoughts were not.

"We should enter their camp and kill the Ventrue Templar tonight," Sihr whispered. Seeing this did not elicit the expected agreement, he quickly added, "All the Templars, if possible."

"But there are so many questions!" Fajr objected.

The tall man's shoulders slowly shrugged. "The questions will die with them."

"But why kill them?" Amala asked.

Before he could get over his surprise at the question, Amala smoothly scaled the nearest tree trunk in an attempt to see where Sir Hugh had headed.

"He's a Templar. They're enemies of the faithful. Their Order is obviously riddled with Ventrue and other Frankish vampires, the enemies of Alamut. Isn't that enough?" the sorcerer boomed up after her, barely able to soften his voice. "His Order exists to slaughter our people. Am I not correct, Fajr?"

Fajr, still busy with his writing, nodded. "In that much, at least."

Amala narrowed her eyes and scanned the web of branches. A few dull yellow glows to the east gave away the Templar camp. Not a huge space. She estimated that Hugh had brought, if not all, then the vast majority of his men with him into the camp, as a show of force. Still, even ten Cainite knights was a formidable number.

She turned downwards and looked at the hooded top of Sihr's head, pleased for once to be taller than he.

"Kill him now, and you do not learn his intent, or that of his masters," she explained.

"That one is his own master," Sihr objected. "You saw how he commanded the crowd."

Fajr looked up from his writing long enough to disagree. "That crowd would follow a talking toad. That's the thing about government, you never really appreciate it until it's gone."

"Sihr Haddad," she said. "Surely you know it's not enough simply to kill someone. You also have to find the right person to kill. Who knows what forces may be behind him? Killing him might just as easily provoke an assault on Muslim lands. Another reason I want to learn what he intends to do with these refugees."

"Very well," the sorcerer conceded, but his displeased expression communicated the depth of his growing doubts. Amala regarded his silence with concern. If deeply convinced he should act, Sihr could prove difficult to stop. A chuckle from Fajr broke the tense silence.

"Marvelous," Fajr clucked. "We shall have to have a plan. I love plans."

Wordless, Amala turned her head back toward the refugee camp and watched, impressed at the effect the knight was already having on the Greeks.

Among them, Kosmas Pangalos, an oddly light feeling filling his chest, muttered the words of Sir Hugh to himself over and over, as best he could recall, trying to lower his voice an octave in imitation. Then, along with some others, for no reason that could be named, he began to tidy up what he could of his small area of the vast, and still growing, camp.

Chapter Six

Fingering the rough cloth of his disguise, Sir Thaddeus Abelard, a second squire in the Order of the Bitter Ashes, remained half in the shadows of the marble colonnade that lined one wall of the lush room, fighting to conceal his disdain at the bloody feast. Here in Adrianople, the impending arrival of the Latin armies had engendered a false bravado on both sides of the mortal veil, and this dark bacchanalia was but one result. Outside, Abelard had witnessed nobles, merchants and craftsmen scurry about in a fervent imitation of normalcy. Here, in the main hall of a vast noble house, the Cainite Prince Licinius was likewise bent on pretending that he and his power remained untouched by the groaning of men's machinations.

Blood, from willing participants and frightened captives alike, flowed freely, tugging at the hunger that divided Abelard's soul. He'd been careful to arrive well fed, however, so he felt mostly uncomfortable at a largess his devoutly chivalric mind saw as bordering on animalism.

Despite his disdain, there was much Abelard admired about Licinius. In the days prior to the Fourth Crusade, the Roman Lasombra had studiously avoided allying himself with any faction, waiting to see how mortal events played out. While he had sympathy for the Latins, his true allegiance lay with any force that would keep Islam at bay. His great fear was not occupation by the current conquerors, but that the Muslim tide would grow to destroy commerce on the Mediterranean æ and thus his own connection to the wider Cainite world.

But the prince and his fate were not what brought Abelard here. It was instead his strange guest, the Ventrue Templar, Sir Hugh of Clairvaux, whose performance at the refugee camp the previous night was fast becoming the stuff of legend. Already this evening Sir Hugh had caused a flurry of talk by refusing to recline on one of the many comfortable couches, insisting instead on a simple wooden chair. The five knights that accompanied him refused to sit at all. Abelard felt a sense of camaraderie with them, noting their uneasiness in the face of these orgiastic excesses.

He willed the slight pleasure to his lips as a smile, meant for those nearby to see. Members of his Order traveled incognito, and his masquerade as a Cainite monk had been hastily assembled. He might yet be taken for one of the desperate refugees and ejected. They could even seek to punish him, and the results of such a conflict, though Abelard was certain he would prevail, would be terribly unfortunate. As such, he wanted as little attention as possible, no matter what he was forced to watch. He concentrated on the scene, hoping that any gaze that happened upon him would be deflected to what he watched.

Servants moved about with effortless courtesy, seeing to the needs of the city's collected Cainites. They wore their finest clothes and lay lazily back on couches and plush chairs in emulation of their leader's stance. They whispered their dry opinions as if life were a play they'd already seen.

This, Abelard knew, was show. The Templar, with his worn armor and dulled sword, with his scars earned ages ago when such things were still possible, had yet to state his purpose. That issue still hanging made true relaxation impractical and the charade of calm superiority all the more necessary.

The prince leaned languorously back on his deep, cushioned couch as if the very end of the world would be, at worst, an inconvenience. He held the rim of a ruby-studded goblet in manicured fingers and absently swirled its dark red contents. When a few strands of his long black hair lazily fell in front of his right eye, he tossed them back with a quick shake of his head, then returned his laconic gaze to the curious Templar who had dared interfere with his seneschal.

"We speak firstly to all those who secretly despise their own will, and desire with a pure heart to serve the sovereign king as a knight. Isn't that how the beginning of your Order's Rule goes?" Marcus Licinius asked.

Abelard nearly gasped at the mocking tone, and was quite surprised when Sir Hugh simply nodded, not showing offense if any had been taken.

"But, Sir Hugh, what is there to despise about desire? Does not its pursuit form the very fulcrum of existence, at least of ours?" the prince said, smiling.

"God is the fulcrum of existence. He exists beyond desire, and to find Him, so must we," Hugh answered. There were a few titters from the crowd before they realized he was serious.

He wants something from Licinius, and is taking pains not to offend, yet feels compelled to stand his ground, Abelard noted. *Licinius, for his part, feels the need to humble him.*

With the two at cross-purposes, it would be a courtly contest of words. Abelard had witnessed these before. Civil though the proceedings might appear, the verbal spars were always in danger of eroding into frenzy should one or another contestant, too slighted or too cornered, lose himself to the Beast. In part, it was a delicate effort to goad the opponent into losing control, but not too much control. Sir Hugh and Licinius were both leaders, more practiced than many Cainites in burying their darker urges for the sake of strategy. It would be interesting to see who prevailed. Abelard favored the far older Licinius. It was after all, his home, his court, and Hugh was here not only as a visitor, but one who had offended the Cainite sense of order by countermanding the prince's will in his own territory.

"I'm terribly impressed," Licinius said, changing the subject slightly, "that so many Ventrue serve in any of the military orders, let alone the Templars. After all, the Church of Rome considers us Satan-spawn, so your glorious nature must remain concealed. How do you deal with the daily prayers? The rituals, rites and obligations that must inevitably be followed when the burning sun is high in the sky? To say nothing of the battles. Would not your failure to show with your arms to fight at dawn brand you a coward among the kine?"

"We make adjustments, and truth to tell, the greater number of us serve in lesser functions: night guards, scouts, messengers," Hugh answered.

Marcus Licinius rolled himself into a seated position to bring his head a bit closer to his strange guest. "Yes, but, not *you*, Sir Hugh. You are no guard, scout or messenger. You claim to be a Templar master, in charge of your own manor house."

"That I am, of a single banner of loyal knights who dwell, when we are able, in a small but devout castle on an island southwest of Tripoli," Hugh answered.

"And please, pray tell my court, how did that minor miracle come about?"

Hugh shifted a bit and furrowed his brow.

"It's a lengthy tale."

The prince glanced at the moon through a large eastern window. It hung high in the sky, above the mists, in a clean heaven just above the city's mountainous walls.

"The night is a child," Licinius said. "There is time for a lengthy tale."

"Very well. During the difficulties besetting Outremer that led to the battle of Hattin and the Holy City's loss to Salah ad-Din, I was but a scout, without ambition. Owing to our proclivities, myself and a small number of my men managed to infiltrate the Muslim camps, providing intelligence to our superiors. My team and I were on a mission when battle was met, returning only in time to watch our fellows slaughtered by Sufi holy men. Through our efforts, by night, we managed to free some from their clutches, and take a small revenge. To answer your first question, as a result of these battles, through the kind machinations of other Ventrue Templar, including my sire, Sir Geoffrey, I became master of a small group now known for and called upon with some regularity, to perform missions of a discreet nature. That status, coupled with our physical distance from the other houses, has enabled us to function freely in His service."

Abelard marveled at the rapt attention Hugh's words elicited from a crowd that had little reason to sympathize with him. *His natural charisma is powerful, suspiciously so. And Licinius isn't getting the humility he wants. He'll become more aggressive now.*

"My, my. Running about in shadows, contemplating assassination, secret missions. You sound more like Assamite murderers than Templars. Perhaps your Order *has* spent too much time among the Saracens," Licinius offered, narrowing his eyes. Remembering themselves, his entourage cackled.

"I respect any foe that in a mere few hundred years has hollowed out the Byzantine Empire," Hugh said.

The prince attacks the Templars, Sir Hugh responds with an attack on Byzantium. In a Latin crowd that would play well, but does Hugh forget where he is? Licinius has found his weakness.

The prince smiled. "So your respect extends to the dread Assamites, who attack our kind from the shadows and feed on our blood with impunity?"

"Perhaps especially," Hugh said. "You've said the word twice now and each time there has been fear in your voice. I would be greatly pleased if the Saracens spoke of the Templars the same way."

"Was there fear? Interesting. I was not aware of it. But tell me, how do you reconcile that respect with your faith?"

"There is no contradiction. In their faith they are deceived. I hope only to bring them to the True God. Alive or dead," Hugh said. A few laughs came from the nobles.

Licinius quickly waved them to silence. "I would just as soon have them burn in any number of their Islamic hells," Licinius said. "Respect for such as they is beneath us."

"It is not wise to underestimate your enemies."

"How does the lion underestimate the mouse?"

"By growing lazy and allowing it to breed until even the great cat is overwhelmed."

Licinius said, "I see no difference between one mouse and a hundred."

Hugh shrugged. "Perhaps that explains, in part, why it was here in your fair city the Goths first bested Rome."

Abelard was shocked. A stunned silence permeated the assembly. Hugh's knights reached for the hilts of their swords.

What is he thinking, bringing up the city's shame at having been the lynchpin of the Western empire's fall? Licinius has killed for less.

Clearly angry, the prince remained motionless for a time, then finally sucked some coagulated vitae from between his teeth and swallowed before speaking. "I'll forgive you that one slight, Sir Hugh, because you are so young."

What? Abelard thought, surprised that the response was not far more grave. Then he realized what he had seen. *I've been a fool, misreading the game completely. Licinius is at the true disadvantage. To move against a Latin now, with their armies approaching, could end up costing him his throne.*

Stefan Petrucha   65

"I was born in 1145 and Embraced in 1179," Hugh said plainly, being careful not to thank the prince for his forgiveness.

"Yes, and it might be wise for you to realize that what power you possess has more to do with the strength of your blood and your sire's status than with your own experience."

Hugh nodded, "Might I ask, how old is the prince?"

Licinius smiled. "Let's just say that I've always considered Constantine's capital to be a passing fancy. I seem, in fact, to have been proven right."

A few laughs and a round of applause from the crowd put things at an awkward ease once more. Licinius swept his hair back and tried again to appear kind.

"You must understand, I'm teasing, friend Hugh, and further, it is my prerogative to do so. Having heard of your treatment of my seneschal at the camp, you seemed to require some humbling. But I have no wish to truly insult or harm you. Already you do me service by quieting the vast mess forming in my lands. And I am eager to hear what more you have in mind. But before that, your refusal to take our food, our women, or otherwise enjoy the comfort of our home, while it may indeed be part of your austerity oath, displeases us no end. Please, let me express my good will to you by doing something for your pleasure. A token. Take a drink at least."

As if out of thin air, a goblet full of warm blood, similar in design to the prince's own, appeared near Hugh's head, in the steady hands of a servant. Hugh glanced nervously around, then accepted the drink. The moment the warm liquid touched his tongue, he swallowed greedily. As the blood flushed to his extremities, a drunken smile formed on his face and he drained the glass without delay. This sign of physical pleasure from their stoic visitor elicited some good-natured laughs from the assembled throng. Lesser silver goblets were given to his men.

Abelard felt some of the tension flow out of the room. *Having shown his strength, Sir Hugh shows himself to be one of them.*

"There, accepting a kindness is not so terrible," the prince said, still smiling. "I would give you bed and a room here as well, but your oath demands you refuse, does it not?"

Hugh nodded.

The prince's voice lost its theatrical tone and took on a more intimate, though equally practiced, timbre. Abelard had to move forward in order to hear.

"As much as I am sympathetic to their plight, as much as we are all deeply, deeply wounded by both the loss of Michael and our sweet sister Constantinople, what can I do? The sheer number of these refugees, so close to my domain, attracts attention at a time when attention is not a desirable thing. What's worse, they are disorganized, in their numbers and within themselves. One might as well converse with rain, and I do not care to debate the weather. I find you, on the other hand, though untamed in some respects, at least able to respond. Disregarding your earlier disrespect, I would learn of your plans here."

"Very well," Hugh began softly. "The latest crusade turned to hell when it abandoned its original purpose. The righteous must now steer their swords true. My men will be with me, and I daresay there will be many among the refugees more than willing to loosen at last their ties to a lost dream in exchange for His True Kingdom. Do you follow me, Licinius?"

"You propose leading your own crusade?" Licinius said, aghast. "Do your Templar masters know of this?"

This man is mad. Abelard thought, shaking his head. *There is nothing more to be said for it.*

"Innocent III, patriarch of Rome, is the Templars' true commander. His desire to recapture the Holy City has already been made plain. I consider that all the directive I require," Hugh said.

Licinius regarded the odd, curly-haired creature before him, unable to decide if Hugh were a mere fool deluded by an infantile grasp of hollow ideals that time would destroy, or some sort of mythical beast that had no place whatsoever in the world.

Hugh waited, an uncharacteristic, child-like uncertainty manifesting on his features. Suddenly, Licinius placed a reassuring hand on his shoulder as he said, "Friend, Hugh, I am grateful to announce that we share two purposes, both near and dear to my heart! First, the removal, uh… let us say the *redirecting* of our fellows, then an assault on the heart of all our problems, the cursed Muslims! To this end, you shall have whatever help I can muster."

Hugh appeared genuinely surprised and gratified by the prince's response.

"Anything that stems the Muslim tide," Licinius beamed. "Anything at all."

Hugh fell to his knees, clutched his hand to his chest, and looked up at the prince. "My thanks, great sir," he said.

"Think nothing of it, good Sir Hugh," the prince responded, barely able to keep from chuckling.

All slights forgotten, the assembled group, well fed and entertained, fell to talking as more fresh drink was supplied, both in goblet and in vein. After a suitable time passed, Abelard moved out from the row of colonnades and drifted toward Sir Hugh. The knight had been uncomfortably cornered by a squat noblewoman whose face was covered in makeup and whose round form was covered in gaudy orange satin robes whose expense far outweighed either their usefulness or their beauty.

"How *does* one kill an Assamite?" she purred.

Abelard stepped close to the conversation, hoping to be taken by anyone watching for one of the knight's familiars. If things went as he predicted, Sir Hugh would not give him away. Before the woman could speak again, he tilted his head sideways towards Hugh's ears and spoke in a whisper.

"I know of the Mandylion," Abelard said. "I know your Templars have it."

Hugh stiffened. Though across the room, Gondemar veered sharply towards his sire, as if the connection between them had no need for words or physical proximity.

"No harm, good Sir Hugh," Abelard reassured him. "Come for a walk through the city with me, so we may talk in private. There is no danger from me, but bring two of your men if it pleases you."

Wary, Hugh signaled Gondemar, who raised two fingers on his right hand, indicating at once exactly which two would be charged with keeping watch on Sir Hugh. Occupied with his flock, the prince barely noticed as Hugh and Abelard made their way to the stone arch that led to the front entrance hall. The two chosen knights fell in behind, keeping a respectful, but watchful, distance.

Abelard led Hugh in the evening air as they strolled the centuries-old Roman streets, rich with religious complexes both Christian and pagan, strong stone bridges, old bazaars, caravanserais and palaces. A fog had rolled in, lending the city a pleasingly supernatural air.

Once certain they were alone, Hugh, still stiff and prepared for a fight said, "Who are you? And of what concern to you is the holy shroud?"

"I am Sir Thaddeus Abelard of the Bitter Ashes. Do you know of our Order?"

Hugh's eyes went briefly wide. "I know you collect and preserve holy relics. If you have any designs on the Mandylion, then know it is no longer in my possession, but in the care of the Templar Order...."

Abelard raised his hands in supplication, "And there my Order is more than content that it remain. We modeled ourselves on the noble Templars, after all."

"Why are you here, then?" Hugh said, still not relaxing his guard.

Stefan Petrucha   69

He spoke softly, in an effort to soothe. "Perhaps you know that, in addition to seeing to the safety of such relics, it is also our mission to offer spiritual guidance to those who bear Caine's mark, whether it be to aid them in their battle against the devil within or without, or, should their condition be too much to bear, to help them find the strength to meet the day," Abelard said. "I am here to offer counsel."

"Ah," Hugh said, nodding. "Thank you, brother, but I have other counsel I keep." He turned away, expecting the conversation to be over, but Abelard called to him.

"Of what nature, Sir Hugh?"

Hugh wheeled back just long enough to say, "A private one."

At first the ashen knight thought to let it end there, but there was something forlorn about Sir Hugh's figure as it stepped away.

Mad or no, my oaths forbid I let him go like this, Abelard reasoned. He stepped quickly up to Sir Hugh and blocked his path.

"I heard your plans to begin a new crusade. The road between desire and reality is long and hard. How do you propose to make the journey?"

Talk to me.

Hugh studied the lines in his face, trying to decide something. "Someone should know of this. Someone should endeavor to understand. Very well, I shall try."

Their walk continued across a long Roman bridge that spanned the river Maritsa. There they paused as Hugh's gaze wandered out over the flowing water.

"Abelard, you know of the shroud?"

"I do. And how the face upon it formed the basis for every image of the Lord in all Byzantium. Did you touch it?"

"Yes," Hugh answered, sadly. "It burned me and has yet to heal."

"May I see the wound?" Abelard asked.

Hugh was taken aback, but seeing what he thought was sincerity in Abelard's eyes he acquiesced and removed his glove. Two smooth spots on his index and middle fingers indicated where the relic had graced his hand. Hugh wasn't sure whether the wounds were permanent, or if, desirous to keep them as a prize, he'd simply willed them not to heal.

Suddenly, Abelard lurched to his knees, grabbed Hugh's hands and pressed the Templar's fingers into his forehead. There was a hiss as Abelard's face contorted. He closed his eyes, strained, but ultimately pulled away, a blissful look on his face. Hugh did not move.

Perhaps he is not mad, Abelard thought, rising. *Or perhaps madness is not always an end to things. Once Rome itself was mere madness.*

"Even God's pain is a blessing," Abelard said, smiling. They locked eyes for a moment as a mutual faith passed between them.

"You believe in God, then, Abelard?"

"Of course," he answered.

Hugh slipped the glove back on and smiled a strange little smile.

"What if I told you that of late I enjoyed a very specific relation to the divine? Would you entertain at least the possibility?"

Abelard shrugged. "I have seen many things I do not understand. That certainly does not make them false. When God wills it, my understanding will come."

Hugh smiled. "Perhaps then, it's appropriate that you be the first to hear of the source of my glorious purpose. I am a servant of Christ, blessed with the blood of Caine to fulfill His will, but I never felt His touch, or knew His will so clearly as I did in the Church of the Apostles, when the Queen of Heaven herself appeared and filled me with purpose most divine."

"The Virgin Mother?" Abelard was aghast, and found himself tumbling back to his original assessment of the Templar.

Hugh's voice grew distant as his meager language struggled to convey an experience unequalled in his life. "She was as a stone aflame, and spoke with a voice at once as gentle as the flapping of an eagle's wings, and as strong as the rush of a thousand rivers. In all her glory she came to me, all things within her, the vault of heaven, the firmament, and all the beasts and men therein, including myself. Outside her, alone, I was but as an insect. And then, entering me as a man might his wife, she deigned to mix her essence with my own."

"Are *you* divine, then?" Abelard asked cautiously. *Perhaps he should be destroyed.*

Hugh shook his head, "Michael's sin, not mine. I am but the vessel for a truth placed within me by a far, far greater hand. Nightly she comes to me now, filling my dreams with such sweet energies that they rival the world for my full attention. Can you understand this, Sir Abelard?"

"I understand your passion, Sir Hugh. But surely you understand that astounding claims require astounding verification," Abelard said.

Hugh nodded, clearly disappointed his revelation had not been met with immediate acclaim.

"I did not say that I do not believe you, Sir Hugh," Abelard quickly added, putting his hand on the knight's shoulder for comfort's sake. "What a great burden this must be for you to bear alone."

"It has been," Sir Hugh said.

He is open to me now. I cannot abandon him.

"There are certain oracles my Order has access to. With your permission, I will consult them on your visions. Should they prove true, this would be glorious news indeed, yet should they prove the false shading of some demon…"

"The visions are not false," Hugh said, gritting his teeth, as angry now as he had been vulnerable a moment ago. Immediately, Abelard raised his palms again.

"Then the oracles will confirm them. Perhaps even the Order of the Bitter Ashes will be compelled to join your crusade." He knew this was highly unlikely, whatever the oracles might say, but wanted Hugh to see the potential for help.

"Their assistance would be a great boon," Hugh said.

"Then let me help you," Abelard urged. He watched the knight's face, confident he would soon have his agreement, but then a haze of shifting dirt in the river, as if something were disturbing the soil below the water, caught his eye. Scanning the river, Abelard again thought he caught a glimpse of movement. No sooner had he furrowed his brow, however, than the brief silence was insulted by the high-pitched shriek of a female voice.

"*Shoef!*" it cried.

Though Abelard did not speak Arabic, Hugh did, and instantly drew his sword.

From the rooftop of a nearby warehouse, a shrieking female figure pointed frantically to the dark river waters. Before Abelard could ask what had been said, one of Hugh's men leapt forward. As he did, a crossbow bolt caught him in the shoulder, piercing his chain mail. In seconds, he fell to the ground in a sickly sweat.

"Poison," Hugh said.

Abelard noted there'd been no rush of air accompanying the bolt. He recalled tales of Assamites being able to strike in absolute silence.

Hugh searched the river for the source of the attack. There, perhaps ten yards from where they stood, a black mass had surfaced. The moment Hugh saw it, before he could tell if it were man or woman, the figure turned to dive beneath the surface again. Abelard marveled at the knight's prowess as he, without even thinking to shed his armor, snarled and leapt into the river. The attacker was already little more than a swelling in the water's surface, rolling quickly downstream, but undaunted, Hugh swam after him, and, as far as Abelard could tell, was catching up.

The stamping of feet turned Abelard back to the street. Ten of Licinius's armed men, who'd been following discreetly all along, burst on the scene. Out of a combination of general concern, and a desire not to be asked many questions, Abelard knelt down by the felled Templar. The second knight had already rushed to his aid and was pulling the bolt from the man's shoulder. Staring at the wet tip, he regarded the mix of blood and black viscous substance that covered it, then gave it a quick sniff. He then looked at his brother knight's shoulder wound.

"Rest easy, Brother Appeles," the second Templar said. "It seems the Saracens wish you to sleep a while. Your strength will return shortly, I think." He reached for a tincture carried in a small pouch by his side, then poured some liquid into the wound. The fallen knight moaned as the medicine bubbled on the open hole in his shoulder. As the wound sealed, he gave himself up to unconsciousness.

"Assamites use a variety of blood-poisons on their weapons," the Templar explained to Abelard. "I have experience with this variety—it saps the strength, but a hardy soul like Appeles will recover with proper care."

They care well for one another, Abelard thought, reminded of his own Order.

Hugh's head burst from the surface, a hundred yards downstream. His prey had escaped, but now his thoughts were elsewhere. "We were warned!" he shouted. "Find the woman!"

At the sound of his voice, all eyes turned back to the rooftop, where, next to their mysterious female ally, another dark figure appeared. This one, scimitar in hand, was slicing so deeply, quickly and deftly into her abdomen that the woman didn't have the time or the energy to cry out. Spitting, the figure kicked her off the roof's edge, then dashed off. Licinius's guards hurried after the attacker, leaving the woman behind.

Hugh pulled himself from the ebon waters and raced up to the fallen woman. Comfortable that the fallen knight was in good hands, Abelard followed. The woman's skin was dark, but not terribly so. Despite the inexpensive green cloth of her peasant tunic, Byzantine in make, her round head bore delicate features unlikely to belong to any peasant. Though clearly an Arab, she wore no veil. Her insulted torso had been all but disemboweled with a peculiar pattern of cuts. A mortal would already be dead, but the woman was Cainite, as evidenced by her body's twitching efforts to heal itself. Without help, she would not die, but the near-death sleep of deepest torpor would soon result.

"*Banu Haqim*," Hugh said, using the Arabic term. "The pattern of strikes is theirs alone." Then, fearing Abelard did not understand, he added, "Assamites."

Abelard nodded. "Your reputation grows."

"Assamites need no new reason to attack Templars. My head or the head of any of my men would prove a great prize. I'm only sorry to have brought such discomfort within the walls of Adrianople." Hugh glanced around and took in his man, as well as Licinius's guards. "I can tell by the look of concern on my man's face that he, like myself, thinks it wisest we withdraw for now."

Hugh moved to lift the wounded woman. "Perhaps we can learn more, or at least offer her thanks."

"And regarding the matter of which we spoke?" Abelard asked.

Hugh nodded. "Consult your oracles. I look forward to hearing what light they may shed."

Abelard smiled. *There is hope for him yet.*

He was about to leave, but as Hugh lifted the woman, he saw a small doll, the relic of a childhood not quite yet forgotten, tumble from the folds of her tunic. It was a crude construction, poorly sewn, stuffed with grain, with a second piece of darker cloth fashioned into a crude dress. Her face was mostly black dye, save for two small ebon stones that formed the eyes. Hugh nodded toward it, and Abelard scooped it from the earth and placed it in the knight's free hand.

Abelard watched as Hugh walked off, carrying the girl, while the other Templar followed, carrying their still unconscious comrade.

"I will pray for you, Sir Hugh of Clairvaux," Abelard called after him.

"And I for you," Hugh answered back.

***

Outside the city walls, far from the refugee camp, in a patch of poplars, the ashen knight found his clothes and armor exactly where he had left them. He shook off the monk's habit he'd worn as a disguise, looking forward to feeling the familiar protection of his mail. Still, Sir Hugh was vexing him. Strong and devout, the Templar might one day prove a candidate for the Order of the Bitter Ashes, provided these false visions were put to rest. Then again, there was always the possibility that the Blessed Mother had deigned at last to speak to, and through, a Cainite, in which case, Sir Hugh was already locked on a divine course.

What a marvel that would be!

Ultimately unable to decide whether Sir Hugh's visions could possibly be real, Abelard longed to hear what his oracular elders would say, and hoped he would not look foolish before his fellows.

Naked now, a sudden feeling of emptiness reminded his hunger of the ruby feast he'd witnessed, and exactly how long it had been since he'd fed. He was days away from his own camp and the willing human providers who waited there. Feeding in the city or the camp now would be both pointless and reckless, so he decided instead to do as he had many times before, and contain the hunger through prayer.

Without his armor, Abelard's knees found the soft, leaf-covered earth. He clasped his hands and let his vision blur as he turned himself within.

"Holy Mother, I pray, look upon your humble servant in his time of need and provide me with the fortitude to still these restless urges...."

Holy Mother? It is my habit to pray to Jesus for strength. This Templar Hugh has invaded my thoughts more than I guessed.

He shook the idea clear and meant to return to his meditation, but then, as if in answer, a ghostly figure appeared among the trees' stiff white lines. At first he took it for one of the poplars, but it moved, and, despite its sheer whiteness, bore the features of a woman. The Grail Knights, those blessed beings of his own Order allowed to sup from the holy cup, acquired such an angelic countenance. Could it be?

"Who are you, phantom?" Abelard asked.

"I am Mary," it hissed.

"You are not," he knew at once. Abelard stumbled for his sword, but she'd already reached him, flying, head first, across the distance between them until their faces were inches apart.

A cloud of grotesque humors rushed from her skeletal mouth, a wind of plague, infesting the ashen knight's mouth, throat and lungs. As he made himself cough in a feeble effort to dispel the cloud, he caught of glimpse of the creature that attacked him, standing back and giggling.

The hunger his prayers had meant to contain now welled to the fore unbidden. Snarling, he lurched forward. He only realized how weak he had become when his legs fell out from under him and he found himself staring at moss-covered leaves. Raising his head, he saw her, still smiling, as she shook her head, "No," as if with that gesture she were providing the answer to any question he'd ever had.

Strength fled his muscles. Faith in the Lord fled like a thief in the night. Even his rampaging craving, which once he'd likened to Satan, grew distant and small.

When he lowered his head again, from weakness, from despair, he heard the leaves rustle as she stepped slowly forward to claim him as prize. Eyes closed, he felt her bony, gumless teeth find his neck, but by then could not bring himself to care at all. Sir Hugh, the Order of the Bitter Ashes, and the world would have to do without him. His only regret was that he'd never found the strength to face the sun one last time before his final death.

Chapter Seven

A strong hand, not used to being gentle, grasped and shook her shoulder. "Back with us yet?" a calm mellifluous voice asked in Latin.

In response, she mumbled something in Arabic. Even she wasn't sure what it was.

"Can you hear me? Are you awake?" the voice said again, now speaking, though with light difficulty, in her native tongue.

After a valiant effort, she opened her eyes all the way. Her reward was the image of a brawny man hovering over her, dark-haired, square-jawed and powerful in limb. He was dressed in chain mail covered with the mantle of a Templar. She recognized him.

"You speak Arabic?" she answered, whereupon she realized how dry her throat was, and coughed. The cough made her aware of her body again. There was a sharp pain in her abdomen, where the longer, deeper scimitar gashes had not yet healed. Sir Hugh leaned forward and, cradling her head in one hand, pressed a wooden cup to her lips with the other. She took the few tiny sips within, then scrunched her face in a slight scowl that there was no more.

"You'll have to forgive us if we don't quite trust you enough yet to supply you with any more than the blood your body needs to heal," Hugh said evenly.

She nodded, understanding. As more of the tent came into focus, she saw a second figure by the entrance. Slightly shorter, but far more grim, he turned angrily toward her and she tensed involuntarily, knowing him as well.

"As Templars we've learned many things about our enemies, at the cost of our lives and our fellows. The Arabic language is just one. The prodigious ability of the Assamites to disguise themselves is another," Sir Gondemar said sternly.

He looks stupid, but he's not. Remember that, she thought.

Methodically setting the cup at the exact center of an upended crate, Hugh settled back on a small wooden stool and clasped his hands. Patiently, he watched as she further took in her surroundings. She was naked, laid out on a soft bed of leaves topped by a rough olive-colored cloth, her modesty shielded by an equally rough blanket. They were in a fairly large but spartan tent. To the side were a few small crates doubling as tables. One had a pile of crude, bloodstained cloth on it that she recognized as her rumpled peasant tunic. Another, near her head, supported an oil lamp. A plain wooden crucifix hung on one wall—and that was all.

"You're in a Templar camp," Hugh confirmed.

"But you are Cainite," she said, her voice a bit stronger now. As she tried to lift her head, she moaned.

"We are with the Lord and, like you, enjoy His special mark," Hugh said, as if that were explanation enough.

"And you?" Gondemar asked abruptly. "Are you Muslim?"

She shook her head firmly and said, "Christian."

"Of what blood?"

Give him the story, she advised herself, *as quickly as possible, so he can either accept it or raise his questions now.*

"Brujah. I was Embraced in the year 1102 and lived for many years near Galilee."

"Not far from Outremer at the time of the First Crusade? A convert from Islam, then?" Gondemar asked.

She nodded.

"When did you abandon Allah?"

She raised an eyebrow at the question. Hugh raised his hand. "No one seeks to abandon God, Gondemar. The Lord has created a world rich in variation. Even we, in our best moments, recognize He goes by many names and takes many forms. The proper question is, when did you find Christ?"

Assamite

"When did you find Christ?" Gondemar repeated.

"The autumn of 1105," was all she managed, as if the event were too important to belittle with words.

Though not smiling or betraying any other emotion, Hugh sounded sincere when he said, "It is always a blessing to welcome another sister to Christ. What is your name?"

"Amala."

"Amala," he answered, rolling the sound slowly on his tongue. "I thank you for your efforts on our behalf. How did you come to help us, Amala?"

"I left Constantinople in March, before the siege. While my accent and appearance were accepted by the Greeks, the Latins mistrusted me and I feared for my safety. I was living in Adrianople, unknown to the prince, and moved freely between the city and the refugee camp where you saved that family. I was trying to eavesdrop on your conversation with that monk when I saw the attacker," she said. Rallying a bit, she forced herself up onto her elbows so she could meet his steely blue eyes. "You are the first fit leader in the name of Christ I have seen in many years. I am pleased they did not kill you."

"Eavesdropping?" Gondemar snapped. "What were you trying to learn?"

She looked down, embarrassed. Hugh reached out, put his hand under her chin and gently lifted.

"Answer," he said softly.

"We are creatures seldom driven by the aesthetic or spiritual. Many Cainites pay lip service to the Lord, only to prove slave to our base longings. You are not one of them. I wanted to find out what you are."

Noting his sire's warm response to the flattering words, Gondemar gave Hugh a worried little smile. "Yet another lost soul falls prey to your charms."

Hugh pressed lightly on her upper chest, laying her back down, then folded her arms gently over her breast.

"I believe you, for now," he said, almost in a whisper. "But I have many, many things to do, and many, many more questions. We will talk again after you've rested more."

I have some time, then, she thought.

With that, Hugh rose. As he walked toward the tent door, Gondemar stopped him and nodded toward the girl. "Guest or prisoner?"

Hugh smiled a bit. "A guest. A guest who must be tended *carefully*."

With that, he vanished beyond the tent flap. Gondemar sighed. He returned to the woman, pulled back her blanket with a tug, and gruffly proceeded to examine her wounds. They were healing but, with her deprived of a full meal, very slowly. In spite of himself, he paused in his clinical inspection just for a moment, when he spotted a glowing drop of fresh blood welling in the tear of her injuries. Unconsciously he opened his mouth, showing wet teeth with a string of reddish saliva beading between upper and lower lip.

"Templars are chaste, yes? You do not diablerize?" she said, referring to the drinking of another Cainite's blood until death.

Gondemar snapped his head up, angry and embarrassed at losing control, even briefly. "Indulging in any form of animal lust is considered a paean to the devil and a distraction from our service to the Lord."

With a sneer, Gondemar turned his back to her. Picking up a glass, he poured a small bit of red, viscous liquid into a wooden bowl and stiffly handed it to her. Her nostrils flared at the smell of blood and she took it without question. Watching her drink greedily seemed to reassure him. She guessed that he expected Assamites, or other such duplicitous agents, to have more self control. For her part, as the vitae winnowed its way through her veins, she tingled with a familiar delight that made it easier

82   Assamite

to push away the pain. She licked the bowl, then her lips, enjoying the dregs of the small repast.

With a sudden softness that surprised her, Gondemar said, "We are not as intolerant of different accents as many of our countrymen. You may well be all you say, and if so, I apologize; but we must remain on guard. There has already been one effort to kill my sire. I am to ensure there is no other."

Then she remembered, *Sihr and Fajr, did they make it out?*

"Has there been any progress in catching the assassins?"

"No. Prince Licinius swarms the streets with his guards. It has become something of an obsession for him, a needed distraction from the coming Latin armies, I suppose. He has even sworn he will bring one back for interrogation," he said, then added with a smile, "If I yet breathed, I would not hold it in anticipation."

With that, he turned down the lantern and stepped toward the entrance. His silhouette framed by the canvas flaps, she called, "Sir Gondemar?"

"Yes?"

"I had a small…" she began, then her voice trailed off, as if she were ashamed or afraid to complete a thought that mere seconds ago had been of great import.

Gondemar frowned, bemused. "Do you mean the toy Sir Hugh brought here with you?"

Her eyes lit. Still amused, Gondemar stepped toward one of the boxes, pulled the ragged plaything out by its straw hair and handed it to her. As she grasped it to her chest, he noted how the tension slipped from her form.

Eyes closed, she asked, "If I am a guest, as Sir Hugh said, must I remain in this tent?"

Despite his generally dour countenance, between her reaction to the blood, the doll and this odd new question, Gondemar let go a laugh that made his sleepy eyes twinkle.

"You are free to go as far as you can walk. With the scant blood we've provided, it'll be at least another night before you're healed enough to do anyone damage, except yourself."

With that, he left her.

Alone, her fingers quickly found a small vial hidden within the doll's belly. It was filled with a thick, argent elixir Sihr had given her. The sorcerer had been reluctant to part with the substance, the product of a difficult alchemical process, but his sense of duty had prevailed.

She uncapped the top, letting loose a pungent odor. Before the smell filled the tent, she made quick work of it, pouring it down her throat in a quick gulp, as the sorcerer had instructed. It tasted loathsome, burning the length of her throat as it trickled into her stomach.

At first, she thought it had no effect. Simply clenching and unclenching her fists brought spasms of unbelievable misery. But, after an hour, with diligent effort, she managed to sit up. At first she swooned, and feared that, despite the healing potion, her insides would spill onto the blanket and leaves, like the dried oats that gave the doll its gangly form. When the dreaded collapse did not occur, she concentrated instead on standing. Pivoting her body, she pressed her feet against the ground. The bare earth was cold against her soles, but she pushed forward, taking the blanket with her. Upon rising, she stumbled, but managed to balance. After that, moving about and dressing was increasingly simple, her limbs feeling more supple. The green tunic, never soft, was stiffer with dried blood, but at least it provided both a small measure of warmth and some protection for her modesty should she be seen.

Sihr had mixed the brew well. By the time she tried to lift the rear canvas of the tent, even bending over, though not without pain, was fluid and simply done. As for the soldiers that lived in the camp, moving about unseen should be no problem for a Child of Haqim, able

Assamite

even in her weakened state to wrap shadows about her like the stealthiest natural predator. Though there would be no immediate threat even if she were, by some miracle, spotted, it would be awkward to be seen walking this far ahead of Gondemar's imagined schedule.

Slipping along a rear row of the tents, she came upon an open row that gave her a cross-view of the area. In stark contrast to the squalor and deprivation of the refugee hovels, the Templar camp was meticulous. Surrounded by rough hills and forest, the area had been chosen for its flatness and scarcity of trees. A series of clean, square, pyramid-topped tents, perfectly equidistant and in straight rows, lay along it. Fires, for light, warmth and cooking, were evenly spaced. Outside one, the human children Sir Hugh had saved from the refugees played while their mother happily cooked dinner. It looked to Amala as if they were growing quite accustomed to their new surroundings, and probably feeling safer here among these Cainites than they had among the mortal invaders in Constantinople.

Nearby, a corral for the knights' well-groomed horses had been built from felled timber. The presence of an armorer's bellows outside one tent told her this was no temporary rest spot—they planned to stay for a while. As she maneuvered behind that tent, she heard scraping metal, indicating that even now someone was at work repairing and cleaning weapons.

A precaution, or does Sir Hugh prepare for battle? she wondered. The desperate Greeks had no surfeit of hatred for the Latin invaders and her own ruse had planted the seed of an Assamite attack. But if the Templars were concerned about attack, they did not show it. The watch was relaxed.

Still pained, she slipped along the tents' backs, until, in time, she came to the largest among them. It was of the same basic canvas as the others, but rectangular, with a series of frills along its pyramidal top. Its central location, greater size and the two footmen keeping guard in front convinced her she had found her target, the tent of their leader, Sir Hugh. Unlike the others, several lengthy tears in it had been left unrepaired.

A souvenir from their battles, she reasoned.

As if a gift from Allah, one long tear in the rear afforded a relatively unencumbered view of the interior, a fact of which she took quick advantage. Inside, Sir Hugh sat on a rough stool, wearing no armor or clothing save the mantle of his Order. He was in deep thought, both index fingers pressing the bridge of his nose. Every now and then, he spoke. When he did, an older man who sat at a table with ink and pen scribbled furiously on parchment.

Close though she was, she only caught a few words: "twisted sack of Constantinople" and "your caring hands." Some phrases brought more concern, such as "lead all Caine's children home" and "split asunder the thick-boned back of the elephantine Islamic Beast," but between the wind and the camp's other sounds, she could not make out a clear sentence.

As she listened, the hair on the back of her neck rose. For an instant, not in the camp, but in the woods that surrounded them, she glimpsed a shape from the corner of her eyes. It seemed a stocky man, or perhaps even a beast, in a cape, so she quickly twisted her head to see more clearly. One instant it was standing there, watching. The next, it was gone, as if it had been only a trick of the clouds covering and uncovering the moonlight. She remained motionless for the longest time, moving only her eyes, her glance darting from dark point to dark point, this time unable to find anything out of the ordinary. It was possible another Cainite was lurking about the camp in much the same way she was: Children of Haqim were not the only vampires able to move about unseen, although most Ventrue like Hugh were thankfully unable to do so. She doubted, however, that the mysterious watcher had seen her, and she had no way to track him at this time. She had little option but to carry on, keeping up her guard.

A sound within the tent brought her attention back to it. Hugh had mumbled some orders to the scribe. The scribe rose, stepped and, clutching his fresh papers in hand, issued some orders of his own. After that, a flurry of activity ensued. Amala peered along the side of Hugh's tent as crated works of art were loaded with the greatest of care into the false bottom of a wagon. Nearby, four knights covered their armor with humble peasant robes, making ready to accompany the precious cargo to the nearest port.

Valuable though the cargo might be, Amala's thoughts remained locked on Hugh. She was surprised he didn't oversee these preparations himself. Quickly, she looked back through the tear in his tent and watched, surprised.

What in Haqim's name is the matter with him?

The muscular knight was barely able to stand for his shaking. He rubbed his temples repeatedly and paced the length of his tent. After a few moments of increasingly frenzied walking, in some strange agony, he slumped down on his own sparse bed of leaves and blanket.

In moments, the small patches of bare leg and chest exposed by the folds of cloth were covered with blood-tinted sweat. He rolled to and fro, eyes tightly shut, as if even the oil lamp's dim light were a dagger. Slamming his mouth shut, he gritted and ground his teeth. Then the twitching of his body suddenly stopped and his mouth opened, letting loose a torrent of whispered words that seemed more conjured than uttered.

Unable to hear, and deathly curious, Amala tossed a small pebble inside, to the far wall of the tent. It hit the canvas with a thud, then landed on one of the crates, loud enough for anyone conscious to hear. Hugh did not acknowledge the sound in any way. Satisfied he was insensate, she raised the flap and slipped inside, taking a heavy stone that lay on the ground. If he awoke and saw her, she could quickly crush his skull.

As she got closer, she was able to make out some words in Latin: "We created man. We know the promptings of his soul, and are closer to him than the vein of his neck."

Though she spoke Latin, it was not such second nature that she could at once recognize its source. Her brow furrowed, trying to recall the phrasing. She was sure they were fragments of some Christian or Templar platitudes, but they sounded oddly familiar.

He spoke again, faster: "Cool your fever with water, for it is from the fires of hell." Then: "He is the first and the last, the visible and the unseen. He has knowledge of all things."

Recalling the Alpha and Omega, she again concluded his mumblings were some remembered bits of apocalyptic text that the Christians loved to tremble before.

Sihr was right. It's likely in this madness that he answers to no one. Should I kill him now then? A better opportunity may never arrive. With the others outside busy readying the cart, if I act quickly, we could all be miles away before anyone even knows he is dead.

Satisfied this was the right choice, she raised the heavy rock above his bare skull and prepared to bring it crashing down with all the swift and deadly force her muscles could provide.

But then Hugh grunted, moaned and spoke again, this time in fluid Arabic: "Fight for the cause of God against those who fight against you, but commit not the injustice of attacking them first."

The familiar enjoinder held her transfixed. This was not the New Testament, or any part of the two older books. This was the Qur'an! Round eyes widening, she went over his earlier phrases in her mind and realized, with great embarrassment, that they too, though spoken in the Latin tongue, were the words of Muhammad, may Allah commend and salute him.

"Yea, if you remain firm, and act aright, even if the enemy should rush here on you in hot haste, your Lord would help you with five thousand angels, making a terrific onslaught," Hugh muttered. A single carmine bead of sweat rolled down his cheek into his mouth, making him cough.

Why would a Christian Templar quote the holy word?

"Whoso has done an atom's weight of good shall see it; and whoso has done an atom's weight of evil shall see it."

She watched for a few moments as the sweating figure of Hugh writhed below her, helpless, in pain, still quoting scripture.

"…And the Last Day, and the angels, and the Book, and the messengers…" he muttered.

Coincidence? Portent? Hugh's voice was distant, as if it weren't his own, as if it had somehow slipped into his body while his guard was down. If he truly was possessed, then by who or what? A shudder went down her spine as a stray thought occurred.

Might it not be Allah Himself that speaks through him now?

The notion wedged its way into her mind like a burrowing animal, only to be put down as sinful nonsense.

Whatever the hand behind it, Sir Hugh's voice dropped lower and lower, and soon fell to silence. As quickly as it had come, the fever broke and the red beads of sweat on his brow evaporated. Soon, he would probably awaken from this strange slumber, and her moment would be lost. Amala was frozen.

What could it mean?

Nothing more perhaps than that he read the Book to better know his enemy. Or perhaps he now recalled, in his fevered state, the prayers of a Muslim he was torturing. Or…

Her original, foolish thought returned, and she banished it once again. Nevertheless, against all reason, against the begging of her seasoned mind, she lowered the stone and slipped back out.

Outside, a cool wind wafted through the space between tents, sending the edges of some of the cloths flapping. The cooler air sobered her at once, and she was forced to wonder if her own mind had been somehow weakened or distorted. Perhaps it was altered by the potion that had so quickly mended her wounds, or perhaps there was something about Sir Hugh himself that conjured a deep sympathetic yearning from any who came near. It was not, she now decided, so odd for him to know the Qur'an. He was, after all, a Templar, and one who'd spent much time among her people. Still, it was so odd he should quote that particular *sura* at the very moment she would have slain him. Could he have been, if not completely, than perhaps partly awake?

Or was it a warning from God not to act?

Her questions were soon complicated by more immediate concerns. The cart was now fully loaded and ready to leave. Once it was gone, someone would be checking on Sir Hugh, and Gondemar would eventually return to check on her. If she could keep her torso out of his sight for the rest of the night and the following day, the sudden change might draw no suspicion, but now, mere hours later, it might end her charade. She was loathe to give up her hard-won position within the camp and wondered how she might continue the masquerade, to learn more about the transformation that had overtaken Sir Hugh.

A sound, not from within the camp, but the forest, shattered any plans. She whirled in its direction and this time plainly saw the figure of a burly man hiding among the poplars. At first she simply thought to watch him further, but her reflexes were still too slow, and he, likewise aware that the cart's exit would soon return more guards to their posts, had decided to leave. Thinking he might be connected to what was happening with Sir Hugh, she thought to follow and find out who he was.

Assamite

As she pumped her leg muscles Amala discovered at once the potion's limits. After but a few steps, pain shot up the whole of her form, outlining in particular her recent wounds. It was not enough to stop her, but certainly enough to slow her down.

Even so, she was gaining on the figure. Though it kept running, it appeared unaware of how close she was. The distance between them almost gone, she could make out the thick apish shape of his head and bristling locks of hair. She was thinking he might be little more than a curious refugee, when the cramps in her sorcerously healed muscles redoubled. She stumbled, and by the time she recovered, her quarry was nearly disappearing into the distance.

I can still catch up, she said with an inward grin, looking forward to the challenge. Unfortunately, she was still not alone, and her loud stumbling had ruptured her ability to blend with the night. As a result, five dark-robed figures rose from the shadows of the caliginous woods and circled her. Amala cursed herself for behaving like a novice, keeping her attention fixed on her target while utterly ignoring her surroundings, not even noticing until now that her chase had taken her straight toward the refugee camp.

"Who are you?" she barked at them.

With the night's silence broken, the five looked nervously about. They did not wish to be discovered either, but Amala's cry had ruined that. With no other option, they quickly decided to make their own presence more widely known.

"Kill the Saracen!" one shouted in Greek. "Her death will make a great gift for Sir Hugh!"

"Yes! A gift!" The others hissed and pressed forward, their thin blades drawn.

No sooner did they cry out than the men in the Templar camp heard. With a clatter of chain and sword, a score rushed forward. She could make out Gondemar's voice among the ghouls.

Amala's choices now were few. Even weaponless and wounded, she might best the newcomers, but that would clearly reveal her combat training, and mark her as a threat. With the Templars nearly on the scene, she chose instead to sink to her knees and feign terror. Then she quickly slipped her hand beneath her dress and used the nail of her thumb to cut open the largest of her wounds. Blood flowed freely, wetting her tunic anew. Her head swooned.

"All of you! Stand down and name yourselves!" Gondemar bellowed. The men that had accompanied him unsheathed their broad swords.

The five Greeks were taken aback. Their blades still pointed at Amala. The tallest turned his head toward Gondemar and spoke in broken Latin.

"Our weapons are not meant for you, sir. We represent the heads of some of the more noble families currently residing in the camps. There are many rumors about your presence. We came simply to welcome your master and inquire of his intentions. Upon approaching, we saw this dark-skinned demon sneaking away. We assumed she'd meant you ill," he said.

"The woman is known to us, and will be dealt with soon enough. But tell me, noble representatives, why do you also slink about in shadows rather than present yourselves appropriately?" Gondemar asked.

The five looked to each other, uncertain who should fumble out an answer first.

"I think can guess that much, Gondemar," Sir Hugh said, stepping onto the scene. Even here, with no armor, he almost glowed, eliciting both confidence and fear. "We are Latin, they are Greek. Like the wounded Amala, other than that base distinction, they don't know us and rightly fear what they do not know. So they sought to gather some intelligence, both for themselves, and to lift their standing with the other refugees. And the best way to hear what someone would rather you didn't is by not announcing your presence. Isn't that right?"

Embarrassed and a bit uncertain, the tall Greek nodded. "But be assured, our intent was never to offend," he added in their defense.

"I am certain that curiosity and not malevolence was your main motivation," Sir Hugh said, scanning them all carefully with his azure eyes.

Amala noticed that his very presence was already having an effect on them. At first they had shifted about uncomfortably, clearly wanting to assume a more arrogant posture before this invader. Now all but one, made even more uncomfortable by the sudden calm of his fellows, were fascinated. Aware of Hugh's influence herself this time, or perhaps because it was not directed at her, it seemed to Amala somewhat less potent.

"Our apologies, Sir Hugh. These have been trying times," the tall Greek said.

"I not only accept your apologies, I will reward your curiosity. Gondemar, step forward. I wanted to discuss this with you at length in private, but it appears that providence has provided a more public opportunity," Hugh said. An anxious Gondemar did as he was asked and stood at Hugh's right hand. One by one, Hugh made eye contact with the Greeks as he spoke, level in tone and clear in intent.

"I say to you now and will repeat to any who ask that the crusaders' presence here is a travesty, a terrible mistake that Pope Innocent has repudiated by excommunicating them all. It is my intention, with the help of all good Christians, both Latin and Greek, to reclaim the reins of history, correct this mistaken endeavor and once more turn the path of our righteous rage toward Egypt," Hugh said.

"Egypt?" the Greeks muttered among themselves.

"Egypt," Gondemar repeated slowly, rolling the word on his tongue and the thought in his mind.

Egypt?! Amala thought as despair filled her heart. *How could I not have slain him?*

"The kings who led the last crusade, those stalwarts Richard the Lionhearted and Phillip Augustus, agreed that, while recapturing a city as remote as Jerusalem could be done, it could never be held long with the rest of the land so lousy with the Saracens and their allies. As was the original intent of this Fourth Crusade, Egypt must be taken first, to split their back," Hugh said.

He pointed east, toward the fallen capital. "In Constantinople, where now the Latin mortals scrape out what meat remains in the petty husk of your empire, you lived a dream. Be thankful that you have at last awoken, before it was too late! The pillaging and destruction you fled is a mere simulacrum of the eternal perils that await if you do not now seek to take back the glory of His name in His land."

Lowering his arm, Hugh nodded toward the camp. "Out there you have nothing, no choice but to wander the wilderness as the tribes of Israel once did. Here, with me, in this moment, in this time, in His name, and by His command, I will give you direction, opportunity, leadership and the chance to reclaim what you have lost."

Though clearly shaken by his words, the taller Greek spoke. "Who sends you to us?"

"No less than the Blessed Queen herself. She appeared to me and laid out this great mission. She will melt the hearts of those who can help us with supplies and men. She will put fear into the bones of our enemies and success within our hands. And so I ask, brothers in Christ, in her name, will you now swear to me?" Hugh said.

Gondemar and all the knights immediately clapped their hands to their shoulders.

"As always, my master," Gondemar said.

There was a moment of utter silence before four of the five Greeks dropped to their knees. Shaking with joy, the tallest said, "I, too, do so swear." Three of the others repeated the words almost beneath their breath. Hugh turned to the Greek still standing, who regarded him with a wry and defiant look.

"I have lived a long time in the great shade of Michael's city, Latin, reveling in its culture, supping on its vast delicacies. There, for centuries, I have grown strong, wise, and unaccustomed to bowing or swearing fealty on request. I have no desire to go to war, and only questions for any who claim to speak for God and to serve our best interests, particularly those who pillage our treasures while claiming to right the wrongs visited upon us. You have yet to prove yourself to me or mine, Sir Hugh," he said.

Hugh's face filled with sympathy. "I understand. I too have been full of doubt, appalled by rampant hypocrisy. Were there more time allowed me by the Queen of Heaven for these great tasks, or you a more powerful force in this sad world, perhaps I would take the time to convince you otherwise. But, as it is…"

In the space all expected he'd left for the next word, Hugh swung his sword and sliced the lone dissenter's head clean off at the neck. The body shook, smoked and disintegrated, untold age claiming its due at last. While they were still recovering from the shock, he waved for the others to stand, which they quickly did.

"Go back to the camps, where I will allow you to speak for me tonight. Take a count and then begin to divide those who wish to join us into warriors and artisans. My men will begin training and organizing them soon," Hugh said.

"And what shall we say to those who followed him?" one asked, indicating the pile of ash that had once been his companion.

Hugh's cool face betrayed no emotion. "Suggest they not make the same mistake."

The Greeks bowed low, then turned back toward the hill that led to the sprawling abode of the refugees. Once they were gone, Hugh put out his hand and helped Amala to her feet.

"As for you, Amala," he said, "what were you doing in my tent?"

Chapter Eight

Amala sat, hands folded in her lap, on a seat in the very tent she'd stolen into mere hours ago. A yard from her, Hugh, the man whose pretty mouth had so deftly quoted the Prophet's words, sat on his modest three-legged stool, eyes cast down on an object in his hands. They were alone in the tent, but outside curious and agitated Cainite Templars and scores of their ghoulish men-at-arms were on heightened alert. They milled about, excitedly talking about an attack on Egypt and trying to guess what was going on inside their leader's tent. Sizing up her chances in a fight, Amala was not encouraged. Dressed as she was in cumbersome peasant clothes, and dangerously low on precious blood, she realized how quickly her mission could devolve into a suicidal run.

It was only a matter of time before he accused her of either spying or planning to kill him. In either case, her position was not a strong one. Any advantages, if any at all were forthcoming, by the will of Allah, would be fleeting at best. For example, right now, not far from where she sat, there was a small metal hook embedded in the tent's central pole, used by Sir Hugh to hang his armor. She stared at it, wondering how quickly it could be pulled free and jammed into her captor's eye.

And while he's blinded, I might grab his sword and decapitate him, she reasoned. It was a desperate plan. Ventrue blood had the reputation of making one very hard to destroy indeed.

Following the revelation that he had seen her in his tent, Sir Hugh had been silent, speaking only enough to dismiss Gondemar and the others. Now, the current object of his attention was not Amala at all, but a small, colorful mosaic he held in his hands. It depicted the Madonna and Child, with the archangel Michael above them, cradling both in his wings and arms. Judging by the grand

Byzantine design, it was likely a treasure from Constantinople. Judging from the broken tiles that lined its rough edges, it was just as likely pried from a wall its makers had never intended it to leave. In deep concentration, he ran his fingers along the tiles' smooth surfaces.

With him thus occupied, Amala moved her hand toward the pole and briefly tested the strength of the embedded hook. He shifted, and she quickly moved her hand back to her lap.

His long thick index finger tapped along the edge of the angel's full cheeks down to a small cleft in the chin, indicated by a single tile.

"Look here, the Toreador Michael in his utter arrogance ordered his own features reproduced as the holy archangel. How could such ill-conceived pride survive for so long? Why has its fall brought so many with it? Surely all the newly dead cannot be so guilty as he." Hugh shook his head. "Perhaps he was not always thus, perhaps he was once a truly great creature, who tumbled from a state of grace so high I will never know it."

His fingers moved next to the image of the wide-eyed mother, which he stroked reverently. "And here I suffer from my own pride, holding on to this rather than passing it on to my betters." He looked at Amala apologetically. "Feeling so fortunate to have it in my presence at all, I wish to linger on it a bit more."

As he looked down again, Amala's hand shot out and pried the hook free. As he spoke again, she slipped it into the folds of her tunic. Her hard-won abilities dampened any sound.

His fingers paused in their movement. Under her tunic, the metal hook was cold against her hand. She tested the tip with her finger.

This will do, she thought. *At least I can defend myself if he comes for me.*

"You do know," he asked, addressing Amala directly at last, "that the Greek church fought bitterly for decades over the importance of icons such as these?"

He's testing me. Why?

"I know something of it, yes. 'Thou shalt hold no graven images before you,'" she answered.

"What do you think, Amala? Do we pray to pictures and statues?"

"It is always possible to confuse a statue or a painting with what it represents," she answered with a shrug.

Why doesn't he just ask why I was sent? Is there some subtler torture he has prepared for me?

"Prince Licinius is scouring all Adrianople for the presence of Assamites," Hugh began. "He has sworn, at all costs, to find one."

Ah, here it comes.

"A holy knight, as we speak, consults powerful oracles at my behest. Already I feel myself shifted towards the center of events."

Amala was perplexed. Instead of the expected accusation, Hugh held up the mosaic so she could see it clearly, and pointed to the face of Mary.

"What would you say if I told you I know for certain that *this* is not the Blessed Queen?" Hugh asked.

Amala hesitated. She was growing confused about whether to attack or strive to better express her opinion on the theological issues Sir Hugh was raising.

"I would say it is fortunate that such images hold no distraction for you," she answered finally. "I pray daily to be so strong."

"That is not what I meant," he answered mysteriously. "But you must be curious about these questions. You must think about these things. Otherwise where did you find the strength to oppose your own heritage?"

He hasn't guessed what I am! He still thinks I'm a Christian convert!

"From the Lord," she answered quickly.

With a sigh, he went back to pondering the mother and child. "What did we kill in Constantinople, and why? Men, women, children—slaughtered for crimes of perception? Do we thus treat the blind or the deaf? Do you really think shades of human language matter so much to God?"

She looked about, trying to look confused and frightened by his questions, and said again, more softly, "I don't pretend to know His will."

He looked up again, this time annoyed. "Nor do I, dear girl. Nor do I. The problem is, we all must guess. We *must*. We must make our choices in all earnestness, cling to them with our very lives and never dare look back. Especially a Cainite! These loyalties to ethics, to bodiless thoughts are all that keep us from surrendering to endless hunger! I mean, look at you! Once you were Muslim, and now Christ welcomes you into His body. Is it not as though you passed from the realm of the dead to the realm of the living? Was it not a greater awakening even than when you were Embraced?"

"It is indeed another world, Sir Hugh," she said quietly.

Hugh rubbed his face with his strong fingers, as if trying to massage new thoughts into his skull, or old ones out.

"The Muslims you reject, how different are even they from us in the surface of our worship? To their mind, the Qur'an is to the Old and New Testaments as we believe the New Testament is to the Old. They believe in Moses, Abraham, even in the Lord Jesus, though they reject His divinity. To them Allah and Ar-Rahman are the same as Yahweh; all refer to the one God, with different words from different tongues. Allah the majestic leader, Ar-Rahman the merciful and Yahweh, the cosmos's very being, singing simply that He Is. It's not as though they worship Zeus or Zoroaster. What shades of difference distinguish us, then, so that one slays the other in His name? Why do we fight?" Hugh said.

Amala was beginning to piece things together. He *had* read the Qur'an, so its words on his lips were no miracle. As for his question, they were beginning to set her mind abuzz. But in answer, she said only, "So that we may all be tested and judged."

Just as it is my duty now to judge you.

"Tested and judged," he said, rolling the answer over in his mind. "Yes. We are all tested and judged. Well met, Amala, well met," he said, nodding. "You see? You have thought about these things. But let me tell you what I think. We have prophets, we have kings, we have the Savior, and to us they are very different things. But to the Muslims, Muhammad is both prophet and military leader. He was a conqueror, not just of the soul, but of land and men. Do you know the Old and New Testaments have very little to say about the conduct of war? But the Qur'an has much to say not only on what is right and proper in battle, but also what is strategically best. It is nothing if not pragmatic."

The conversation had been so strangely pleasant, Sir Hugh so intensely sincere, she forgot herself a moment and whispered, reverently, "And more…"

He caught the whiff of deep emotion immediately. "Then you recall your love for Islam! That is good, and exactly what I needed to hear."

Pointedly he leaned forward and gazed deeply at her. "Why were you in my tent, no less than two hours ago?"

It was all a ruse. He only wanted me to admit my love for Allah. That is as good for his kind as any confession.

She once more tightened her hand on the small hook, then tensed, animal-like, prepared to dive toward him.

The tent filled with Sir Hugh's laughter.

"Of course I don't expect *you* to have an answer for that. How could you? How could you even *know* you were here?" he said.

As an expression of deep puzzlement wrapped its way about her features. Hugh rose, walked behind her and put a hand on her shoulder.

"Of course, I have confused you. Sometimes I speak my mind so quickly I've forgotten others are listening." He paused, perhaps pondering whether to go on. "I have visions. There's no simpler way to put it. Some months back, while I thought I was awake, the Virgin Mary appeared and showed me, among many other things, that the state I thought was waking life was little more than another form of dream. Since then, she comes to me nightly. It is as though a second creation is being played out, purely for the purpose of imparting the details of my mission."

With a flurry of movement more appropriate to a great bird than a man, Sir Hugh fell to his knees and grasped both her hands. Quickly, she slipped the hook into the folds of her tunic, prayed it would not fall, then put her hands in his palms. As his huge hands closed about hers, his eyes, so bright and clear, filled with blue fire.

"Sometimes I fly among the heavens, witnessing the very heart of creation. Bright creatures of light lift me and sing to me with their being. Sometimes I hover above the waters and feel the vibrations of chaos lap at my soul. But other times, other times, such as this very night, I am exactly where I seem. Here, lying on that bed of leaves, with my own spirit hovering inches above my body, unable to move, but seeing all. Tonight, in such a state, you were here, standing before me, and I somehow knew that you were about to give me some great divine gift that only you could impart," he said. By the end, he was whispering as if in prayer. He knelt there a moment, staring at her, hoping, child-like, that she would provide the answer he so desperately longed for.

Amala was dazed, enchanted by the sincerity pouring from him, caught between understandings of what was going on and how it impacted her intentions. If this

Assamite

tingling, steady yearning that had risen in her was a fraction of what he elicited from others, Sir Hugh was far more dangerous than any could imagine. But he was so young, in terms of the long-lived, a veritable babe in a benighted world where monsters who had seen Rome and Babylon rise and fall still stalked the night. Could the Ventrue come to this on his own, or was there some other force behind him? A more powerful Cainite? An elder?

Her mind catalogued more and more powerful beings until finally that other, unbidden, foolish possibility came to mind again. Having read the Qur'an, having committed it to some deep part of his memory, could he somehow have been thus touched by Allah?

Is God speaking to him?

Begging forgiveness for her very thoughts, she prayed for any slight sign that she should try to slay him at once.

When she did not speak, he rose abruptly and whirled, showing her his back, suddenly embarrassed. "I realize how strange this all sounds, but the world is God's story, and just as with the work of any great poet, every word, every sound, every moment, is rich in significance and intimately interconnected. Can our meeting be any exception? Think on it. What are you? A convert in a strange land, guided by faith. What am I, if not in the process of my own conversion to some still higher, as yet unguessed-at relation to the divine?"

He forced himself to face her again, as if a mortal suitor proposing marriage. "Do you see it? She has sent you to me so that your path will help light my own. But you must be open to me, to hold back no thought, no opinion, you must be willing to step back along your own road, to recall your love for Allah so you can sketch for me in intimate detail how the miracle occurred and it became a love of Christ. In exchange, I will take you with us on our holy quest."

She turned to look up at him, and felt as if she was truly seeing him for the first time. He was beautiful.

He paused, then smiled widely. "What do you say, Amala? Do you tremble in fear or anticipation?"

"I... will try, my liege," she whispered. There was not, after all, much else she could say.

Hugh was buoyant, as if her ambivalent response had confirmed his intuition with fact.

"Excellent! You will have free access to the camp. There will be some talk, because of your fair sex, because of your heritage, especially I suspect from dear Gondemar, but that will pass. All foolish gossip will fade quickly in the face of the great new deeds that even now absorb our attention."

His hands clasped on her shoulders, he pulled her to standing. As he did, the hook nearly dropped to the floor, but she managed to catch it between her legs, a motion which Hugh took for girlish dizziness. As he walked her to the front of the tent, she quickly bent and slipped it into her hand.

"Go back to the hospital and gather your things. I will have quarters prepared for you next to my own. We will talk again tomorrow night," he said.

Once outside, he bellowed, "This woman is brought to us from God! She is to be treated only with courtesy and consideration!"

Once alone again, outside, it took Amala several minutes before her senses fell back into place and the world once again seemed real—several minutes of walking, of praying to Allah, of looking at the sky, of touching the earth, the grass and the rough bark of the tree trunks. She had to pull herself together quickly. It was only a few hours before dawn and there was much she had to do.

A story from the Qur'an came to mind. A whore who risked her life to save a dog trapped in the bottom of a well was looked upon with favor by Allah and allowed to enter Heaven.

She wondered briefly if perhaps Sir Hugh of Clairvaux were her dog.

***

"Are you mad?" Sihr blurted, barely able to keep his tones low as he watched the vizier thrust his hand directly toward the fire. The sudden speech made Fajr hesitate.

"Hush! We're not completely invisible, you know! And every moment I wait, more of the letter is destroyed!"

Indeed, though a fortuitous wind had rolled the crumpled ball to a less active section of the campfire, even now its edges blackened and threatened to burst into flames.

"I just do not believe a Cainite can..." Sihr sputtered, but by then Fajr had stuck his fingers nearly into the flame and gingerly pulled out the crumpled scroll that had been deposited there seconds ago by Sir Hugh's scribe. The paper, still fraying into red ash at the edges, rolled back and forth between Fajr's wrinkled black hands as he forced air into his lungs to try to put it out. When these efforts only increased the burning, he gave up, tossed it on the floor and stamped it out with his foot.

"I am impressed," Sihr said.

"Better you should be quiet," Fajr answered, hurriedly beckoning the tall sorcerer towards the woods outside the camp. Once they were a safe distance away, Sihr cupped his hands and intoned a few strange words. A ball of green flame, not quite touching his skin, soon materialized, and he tossed it, almost lazily, onto a pile of twigs and leaves Fajr had gathered. At once, Fajr spread out the sheath, trying to make out the scrawled words.

Sihr straightened as the vizier went about his work. He thought of telling Fajr he could have saved the scroll without touching it, or put out the fire by summoning rain, but decided not to insult him. Besides, he was genuinely taken aback by the scholar's display. The thought of burning had always been a dreadful nightmare for him, and Sihr had thought all Cainites felt likewise.

"You put your hands in the fire. That would drive most of us mad with fear. Such control that must require."

Stefan Petrucha

"For some," Fajr said. "But for me the opportunity to achieve a prized piece of knowledge awakens an even deeper obsession. It has nearly killed me on several occasions, at times nearly cost me a finger."

He raised his index finger towards Sihr to remind him of their earlier, less pleasant encounter.

"You take such risks for mere knowledge?"

Fajr shook both hands at him. "Knowledge is never *mere*. It is always power. Oh, you impress yourself with your sorcery, but there is sheer knowledge in this world that would put such tricks to shame."

"Such as?" Sihr asked, genuinely curious.

Fajr smiled. "Such as? Even in this you challenge me? Well, then such as the Sargon Codex. Surely you know of it?"

"I do not," Sihr said.

"It is an ancient text, very ancient—Chaldean, if it exists at all. Many believe it is just a myth. According to the reports I have heard, it would take years of study to unravel its simplest axioms. But the dedicated scholar, they say, can decipher its mysteries and uncover the science of sciences, the key to complete understanding of the universal structure. Such a scholar, they say, would know all that is knowable, enhance his abilities to the utmost, and become all but a god. For that—no, for nothing more than a piece of a piece of that—I would gladly plunge my arm into a fire," Fajr said wildly.

Sihr shook his head. "Yet you yourself say it does not exist. Only a man from the city could take such delight in a mere mental construct."

Fajr waved him off. "And perhaps your problem is that you do not take enough delight in things." Then he laughed and slapped his thighs. "But forget that for now. Let us instead concentrate on the prize we have achieved and read what Sir Hugh was writing to the prince of Paris."

Assamite

Chapter Nine

May 12, 1204

My dear Prince Alexander,

I can no longer entertain any doubt that Heaven exists, for I have walked the streets of Hell. Far worse than any battlefield and more heartless than our own defeat at Hattin, the twisted sack of Constantinople, condemned by our patriarch in Rome for what it was, has forever proven to me that evil, and therefore, good, exist as truly as the firmament in which rests the world. I am sure by now you have heard from those whose gifts with language far exceed my own, of the uncounted sins that occurred on those three dark nights, as Christian slew Christian, and of the terrible loss of the most exquisite objects of art and holy veneration.

Nonetheless, let me bring you the good news that bearing witness to these events, rather than crushing me, has made me all the stronger. I am honored and humbled to be sending yourself and my beloved sire Sir Geoffrey these holy relics and items which, once in your hands, I know will be safe from the wanton destruction and callous hungers of beings who abdicated their sense, their aesthetics and their souls in a frenzy that can only rightly be called demonic. I wish only that I could have thus taken and wrapped the whole city and delivered it to Paris and your caring hands.

Yet, just as the world's corpus is second to His Word, I am likewise humbled, indeed shivering from joy, to also report that the Lord had a most special blessing set aside for me. Within the depths of the Church of the Apostles, among the hallowed bones of many Christian emperors, as I sought the jeweled crown you requested, the Blessed Queen of Heaven appeared to me and filled me with His light and purpose. Having seen her and known her to be what she claimed, I can no sooner deny the commands she made of me than I could my need for blood. Listen, and see if you have the strength to doubt.

As you know, the children of Caine have, of late, been thwarted and taken off guard by the fitful, chaotic movements of the very mortals we were created to shepherd. Now it has fallen upon me to reverse the trend, and take up the reins dropped or set aside by others. By His Word, here, beginning among the sad and desperate refugees of the great city, I am to gather what support I am able and lead all Caine's children home, first to Egypt, to split asunder the thick-boned back of the elephantine Islamic Beast, and then, while it writhes crippled by our righteous blows, on to reclaim the Holy Land itself.

I pray that upon hearing this, your heart rises with gladness and you are moved to send me as many troops and supplies as you can spare. Yet I know the distance between us is great, and you have not seen, heard and felt what I have. So if instead, you read these words and think them madness, I beg you consult what holy oracles you will to test them, that you may learn that I am indeed mad, but that my madness is divine. Even now, she comes to me nightly, in the form of a sweet dream, reshaping me from the inside out, for the terrible purpose I am to be used. How blessed to be of such service!

I shall pray long and hard that these words convey the merest fraction of the glory the Queen of Heaven has shown me, for then I can rest assured that my pleas for aid will utterly bypass both your great mind and your ample heart to commune directly with your immortal soul. I await your answer.

In His service,
Hugh of Clairvaux

***

"And this was just a draft!" Fajr said, shaking the parchment towards Amala. "The finished version is en route to Paris!"

Since Hugh had strangely chosen to lift any restrictions on her travel, meetings among the three Assamites had become easier.

Wondering about the phrase "Queen of Heaven," which she'd heard Hugh use, she tried to take the crumpled parchment from Fajr's hands to read it herself. Surprisingly, he briefly held it fast, as if unwilling or unable to let go. She looked at him, curiously. The vizier smiled, as if his grip had been some inexplicable accident, and released his hold.

Sihr stood as best he could. He'd been agitated since he'd first heard Fajr read the letter, but the cave's height made the tall man stoop. He tossed the rocky ceiling a look of aggravation, as if he could destroy it in a moment, but did not want to make the effort.

"It is clear," he boomed, turning his back on both of them. "We have waited. We have learned. This man and all his followers must die."

"Again, you rush to simplistic conclusions." Amala moved so she could see his face as she spoke. "Planning to attack Egypt and doing so are two different things. The Third Crusade involved a hundred thousand men. I doubt there that many of our kind in all the world, Christian, Islamic and barbarian. Why do you think none of us has ever ruled a sizable kingdom, except by manipulating the kine? Even when Michael was emperor of Byzantium, he had to keep his true nature a secret."

As the sorcerer shifted nervously away, Amala suddenly realized Sihr was refusing to look at her. "What's wrong?" she asked.

"Your veil," he answered.

"My apologies, Sihr," she said. "In focusing my thoughts on our mission, I have forgotten decorum." Somewhat embarrassed, she reached into her rucksack for the slight cloth and wrapped it about her head so it covered the lower portions of her face.

Sihr turned about, shaking his head. "You pray to Mecca, but you go about bare-headed in public, among Templars and other Christians."

Amala was about to respond, but Fajr piped up, happy as ever to show his knowledge: "It is written 'When ye travel through the earth, there is no blame on you if ye shorten your prayers for fear the unbelievers may attack you: For the unbelievers are unto you open enemies.' This is *taqiyya*, established by the great Shiite Muhammad al-Baqir centuries ago. Dissemblement, concealment and precaution.

"In other words, when a good Muslim is in hostile territory and revealing his faith will prevent him from spreading or protecting it, concealment is permitted, even mandatory, without entering a state of sin. Even when the Greeks allowed us to worship freely, there were times, as I lived among them, I found it necessary myself. Recently, to slip past some less avaricious Cainite crusaders, before I met the dogs that sought to rob me, I prayed aloud to Jesus as Lord."

"Really?" Sihr said, amazed. "How was that?"

"Odd," he said. "Very odd. And I judge myself harshly for it, especially considering the ultimate fate of the scrolls I carried. But I also know, as it states in the Qur'an, that it is not by our words but our hearts that Ar-Rahman judges us."

Sihr bobbed his head left and right, wrestling with the notion. "Sir Hugh and his Templars should still die at once. Your new position in the camp gives us great opportunity to contrive an ambush."

Now it was Amala who turned away. "There is a further complication."

"Of what sort, precisely?" Fajr broke in, his quill at the ready.

"I was witness to one of the trances his letter describes. In them, he… quotes the words of the Prophet at great length," she explained.

110   Assamite

Sihr and Fajr were both aghast, but the vizier more quickly returned to form. "Which passages exactly? Does he speak Latin or Arabic? Is the voice clearly his or that of another? Are the quotes pertinent to the situation, or random?"

Amala raised her hand to silence him. "Sometimes Latin, sometimes Arabic. I am not certain of the voice's source. It was one incident. I was taken off guard. If it occurs again, I will be more careful to record the details."

"What does it matter what he says in his dreams?" Sihr said. "His deluded mind probably recalls the pleading words of an imam who fell before his cursed steel. If we do not kill him, it is a repudiation of our duty both to jihad and Haqim!"

"The struggle against idolaters doesn't only mean their destruction. That much I know well," Amala said. She was agitated herself now, feeling the tightening fear of her craving making itself bare. She rubbed her hands together, folding one over the other in an effort to calm and comfort herself. In part, the sorcerer's impulsive display of power had taken her aback, but there were also crucial matters about her history she had kept from them. Now it had become obvious she should drop some portion of her silence, regardless of how it affected her role as the group's leader. The Beast did not care for the taste of vulnerability.

"Before my Embrace, I was Christian," she confessed. "Having seen the Prophet's light, I seek to bring it to others. Even others such as Sir Hugh."

"What?" Sihr bellowed.

Fajr cackled. "You think to convert him? A Ventrue Templar?" Then, considering the notion, he raised his eyes upwards and tilted his head. "Well, it's not entirely without precedent. There is a small pocket of Ventrue in Arabia who call themselves Muslim...."

"Yes, the Hijazi," Amala said.

Sihr was enraged, no longer able to form his objections into words.

Hoping to convince him at least of her sincerity, Amala said, "Muhammad, may Allah commend and salute him, when the angel spoke to him, would shiver, shake and speak in tongues, much as Sir Hugh does now."

Sihr exploded. "You dare compare him to the Prophet? You think the angels whisper in his ears to convert him to Islam? Better they should be stabbing him in the brain with the bones of those he has slain! Are you mad? Why not have a *muta*, a temporary marriage, between the two of you as well? Fajr can perform the service, and Gondemar will be the witness!"

Sihr made a sudden motion towards his head, which Amala misinterpreted as a possible attack. As a result, she instinctively reached for the hilt of her sword.

Sihr glared at her. "That is not something you want to do."

"Do you give the orders here now, nomad?" she said, sharply reminding him of his vow to the elders at Alamut. Sihr tensed at her rebuke. Amala swore she could actually see a fearsome, unthinking brute rise in his eyes to vie for dominance over the sorcerer's next move.

Fajr must have sensed it to, for he leapt to his feet and stood between them with his hand on Sihr's chest. He spoke as quickly as he could.

"Now, now, now, now! Let us not fall upon one another like dogs!" Fajr said. Then he turned to Amala with the tone of a reproving parent. "Ventrue blood carries a powerful charisma with it, a presence that draws the hearts of those near to follow. Sir Hugh enchants whomever he meets. Might not you be thus enthralled?"

"I am aware of his influence, but..." she began. Fajr cut her off. Amala noted a slight smile forming on Sihr's lips.

"You are aware, but can you be certain he does not influence you?" Fajr demanded.

"No."

"Ah." Finished with her, he wheeled toward the giant in the room. "As for you, my fine desert friend, as our leader has rightly pointed out, a 'crusade' of Cainites isn't going to be terribly dangerous unless it is a strike against a specific target! Under the circumstances, don't you see where it might be worth staying close to Hugh to uncover the details of his plan?"

Sihr locked his eyes on a point in the cave's wall, but said nothing.

Fajr rephrased his last sentence. "You see, don't you? You are intelligent. You see how we are in a unique position to… to study, yes? You understand the importance of knowing your enemy fully. Surely…"

"Yes," Sihr said finally. "My apologies, Amala."

Relieved, Amala sat on the floor, folded her legs and stared into the small fire. "And mine, for goading you. With the Latins and the Greeks so busy with one another, I anticipated a far simpler mission. The complexity of these times overwhelms me. I barely understood the old order; now history's sands shift one way, its winds another, and some rough new creature is being born. But regardless, I am the chosen commander of this mission, and must consider that the easiest answer may not be the best. We should do well to remember the wall."

"The wall?" Fajr asked.

"An obstacle more easily removed with patience than deeds," Sihr explained, his own tone considerably softened.

She shrugged. "I do not necessarily believe Hugh is being converted by Allah's angels, but I'm convinced something moves behind him unseen. If that something is not divine, then there is another actor threatening us, an actor who may escape unless we draw him out."

"There," the vizier smiled and slapped Sihr on the shoulder. "You see? It is best we study."

Amala nodded.

"No," Sihr said. "There is a third option."

"Oh?" Amala said.

Sihr removed a ceremonial bowl with brightly painted figures on it.

"I will require some blood from each of us," Sihr said. Fajr was cautious, but Amala put her hand out towards the sorcerer. He gave her a gruff smile, then sliced at her palm with a quick move of his dagger. Squeezing her hand, he let the precious vitae drip into the bowl. Seeing that the sorcerer meant no harm, Fajr supplied his hand as well, and soon the blood of all three mixed in the wooden container.

That done, the sorcerer headed out of the cave. Amala and Fajr followed without invitation and found him using his fingers to smear the rich, red liquid into an intricate pattern of markings on the dry earth.

"It's lovely," Fajr commented. "An augury of some type, no?"

"An aid to reading the stars, in fact." Sihr sat in the middle of the now-complete sigil. "They will not reveal whether or not the destruction of this Hugh of Clairvaux would be in our best interests, but I can determine just when the best time would be to make the attempt. Up until that time, it is perhaps best that Amala study this Templar and his motivations."

"And if the moment is soon? Even tonight?" Fajr asked.

"Then we strike before the opportunity is gone," Amala responded, well aware that she had let one perfect chance go by already.

"Shall I proceed, then?" Sihr asked her. She nodded.

The spell was not an easy one. He cracked his fingers, stretched, then muttered strange syllables that sounded vaguely Arabic, but clearly were not. Over and over he repeated them, with minor variations, until their odd cadence filled the air. As he spoke, the harsh, cracked edge to his bass voice changed to a calm, fluid series of tones.

Then all at once they recognized the clear question, "When would be the best time to destroy Hugh of Clairvaux?"

Upon completing the sentence, Sihr's massive form rolled forward, as if suddenly exhausted, or even asleep. When he rose, pain and disappointment were written on his face. Clearly the answer had been neither what he expected nor what he had wanted.

"*Thw al-Hijjah*; for the Europeans that would be about the beginning of August," he reported.

"Then it *is* best we study," Fajr said. "Your own blood magic reveals it to be so."

Again, Amala nodded. "I will return to the camps. Sir Hugh speaks of his first encounter with this Queen as occurring in the Church of the Holy Apostles. You two must journey back to Constantinople to see what you can learn there."

"The city?" Sihr said, clearly disappointed. Then he fell to brooding.

Chapter Ten

May 20, 1204

Cursing the darkness for want of a torch, the five slightly tipsy soldiers tumbled more than marched after their sergeant, Opizinus Scafficii. Once mere crusaders, they were now part of the advancing armies of the newly crowned first Latin Emperor Baldwin. They'd had an easy time of late, marching from town to town and accepting the quick surrender and oaths of fealty of those within. The last town, Lalapasa, with its merry Greek taverns and welcoming wenches, had proven a little too enchanting, and the trio had overslept as their unit moved on. Now they were so desperate to catch up before they were denied a share of the modest looting they'd taken part in, they'd walked through the day and into the night, pausing only to indulge in a skin of wine, for the sake of "bodily warmth."

Scafficii, their cheery Venetian leader, swore to the Lord Jesus he'd been on these very roads not less than a decade past. As the sun set, he had recalled in great detail a clever shortcut, certain it would put them in the army's camp within an hour. That was at least two hours ago, and now they stumbled blindly along, barely able to keep track of one another, jumping at sounds they feared might be wild animals, hoping for some sign of light. Scafficii, confident they'd find something soon, bade them all to wait while he stopped by a mossy oak to relieve his bladder.

"Trust me, boys," he said, shaking himself dry. "As sure as God is on our—"

Then he just stopped.

"Sergeant?"

There was a brief rustling, followed by a long patch of silence.

"Help! The devils are—!" another cried. In an animal panic, the three remaining soldiers awkwardly drew their swords and swung blindly about.

As it was, "A blade—!" were the last words uttered by any mortal in the area.

After a while, Fajr lit a small torch to make their work on the bodies easier. Sihr Haddad, wiping the fresh blood from his mouth as he stood, said, with no small distaste, "I do not care for the turns our mission takes."

Indeed, their quest to Constantinople and the Church of the Holy Apostles had done nothing other than provide Sihr with an even greater hatred for cities. A search of the now-desecrated, abandoned church proved fruitless. Though Fajr had guessed the above-ground tombs were meant for the tourists, and there were doubtless other crypts hidden somewhere in the structure, he had no way of knowing where they lay, or, for that matter, where Sir Hugh had had his first supposedly holy encounter. Gathering intelligence was likewise impossible, with most of Fajr's sources having fled. Those few who remained spoke excitedly of Sir Hugh, but knew even less than the vizier did.

Now, annoyed at having been taken to the city in the first place when his instincts insisted he should be killing Templars, Sihr had taken to questioning the motives of their leader.

"How do we know Amala isn't the one who will be converted? She says herself she was once a Christian," he said.

Ignoring him, the vizier shook his head as he went through the soldiers' meager belongings. "How could anyone wander so far off the road by accident? Miles from their regiment and they decide to head in the wrong direction? Were they drunk? Or simply stupid? It's a wonder these Latins found the Byzantine Empire at all!"

A small locked chest vexed the vizier. He tried to pry it open with his dagger, but could not. Seeing his frustration, Sihr waved his hand at it, twisted his fingers, and moved the simple mechanism with his will. The box popped open. Fajr nodded Sihr his thanks, but was disappointed to find only some identification papers within.

The vizier plopped himself on the ground and collected the sergeant's blood in a small bowl. "At least we now know Baldwin is emperor," Fajr mused. "His partner Boniface must be bristling at the loss. I wonder how long he'll be able to hold things together. A week? Two?"

Chuckling to himself, he withdrew his notebook and pen and, using the soldier's blood, since it was the only liquid handy, scribbled away.

"There must be *some* force behind this Templar's visions. But what could it be? An elder?" Fajr mumbled as he wrote.

Meanwhile, the grim sorcerer paced in anger.

"Did you even hear me?" Sihr asked.

Fajr turned his eyes towards the agitated sorcerer. "Do they teach such disrespect for the chain of command in the desert?"

Sihr bristled, shook and then jangled one hand angrily in the air as if trying to banish the negative feelings from his heart. As the warm blood in him quelled his hunger, he sat himself down on a rock and began scratching shapes in the dirt with a small stick.

"Even so, vizier, do you believe Amala wears a veil in her heart?" he asked almost absently.

Fajr shrugged. "Only Ar-Rahman knows, but let me give you some advice. Sometimes, my friend, on the spur of the moment, you make marvelous decisions, such as when you suggested these crusaders were traveling too close to our little cave and we should stop them. That was a good decision. Now, though it is a shame to kill the kine, we have food and know that Baldwin is emperor, though why my friends in Constantinople did not know this, I cannot say. To continue to try and further impugn the integrity of a woman we are bound by oath to follow, this is not such a good decision."

Sihr waved a disdainful hand at the corpses that lay just outside the fire's range. "What import is there to this? Who cares which mortal sits on what throne?"

Fajr twisted his head sideways and marveled at the statement. "You have spent far too much time in the desert, Sihr Haddad. How could you choose to live alone? How can you keep your hunger at bay without the warm buzz of talk in your head? How can you refine your mind without the great libraries that cities have to offer? How can you prefer the sameness of sand and sky to the golden domes of Constantinople?"

Sihr laughed. "You speak of distractions, tricks to bide the time. I have faced my hunger so often that we know each other better than any mortal man or woman can know one another. As for my mind, the desert caves have forgotten more secrets than all the world's libraries contain. And your gilded mosques and churches? Sad imitations of the mountains and celestial orbs. There is no greater beauty than the desert at night. It is God's heart revealed. My hunger melts to nothing in such moments."

"But you are here," Fajr said.

"I have noticed as much," Sihr nodded, in an attempt at humor.

"Why?"

"The desert sky said it should be so. Visions I cannot begin to describe, unmistakable portents bade me to reconnect with my clan and the world of man. I had no choice but to obey. I do not know if this is for my personal edification or if there is some task I must perform. In any event, it has been a trying experience," Sihr said, in even tones filled with sadness. Shaking the memory of his home from his mind, he added, "Now tell me why it is important that this Baldwin has been chosen as emperor? And, for that matter, what it is he is now emperor of?"

Feeling a nascent bond with the sorcerer, Fajr grinned. "My friend, he is emperor of whatever they decide to call the remains of Byzantium! Probably the Latin something-or-other! First of all, it's a surprise to me at least that the Latins are already this far north. I'd thought Constantinople would keep them all busy for a time. Its importance to us is that the new human order is being established rapidly, which means the Cainite order will follow suit. I expect that Sir Hugh of Clairvaux will be playing out whatever part he has in this sooner rather than later."

"Then this is all the more reason not to trust the conclusion of our mission to this convert," Sihr said.

Fajr rolled his eyes. "You judge her too harshly. Would you slay someone who spoke the word of Allah?"

Sihr raised his head. "If he were a Templar planning to raise an army and invade Egypt? Yes!"

Fajr shook his finger in the air. "You have a point, I admit, but she is right to wait for now, as shown by your own magic. As for Sir Hugh's trances, I would expect at least some curiosity from someone who had experienced visions of his own!"

Sihr's eyes went wild. Fajr immediately realized he'd said the wrong thing, and wished he could somehow yank the words out of the air and back into his mouth.

"You dare compare his addled babbling with my most sacred moments?" Sihr shouted, rising.

"No, no! Please! My foolish tongue misspoke! I know this is a grave game we play! Didn't I tell you how that maniac, Hugh, swimming in his full armor, nearly caught me? His hand was on my foot! He almost caught me, I tell you! And what would his Templars have done with me, then? I know this is a dangerous game," Fajr said, trying to think of as many words he could for "I'm sorry!"

The enjoinders fell on deaf ears, however, as Sihr stood, whirled and walked off toward the place his black horse waited, his worn burgundy cape flapping behind him. With a surprisingly agile leap for a man his size, he managed the beast's back in a flash.

"Wait! Where are you going?"

Whatever command he issued the horse, Sihr rode towards the black forest. He did not turn back, but said, "The augur indicated the time of death for Sir Hugh. It indicated no such time for the death of his fellows."

Fajr stumbled after him, debating whether to take his own mount or to hold to the hope his words could stop him.

"Don't be a fool, Sihr! You risk exposing us all!"

But by then the sorcerer was too far off to hear.

Alone now, Fajr glanced at the darkness where Sihr was headed. He could try to follow, but the sorcerer's charger was fast and tough and Sihr was a master horseman. In city streets Fajr might have had the advantage. In the wilderness, he would never catch the Bedouin.

Instead, he glanced back at the three bodies, still wet with blood. Heeding the call of his thirst, he decided to drink what was left.

***

Sihr's horse soundlessly galloped in the direction of the Templar camp, his vows of fealty left as far behind as the flustered vizier. He felt truly alone again for the first time in many weeks. The solitude, like the dark, blanketed and comforted him, making him feel more in control again, but the familiarity of such comforts soon became a painful indication of failure. After centuries alone among sand dunes, caves and animals, he'd emerged from solitude to embrace the very sense of community of which the vizier spoke. Yet his control, when challenged, slipped from him quickly. It was the first time the Beast had decided for him for as long as he could remember, and he was barely aware of it.

I am giving them every reason to be afraid of me, he lamented.

The distinction in weight, feeling and texture, between natural instinct, intuition, and the primordial hunger that communicated nothing but its own need, was as clear to Sihr as the difference between night and the long-unseen day. But how could they trust him on that point now? Worse still, perhaps, though he yearned to prove himself acceptable to his fellows, he retained his conviction that allowing the Templar's plans to proceed for any reason was a mistake.

It was another mile before the sorcerer realized he was not so much concerned that Hugh's visions were true, but that his own might be false—a possibility he'd never before entertained. His once-absolute trust in the messages he saw in the sands and stars, which had been his guides both to survival and the acquisition of arcane power, was fading. This then was the dark side of community—that the voice of another might challenge the very foundation of the self. Until he had emerged from the desert he had had no such other to insist on forming a consensus view, or indeed to wrest from him the very reasons he had emerged in the first place.

As he and the horse slipped through the varying shades of black, the camp's dim glow and the tips of its tents grew visible, glowing beyond the natural brush like the rude intervention of a city on nature's course. He could still turn back, he should, but something would not let him.

He came closer before slowing down, perhaps too close. They had been fortunate in encountering no difficulty in concealing themselves thus far, but there was always the danger that, as word of Sir Hugh's unholy crusade spread, they might attract Cainites with keener senses than Gondemar and his ghouls sergeants.

He paused his steed at the camp's edge and sneered at the banal evenness of its perfect lines. *They imagine their*

122   Assamite

Order and rules to be somehow closer to God than the grit and earth from which Creation itself rose.

He felt his hunger grow again. It would be easy to tell them differently. With the rage and the teeth Allah had given him, he could show them the truth in a mixture of pleasure and pain.

A sudden rustle, hooves on earth and twig, reached Sihr's ears. It came not from the camp or the hastily cleared road that led through its center, but from a spot a hundred yards to the east. Thankful to be diverted from his inner turmoil, he steered his horse towards the sounds.

A knight, looking strangely familiar, led a group of ten men on horseback out of the camp. Sihr wondered at once why they weren't taking the main road, and why they were trying so very hard to be quiet. As they moved east, farther from the camp, Sihr shadowed them. He was not quite as skilled in the arts of moving invisibly as Amala, but centuries in the desert had not left him without his ways.

Your target is here, Sihr, at just the right time, a voice whispered in his head. *Show him the truth.*

Sihr rubbed his brow, realizing this was no vision that spoke to him, but a yearning as old as Caine to which his own mind lent vocabulary and tone.

Begone! he shouted inwardly, but it laughed. Sihr turned his attention to the group.

The ghouls and thralls were of no concern to the sorcerer; they could be dealt with simply by blade or sorcery. As for the Templar leading them, Sihr thought of a dozen ways he might make him die. Blood-poisons, culled from the deepest physicality of his being, could slow or damage him. A blast of mystic fire on his chest might drive him to frenzy, startling his men for a precious few seconds and giving Sihr time for a decapitating blow. He'd heard tales in Alamut that the Ventrue were devilishly hard to destroy, that their tough, dead flesh could turn aside sword-blows and even fire, but he was sure his sorcery would be a match for any Frank.

And then you could drink.

For a second Sihr was afraid he'd been spotted, but instead the Templar turned to a man at his side.

"Do not look at me that way! I betray no one!" he barked. Sihr recognized the voice as Appeles, the Templar who'd taken Fajr's poisoned crossbow bolt. But why was he speaking of betrayal?

The group stopped advancing, and made a small circle of their horses.

"Please, you mistook our concern for judgment, Sir Appeles. As always, we shall follow you to the earth's ends," the man beside him said, his face and voice filled with the blind loyalty of a ghoul, bound by the addictive blood of a vampire.

"He has exceeded his authority, acting without even the knowledge of the Order or the Church. He recruits the Greeks as if they were somehow not fallen from the true Church!" Appeles said.

"Yes," they reassured him. "He goes too far."

"Without the Order there is only darkness!"

"Yes, we do right to try to stop him," they said, smiling.

"It is the Beast's road."

"Of course!" they said.

Appeles nodded, then turned to go on.

He is comforted in his actions by puppets. Just as we are all sometimes deceived by false voices, Sihr thought, braced by the exchange. He fell back and let them continue on their way. Clearly, it was best if the Christian authorities— mortal and immortal alike—learned of Sir Hugh's plan. Stopping Appeles would be a disservice.

But they still do not know the truth! Don't let them go!

But by now, having heard the sheepish piping of Appeles's retainers, the Beast's ruse was so obvious the ancient sorcerer was able to banish it quickly, with the vague promise of some food before dawn.

There were lessons here, not to be scribbled down for some strange posterity as Fajr would have it, but to think on and incorporate into his being. By following his instincts, Sihr had at first imperiled his goals, yet instead, by holding back in the moment, obtained important news. Not only were the Templars not behind Hugh's strange efforts, they might even seek to stop him.

Pleased, he hung back and watched the glints of their armor recede in the night like misshapen stars.

***

Miles away and hours later, near the fringes of Constantinople, the morning sun found the dead and drained bodies of most of Brother Appeles's entourage. What remained was riddled with a strange plague that soon passed to the scavenging animals that fed upon them.

Appeles himself clung to his existence, but only barely. His sword by his side and his armor torn by savage combat, he was propped against a tarnished marker on the road to the city gates. A film of black, bilious fluid coated his face and chest, and he slept in the oblivion of torpor. He had not moved for several hours.

When the rays of the eastern sun first touched his flesh, nothing happened. A Ventrue of powerful blood, his undead flesh was more resistant than most. But it took only a minute or two for the first wisps of smoke to rise from his torso. His exposed flesh blackened like wood in a bonfire and small licks of flame burst from the tears in his armor.

The pain of the sun, anathema to all Cainites, finally forced him from slumber, but could not compel him to action. Instead, looking at the impossible brightness of the sun, his very eyes boiling away, he pushed one last request through his parched throat and cracked lips:

"Blessed Mother, please forgive me."

Chapter Eleven

May 27, 1204

Kosmas Pangalos winced as he looked down at the sword he'd just split in two with an ill-placed hammer blow. Paumer, the barrel-chested, red-haired Templar armorer charged with teaching him to become a swordsmith, clenched both hands and shook them.

"Too hard! Too hot! How many times must I tell you? A balance is required! A balance! Pay attention to the materials you work with!" he said. "Again!"

Kosmas shrugged sheepishly. At least this time Paumer didn't look ready to surrender to his frustration and tear Kosmas limb from limb, as he had with the first three swords he broke. But Kosmas was keenly disappointed at himself, both for failing to learn the new trade and, perhaps even more to the point, for ever having mentioned he was a maker of kettles.

"I beg you," he said. "Let me give up! I am far too stupid to master such a subtle task!"

"Agreed!" Paumer said. "But there's a shortage among you Greeks of the skills needed for war, and since neither of us makes these decisions, you will try yet again."

Unhappy as he could be, Kosmas pumped again at the bellows that heated the coals. He paused, hoping to change the subject.

"Perhaps there's a bit of news you could confirm for me, good sir?" Kosmas asked his teacher.

"And what might that be?" the armorer asked, raising an eyebrow.

***

So, Prince Licinius has caught himself an Assamite, Lucita of Aragon mused as she watched Adrianople's thick walls through the window of her carriage. She'd heard three different versions of the capture, each told with the utmost sincerity and gravity. She preferred the one where Licinius himself dealt the final blow, perhaps because it was the most ludicrous, but was certain all three were fabrications. Most likely it was luck that had delivered the Saracen into his hands—but why should Licinius admit that, when he had such a prize to strut about?

A sudden lurch snapped her back to her rough environs. The plush, deep pillows meant to smooth the bumpy ride were failing utterly. The expertly crafted and finely adorned carriage that carried her was being rattled nearly to pieces as its four-horse team pulled it along the rough space of rock and fallen timber that barely passed for road. Though dour for much of the journey, Lucita grew pleased as she saw the shadowed outlines of Greek footmen on the road, guarding the refugee camps' outskirts. Recent reports led her to believe that conditions here would not allow for even a modicum of security, so things were indeed changing rapidly. That fact clearly brightened the prospect that her mission here might have true import.

Two years ago, she'd been part of a Lasombra delegation in Venice trying to exercise some influence over the course of the crusade that had eventually come to Constantinople. She'd failed to have much of an effect then, but perhaps this time would be different. She had little desire to report another failure to the elders of her clan, or to her sire in Castile.

As the wooden wheels of her carriage stumbled along, bringing her deeper into the camp, her spirits rose even more. Far from the anticipated social ataxia, there were group fires, corrals, even some tents where merchants displayed wares. Men and women of different dress and stature—ghouls most likely—were cooperating with one another in the repair and maintenance of the meager shelters. Cainites of every stripe worked to coordinate the efforts of their thralls. Perhaps most exciting, weapons and armor were being cleaned, repaired and forged.

It was a short trip from there to the Templar camp. The hill separating the two sites was quite steep. More than once, her servants had to push the wagon's wheels over roots, rocks and other obstacles that even the four horses could not manage. Lucita grew quite bored with the delays, but when the camp appeared over the rise, with its smooth flat roads and orderly layout, looking the part of a small capital city, she let out a gasp.

Introductions were made to those knights guarding the main road, after which she was welcomed with all the courtesy due her. And why not? Sir Hugh already knew she represented powerful Lasombra elders whose support could greatly benefit his efforts. The Templars provided Lucita with a private tent not far from Hugh's own. Inside, she found many comforts—pillowed chairs and an ornate table, much more luxurious than anything the austere knights allowed themselves. It promised to be a pleasant stay. Already her attendant Dolores had arrived and was beginning to unpack. Lucita would have to remind the silly fool to count the heads of the knights and the men-at-arms, to get a sense of what force Sir Hugh already commanded. Later. For now, she wanted to refresh herself.

"Dolores, have the boy brought here, but be discreet about it," she commanded. The boy in question was one Rodrigo, one of the loyal peasants from home who traveled with her to provide a supply of nourishment. He was still hale and healthy and happy to exchange his blood for the pleasure Lucita's kiss sent through his form, as was only proper.

The wrinkled face regarded her with no expression. "Do you not fear to offend Sir Hugh? They say he safeguards a family of Greek children—"

"I know, I know." Lucita waved her servant off. "But even this holy Templar of ours must feed. And how can Sir Hugh be offended by what he does not see?"

Some hours later, the Latin noblewoman stepped into the cool night and took in her surroundings. As she did, a pretty, dark-skinned woman meekly emerged from Hugh's tent and slowly made her way through the camp. A few knights acknowledged her with bows.

She is no stranger to the camp. This must be Amala, then, Lucita thought. *The Arab woman he spends hours with in supposedly spiritual conversation.*

As the woman walked close by, Lucita whispered to Dolores, intentionally loud, "Look, there's his concubine. Sir Hugh must be about, then."

Amala froze in her tracks. Lucita noticed at once, and with some surprise, that the Arab's black eyes were glaring at her. It was not an appropriate gaze for a peasant who would, by rote, avert her eyes. As if suddenly aware of the strangeness of her expression, Amala looked away and moved forward.

Lucita, her curiosity alight, was not about to allow that.

"Concubine," she said, repeating the irritating term, "announce to Sir Hugh that Lady Lucita of Aragon wishes to speak with him. You're allowed to do that, aren't you, concubine?"

The peasant shook—visibly shook!—and half-turned away. When she finally lowered her eyes and slowly shook her head, the effort of it was clear for Lucita to see.

"No, lady. I am not allowed," the Arab whispered softly. "And Sir Hugh has taken a vow of chastity. I am not in any sense his 'concubine.' May I go?"

"Yes," Lucita said, now fascinated. This Arab girl in a peasant tunic had dared to contradict her. The fact there were Assamites about had been made clear by Licinius's recent luck. Lucita knew the Saracens as masters of disguise, but could their masquerade be pierced so easily?

Hide in plain sight, she recalled her companion and ersatz superior Tomasso Brexiano telling her once. *What a gift this might make for Sir Hugh!*

The moment Amala turned to leave, Lucita's hand shot out and grabbed her by the arm. She resisted at first, and as she did, a small doll fell from the folds of her robe and tumbled to the earth.

Both of them stared at it.

"No. Don't go. Not just yet," Lucita said, raising her head to make eye contact. "Your name?"

The woman could not keep from looking up, and when she did, something electric passed between them that took Lucita aback. "Amala," she said.

"Arabic."

"Yes."

Not breaking eye contact, Lucita said, "What a lovely doll."

In an instant, the heir of Aragon moved to retrieve it. But in less than an instant, Amala's hand was already on it. Lucita leaned down and wrapped her own hand about Amala's. With a gentle, suspicious touch, Lucita tested the strength in that hand. It was firm. Immovable. All Cainites were inhumanly strong and those trained as warriors were stronger still. The fact that this supposed peasant's strength matched her own confirmed nothing, but, importantly, it also didn't disprove Lucita's suspicions.

Not sure what to do, for four long seconds, Lucita ticked off the possible advantages and disadvantages surrounding the untimely death of Sir Hugh. After a few moments, a wicked twinkle appeared in her eyes.

"Keep it, then," Lucita said with a smile.

She would say nothing for now, and wait instead to see how she fared in her meeting with Sir Hugh. The information about his concubine could be the very gift she was looking for.

Clutching the doll, Amala ran off.

***

Once alone, within the confines of her tent, Amala broke out in a bloody sweat, barely able to stand.

That woman knows I am not what I seem, or at least she suspects. Why didn't she speak?

She was furious at herself for being angered by the silly 'concubine' comment. Even an amateur would have spotted its intention. Her conversations with Sir Hugh were growing longer and more suspect, and the Assamite had borne many half-whispered insults and insinuations from the knights. While she disliked the extra attention, she had never responded with other than a demure averting of her eyes. This night, though, much was bearing on her mind, making her feel pressed in to the point where the brutish side of her Cainite nature was increasingly raising its head.

The last two weeks had been a series of mishaps. The mission to Constantinople had failed; then Fajr had related the story of his disagreement with Sihr, and the sorcerer's subsequent departure and seeming vow to kill a Templar. Next, Appeles, one of Hugh's most trusted knights, vanished with his retinue. Sihr had since returned and insisted the knight was off to reveal Hugh's plans to their Order's command, but the sorcerer had become increasingly distant, spending more time alone, becoming increasingly moody, as if reverting to his nomadic ways. Now word that Licinius had captured an Assamite spread like fire through the region and neither Amala nor Fajr could locate the sorcerer.

If that fool has gotten himself caught, I'll behead him myself!

It could be someone else, perhaps some poor Cainite whose skin happened to be dark, not even a Child of Haqim. Nevertheless, she could not wait much longer for Sihr to reappear. She could ask Sir Hugh to bring her to one of the Romanesque torture sessions on the pretext that her fluent Arabic might prove useful. Whereupon, if it were Sihr, the mission might well end in a bloody mess.

And now there is this woman. Lucita of Aragon.

There was something keenly different about her, something about the fire in her voice, that instantly slipped past all Amala's training and struck her to the bone. Confused feelings of misplaced rage welled in her breast the moment she heard that voice.

Was it just her voice? Was it her gait? Something about this creature seemed so horribly familiar. Her eyes? Her skin? The shape of her skull?

No, she decided as she looked down at the doll in her hands and gently folded its straw hair back in place. It wasn't any physical characteristic. It was the very spirit that oozed from her. This Lucita of Aragon was hard and unyielding—young, but already a creature of steel.

She recalled, in eidetic detail, someone Amala had known in life, another woman old beyond her years.

Interlude

The Present

The story paused, perhaps because the teller had reached a particularly difficult part. With the hesitation long enough for a question, Ruya felt obliged to ask one.

"You said when you began that you were in this story, that it was something you remembered yourself, that you were days away. What do these people have to do with you? What connects you to Sihr, Fajr and Amala?" she whispered.

Fatima spoke evenly, but there was an unmistakable emotion in her voice that Ruya had never been privileged to hear before.

"I met my dear Amala over a century before, before my Embrace, but after the dread Latin armies had taken Palestine in their so-called First Crusade. My father was a warrior in the service of Ibn Tumart, a great man who would grow to found the Almohad tribe that wrested Spain, Morocco and more from the moderate Almovarids. To be further educated in the ways of Islam, Tumart traveled east to Mecca, then Palestine, and my family accompanied him. It was in those lands I spent much of my youth, happy, until the crusaders arrived...."

***

June 12, 1101

The naked, blinding sun sat directly above, the eye of a burning God locked open in a sea of undifferentiated blue. Though Amala's veil remained in place, the flapping material of her skirt slowed her so terribly she had to tear it off. The bondage shed, her long lean legs found their full, natural stride. Her bare feet sent sprays of white sand flying behind her. Easily now she widened the distance between herself and the more ponderous, but stronger, crusader. After a happy laugh at her burst of speed, Amala returned to her even breathing and tried to guess how long it would take to reach the small oasis. Ahead, there was little else to block the view of the horizon, leaving small doubt he could track her, even if she did outrun him. Her only hope to evade him was to reach the terrain that lay ahead, carpeted with thick, fibrous vegetation, and somehow conceal herself within.

An odd thud made her look back. Seeing her increased pace, he had dropped his pack, and he too now picked up speed. By the time the oasis's edge was but fifty yards off, the crusader was catching up quickly. Two steps from a bed of palm trees, he tackled her. She giggled as they rolled together on the warm sand.

Feeling something caught beneath her, she gently reprimanded her heavy young lover. A quick move of her hand freed the doll from the small of her back. Gently she moved to straighten its straw hair and press its grain-filled belly back into shape.

"Andret, you nearly crushed it!" she said, making her round eyes wide as she pouted.

"I'll get you another," he answered, so drunk with the sight of her, he didn't bother to look at the toy. "Three if you like. Or even better, something more befitting a woman than a toy."

"But I like this one. It befits me fine," she answered.

"Well, we wouldn't want it crushed, then, would we?" he said. He gently pulled the faux human from her open, willing hand and laid it gently aside.

A wicked twinkle flashed in Amala's eyes and she stretched her neck forward. She bit gingerly at his lower lip, then pulled him down toward her.

In time, as the sun moved farther down in the sky, and its heat became not quite so base, the motion of their bodies melted into promises for later that night, and Andret left her to enjoy the breeze. Her body felt so alive it was difficult to relax, but romantic daydreams eventually carried her into a light sleep.

Then something cracked, quite clearly, among the trees in the oasis. Snapping her head up, Amala turned towards the sound and saw two dark eyes, glaring coldly from within the late afternoon shadows. At first she had thought it was some predator, a wild dog perhaps. That it was her best friend was little comfort.

"Fatima!" Amala said. "How long have you been there?"

"You were supposed to kill him," the other woman said, moving only her mouth. "To bring him away from the others and kill him. You said it was taking time to gain his trust. You didn't say you were planning to bear his young."

Amala sat up and made a face. She pulled some small twigs and blades of grass from her hair. "Haven't we had enough bloodshed?"

"No."

"But he's horrified by the way they've treated our people here, and sworn to abandon his fellows. I even read to him from the word of Muhammad, may Allah commend and salute him. He's already joined me in the prayers..." Amala said, unabashedly smiling at her dour counterpart. Finding Fatima's glare intolerable, she turned away and occupied her hands by preening the small doll.

"Then let Allah absolve him on Judgment Day," Fatima finally said. "And let death be his reward for his crimes in the here and now."

"Fatima, my sweet, you must believe people can change! We have souls, and by Allah's nature we all yearn for light. Isn't that right, my little one?" Amala said.

"Will you *please* stop talking to that piece of cloth while I'm here?" Fatima said. "Where were the souls of these so-called men when they drove my family from our home? Where were those souls when, as we tried to flee, they slaughtered them one at a time, youngest first, so my mother could see her babes cry to her with their final breaths?"

"And how many have we killed these last few months as we travel, drawing them away drunken from their camps with our dances and wicked promises, only to slit their throats? Twenty? Thirty?"

"Twenty-eight," Fatima said, nodding toward the notches on the hilt of the dagger she kept strapped to her side.

"And how many more must die to appease your need for vengeance?"

"All of them. Do you so quickly forget that, when men like your beloved Andret entered Jerusalem, they killed and dismembered all the civilians, women and children, too?"

"I remember."

"That the piles of bodies were as big as houses?"

"I remember."

"That there were once thousands of Muslims and Jews living in that city and now all are dead?"

"I remember!"

Amala hissed some air between her teeth as she rose. She wiped herself as clean as she could, then put her open hand out to Fatima and waited. Eventually, the darker girl tossed a carrying sack out to her feet. Gruffly, Amala grabbed it and withdrew a new soft tunic more suitable for travel. Rather than return the sack to Fatima, as expected, Amala kept it by her side. Fatima was puzzled and hurt by her sudden show of independence. Almost since they'd met, Fatima, the stronger of the two, had carried the sack. Though they were about the same age, she tended Amala as a mother tended her child.

"So. Will you marry him?" Fatima said, gritting her teeth. "In a mosque?"

"He has a Christian wife," Amala responded, knowing it would further irk the sensitivities of her companion. "But I'm not sure I would, even if he didn't. Though right now I feel as though I would follow him to the very ends of the earth."

"Once you said you would follow me anywhere," Fatima said as Amala let the tunic fall around her waist.

A sad smile played across Amala's face, making her look years older than sixteen. Suddenly full of pity at her friend's pain, Amala walked up and stroked Fatima's straight black hair. As she felt soft fingers brush her forehead and cheek, Fatima closed her eyes.

"You're so certain," Amala said. "You do your family proud, but…" She turned to look at the sky. "I… I'm not so hardened. Perhaps because I do not come from such hard stock, perhaps because Allah has other purposes for me. I was just a child when the crusaders came, but I remember what it was like to live in peace. My family converted, you know, in those days. Yes, I was born a Christian. I know we must fight, but I pray for peace every hour. Tell me, Fatima, do you?"

Though Amala's back was to her, Fatima shook her head.

Amala turned back and smiled: "I would follow you anywhere, my dear, through any desert, into any cave, up to the cold northern wastes, even into the den of one of those blood-drinking monsters they say rule the nights— anywhere except the dark place you are so very intent on heading to," she whispered. "But don't think on it too much. Some things it doesn't pay to dwell on. We both know I only slow you down."

"Only because you choose to betray your people!" Fatima growled, her lower lip quivering.

Seeing no point in further words, Amala shook her head, whirled and strode across the sand, matching her feet to the vague impressions she'd made while running, leaving her shaken friend behind as quickly as she could.

As Fatima watched, still standing in the trees' shadows, a tear fell from one almond eye and ran down her cheek.

Hours later, after the great sphere of white fire had rolled slowly beyond the mountains and the first few precious stones of the night sky twinkled, an eager Amala rushed to a small clearing about a half mile from a crusader's encampment. As expected, Andret was in their usual spot, lying on their blanket, one knee raised, eyes closed as he faced the heavens. She'd sworn she would hold him to his promise of joining her evening prayer.

"Come on, Andret, up with you! We have to face Mecca!" she said cheerfully. In most mosques, men and women were required to pray separately, but under the circumstances she felt no shame in bending the rules, though she would insist he pray two steps closer to the holy city than she.

When there was no response, she playfully kicked at him. Still no response. Suddenly concerned, she knelt and felt over him with her hands, calling his name over and over. He did not move. Near his neck, her hands came across something warm and wet, and then an odd flap in his skin. Terrified, she raised a moist finger to her lips and touched her tongue to it. At the coppery taste, she shrieked long and loud.

"Fatima! Fatima!" she sobbed, throwing herself forward on the dead body of her lover. Heaving, she gasped in the dry desert air, then wailed once more to the dark between the stars.

"Enough! Enough" a voice hissed from nearby.

Andret's sword still in her hand, and a new, particularly thick notch on her dagger, Fatima stepped out from her hiding spot and looked nervously this way and that.

"Quiet, fool! We're not so far from their patrols! They'll hear you!"

Amala continued wailing.

"I only did what you should have done!"

"What I should have done?" Amala cried, turning her red eyes to her dark companion. "This is not about what

Assamite

should and should not be! This is about one thing and one thing only—you!"

"He was the enemy...."

In a sudden shiver of movement, Amala bent down over the corpse and felt about his neck. Finding what she wanted, she yanked the necklace free and held it up for Fatima to see.

"There! There! Can you see the silhouette despite his warm blood? Can you?" she cried.

Fatima fell silent as she recognized a small golden charm of Amala's, one she knew bore the Prophet's name. If Andret had been found wearing it, it would have meant his death. It was clear he had not intended to return.

"Yes, that's right, look! Look! You stupid animal!" she shrieked, shoving the small bauble into Fatima's face. "You were wrong! He was coming to me!"

Still shrieking, she pointed back in the camp's direction and said, spitting as she spoke, "There are a hundred evil men there you could have vented your anger on. How could you be so stupid, so petty, so jealous?"

"I wanted to save you," Fatima said numbly.

Eyes wide with rage, Amala leapt at her, shrieking, "Save yourself!"

Instinctively ready to fight, Fatima lifted the knight's heavy sword. Amala first scratched at Fatima's face, then simply held it still with both hands. The blade between them, Amala's trembling face wet with tears and the dead man's blood, they kissed.

Chapter Twelve

May 29, 1204

Lucita flipped her black braided locks back in an effort to conceal her annoyance and instead to meet the man once more with a wicked twinkle and disarming smile. Though the boy had well sated her, this terrible creature was making her borrowed blood boil.

"Perhaps I am as yet naïve in such things, but I simply don't understand. If you wish to slay a snake, would you lop off its tail or simply behead it?" Lucita said. "Or do you simply follow the rule of these stupid crusaders, who sought Palestine, but took Constantinople because it was closer?" Pretty though Sir Hugh was, and amply charming, she had yet to find his words at all delightful.

With calm deference, Sir Hugh unrolled a map on the table that showed Palestine. Those areas lost to Saladin, as well as the other Islamic lands, were indicated with a series of nearly perfect, straight diagonal lines. Hugh tapped his rough index finger on a small circle that indicated Jerusalem, which was quite plainly surrounded.

"It is well known that the holy city is isolated. Once conquered, the supply lines, even contact with the outside world, would be impossible to maintain. It would be a false victory," Hugh began. But by then Lucita's attention had wandered and she sipped from the goblet Hugh had provided. It, like him, was a pretty thing, a finely crafted golden base that held an agate half-sphere. The dregs of the crimson liquid it held now revealed the fine marble strips of color within. She'd been pleased he served her with such finery, and now preferred to dwell on its beauty rather than listen to his babble. By the time she looked up again, his lecture on the military campaign was at an end.

She put the goblet down, flattened her gown in her lap, and sighed. "As I've said, Sir Hugh, I represent certain powerful Lasombra elders," Lucita began. She'd planned on hesitating a bit, to let Sir Hugh wonder who they might be, but instead, to her surprise, he filled in the missing information himself.

"The Amici Noctis, yes I know, lady. The friendly majority who seek to abandon the smaller Muslim factions within your clan," he said plainly.

"I see," Lucita said. Though there was no real danger in Hugh's possession of such knowledge, she was not used to having it presented as public knowledge, and thought it a bit rude. "May I ask what else you know of me?"

"That you are of royal blood, the Bishop Moncada's childe; that you are quite skilled at diplomacy and driven by an intelligent ambition," Hugh said.

Lucita looked down, annoyed to be so easily summed up. "You give me much credit. I fear I have not given you enough. But tell me, do you come upon your intelligence through the Templars, the Ventrue hierarchy, or some other means?"

A strange smile played upon his lips that told her at once he would not be forthcoming. "It sometimes seems they are all as one. But please do not fear me. We share a love of Christ and a hatred for the Saracens. There is no reason your masters and I should not be allies," he said, meeting her eyes with a steady gaze, as if somehow trying to mesmerize her.

If he was, it certainly wasn't working. Lucita grinned widely back, parting her full lips enough to show her pointed canines.

"Well, there is certainly no reason we should ever be enemies, Sir Hugh," she answered. "I will tell my betters of your plans and of what you have accomplished here."

She half-rose, ready to leave. Hugh stood and pulled the chair out for her.

"And do you think they will give me their support?" he asked, showing for a moment a slight weakness in his eagerness for her opinion.

She brushed her back into his chest as she rose, then turned to face him, briefly supporting herself with a hand on his broad shoulder.

"I am sure they will look upon your efforts with favor, and supply you with whatever you need," she began. As she stepped away, breaking contact, she added, "But only when you are ready to reach Palestine."

Hugh nodded. He held the tent flap open while she departed.

Outside, Lucita stormed along the neat row of tents toward her own. *Such a fool will never get out of Adrianople, let alone across the sea!* she thought. Still, he was drawing more and more support, not only from the refugees, but from established Cainites in nearby cities. Soon, she realized, if things continued, his pull would be felt in Constantinople itself, where, with Michael dead, the delicate balance of factions could easily be tipped, or tripped, in any number of directions. That shift might create possibilities.

Lucita was pleased she'd decided not to mention her suspicions regarding Hugh's dark-skinned concubine, Amala. So pleased, in fact, that by the time she reached her tent and ordered her servants to pack, though by no means absolutely convinced the creature was an Assamite spy, she found herself hoping she was. Smiling, her head swelled with the possibilities for personal growth and power, in a world without Sir Hugh.

***

Sir Hugh snatched up the fine goblet he'd served Lucita with, and, as he stared hungrily at the few red drops left within, found himself squeezing the base so hard, the fine gold designs bent and broke beneath the force of his hand. He tried to let go in time to save it, but it was too late. Free of its gently formed moorings, the agate slipped and crashed to the ground. The rare goblet was ruined. He'd been ill-prepared for another disappointment. The Amici would have been strong allies, but now he thought the Queen of Heaven had only brought their representative here as another test.

How many more such tests will there be, Mother? How many? he asked inwardly.

Sir Abelard had never returned with the promised confirmation. Appeles was missing for, what, now? Fifteen nights. Dead at the hands of Assamites, or perhaps worse, bringing word of Hugh's plans to some Templar masters, at a time when he was ill-prepared to receive their antagonism. It was crucial that he have his sire Geoffrey on his side first—he would know the proper way to approach the mortal Order and the Cainites who used it. And why had his letter to Paris yet gone unanswered?

It was a test, Hugh told himself again.

Just as he wondered again how many more there would be, a spasm of pain took him to his knees and his head filled once more with visions. And though they took him far from the world he perceived, and he remembered them as bliss, he would never call them a relief.

Chapter Thirteen

August 3, 1204

Kosmas Pangalos shuffled uncomfortably among the vast crowd of Cainites, thralls and ghouls who awaited Sir Hugh's signal. His mail armor, though thankfully not forged by his own hand, was terribly tight and constricting, a sensation aggravated by the heavy cloak he'd been forced to wear as a disguise. While those about him shifted with anticipation, Kosmas had been far too uncomfortable for far too long to be happy about it. The only thing that kept the darkling half of his psyche from welling up was the knowledge that going into a rage in the midst of this group would be suicide. Still, it was a tough struggle for the pot-maker.

Worse still, the long blade of the sword he'd been given weighed heavy in his hand. His arm already hurt from having waved it so often in response to the earlier speeches from the elders and princes. It took them ages to give the valiant effort their blessings, and to warn that they be sure to get their proper share of the booty.

Who'd have thought the unbreathing could be so long-winded? Kosmas mused.

Now he waited yet again, this time for Sir Hugh, who seemed not to notice any of them as he stared out at the horizon from his tower balcony. How much longer, he wondered, before he gave them the nod? The longer he was away from the sound of Sir Hugh's confident, commanding voice, the more he thought the whole crusade a bad idea. Not in general, necessarily. After all, what did a pot-maker know about the rights and wrongs of military campaigns? But, certainly, a bad idea for him.

Would the ship be comfortable? He'd heard it was even worse and more tightly cramped than the camps had been before the Templars arrived. Even afterward, the floor of his lean-to never matched the warm pile of straw by the hearth he had kept in his small, dark shop. The memory of home pinched his heart. Was it still there, in the vast city's most modest bazaar, he wondered? Or had it been burned, trampled and destroyed like so many others? If fire hadn't claimed it, his hovel wasn't a likely target for pillaging, so perhaps…

With no significant movement from the stoic figure on the balcony forthcoming, the weary Kosmas glanced lazily about, hoping he might be close enough to a tree that he could reach it and lean against it to rest. At times he was so hemmed in by the crowd, he couldn't even turn his shoulders. Instead, he turned just his head this way and that, seeking some slight vision of rest.

And there, to his right some twenty feet away, was no tree, but a cart. Seven men sat atop it and others crowded about it, but there was a small open area on one side he might be able to reach.

Cautiously he shifted his weight sideways and made for the cart. Encountering great resistance and annoyance, he made his way, pushing, wedging his chest and waist into the small spaces between bodies. Moving through mortals was easy, and the army was composed mostly of thralls and ghouls, but the occasional Cainite he encountered slowed him dreadfully. It was well worth the effort, though, for at last the cart's edge came within reach. He had only to put out his hand, grab it and pull himself toward it. Once there, he could lean against it with impunity, even, if he could manage it, lie down beneath it.

With a smile on his face, his hand reached out and his stubby fingers wrapped along the blessed wood's top edge. With a grunt, he pulled forward. Rather than reaching the cart, though, he found himself directly in the path of a brown-robed creature. The figure, whatever his destination, had spied the same gap Kosmas wished to take advantage of, and the two collided.

Its robes were that of a monk, but that mattered little in a crowd where all were disguised as some harmless something or other. Everyone was at great pains to appear as anything other than the army they hoped they were.

Inappropriately infuriated, the figure cursed at him in some language he didn't recognize, then tried to move forward again. To make matters worse, Kosmas had somehow managed to snag his sword in the fellow's robes. Feeling a sudden tug, Kosmas pulled. The robes tore, revealing for a second a deeply dark skin that even the petty merchant knew was neither Latin nor Greek.

The vision lasted briefly. When Kosmas looked again, the black skin was white, the hair Viking red. The figure even grinned and bowed politely, before turning to make his way toward the tower. Kosmas was dumbfounded. Had he seen what he saw? And what were the words that had been cursed at him? *Elif air ab tizak?* Something like that. What sort of language was that, with its guttural intonations? It sounded more like someone trying to cough up phlegm than proper speech.

He repeated the sounds absently to himself until someone slapped him on the shoulder.

"Practicing your Arabic curses for the war?" the fellow said with a lusty laugh.

"Arabic?" Kosmas mumbled. The slow-moving wheels of his brain set to turning.

The figure was now nearly at the tower's base, an even worse view than Kosmas had. Then a second figure, much like the first, but moving in from a different direction, appeared by his side. Then a third. In unison, they changed. Their colors shifted so they were no longer that of any human or Cainite, but matched instead both the hue and texture of the fieldstone tower. Practically invisible, they climbed. And no one else, *no one* in this vast crowd of undead nobility, soldiers and would-be crusaders had even blinked.

　　　　　　　　　　Assamite

"Assamites," Kosmas said, softly at first. Then again, louder: "Assamites!" When no one reacted, he screamed, pointing at the wall, "*Assamites! Assamites! Assamites!*" He screamed so loudly now that the crowd, starved for something to do while waiting, gave him their full attention. A few people next to him, though as far as he could tell they hadn't seen anything themselves, decided to take him at his word and joined in the cry. Together, they chanted, "*Assamites! Assamites! Assamites!*" while Kosmas continued pointing.

From the crowd's periphery, Gondemar, wary since the boy's warning, searched for the source of the screams. Tensing, he spotted the plump vampire's frantic pointing. At first, as he scanned the area, he saw nothing but the even-sized stones that comprised the structure. There was not so much as a stray shadow shifting between gray and black. Then something along the rough texture caught his eye. A shape wavered as it rose, like an enormous invisible spider rippling beneath the wall's surface. Without a second thought, Gondemar signaled the knight to his left by tapping his upper lip with his index finger twice. Two loud blasts burst from a long horn. All eyes turned to Gondemar. He quickly raised three fingers, one half-bent, then pointed to the tower wall.

In response to his signal, there was a quick shifting in the crowd as bows and crossbows were drawn and loaded. Then, with a quick slash from Gondemar, scores of arrows and bolts set sail in the air, a rain of jet-black lines arcing against the pale colors of the clouds and sky.

Some shots went high, whizzing past the figure of Hugh, to clatter uselessly on the balcony floor. Others missed the tower entirely. Still others went low, impaling a few unlucky soldiers. But, in the end, sheer numbers outweighed skill, and a majority of the missiles struck the tower wall. Here again, most were useless, shattering, splintering against the rock, or lodging in the tight spots between stones.

Stefan Petrucha   147

But, again, by dint of numbers, despite the misfires, the scattershot strategy succeeded. A mere ten feet down from the lip of the balcony, the three figures lost their eerie camouflage. Riddled with arrows and bolts, they tried to keep climbing. Now that they were visible, slowed, even more arrows hit their mark, and the figures soon tumbled into the angry crowd.

Gondemar thought at once to question them and quickly ordered they be taken prisoner, but no one was listening anymore, not even his own ghouls. There was no question in this army what the fate would be of anyone who dared assault their new angel. Having heard how Assamites fed with glee on Cainite blood, everyone was anxious to return the favor. In minutes, there was nothing left to be questioned. It was even impossible to tell if the attackers had been men or women.

The lucky few whose tongues had found the heady blood of their enemy raised their weapons high in the air and shouted, "Hugh! Hugh! Hugh!" The pulsing chant spread among the assembled crowd in a widening circle, louder and louder, until all present joined in. Even Kosmas, who thought he could hold out until the great knight himself had spoken, found himself screaming at the top of his lungs, thrusting the tip of his blade as high in the air as the length of his arm allowed, nearly dislodging his shoulder from the joint.

As the cry rose, Gondemar briefly feared they might attract the wrong sort of attention. But, he realized with a smug smile, they were far from the city, and he had no idea how to, or even if he should, control the raging, delighted mob. The only one who could do that now, Gondemar knew, was watching them all from the balcony, with what he imagined must be the greatest of pleasure.

Chapter Fourteen

June 18, 1204

There had been little to comfort Amala of late; Sihr had yet to resurface, and now it had been several nights since she'd seen Fajr. It was to be expected, since she'd been traveling outside the camp with Sir Hugh as he rallied support, but the fact of it did not aid her faltering spirits. The confident ease that enveloped the five knights as their steeds moved languidly along the wide flat road didn't help much either.

The night before, they'd been attacked. Twenty witless rogues provided the Templars with little more than a minor distraction and pleasant repast. The knights' unleashed ferocity hadn't surprised her—Sir Hugh actually snapped one in two with his knee and arms—but their sword-skills had. She calculated she could take as many as three of them, and perhaps Hugh as well, but no more.

This night, the hilly woods subsided into more open, flatter farm lands, where such ambushes were more difficult to engineer and thus more unlikely. As of sunset, they were north of Constantinople. While there was some foot and horse traffic as they passed over the Bridge of Justinian, once they traveled due east rather than south into Galata, the city's Genoese district, the passersby thinned to nothing. The square tops of a few genteel estates could be made out above the treetops, and the knights wondered which might be their goal.

Amala shared a horse with Sir Hugh, her arms wrapped tightly around his waist, agitated all the more by the comfort she found in his physical nearness. Though a fine rider herself, even by Assamite standards, the Byzantine tunic and heavy, dark blue stole he'd given her forced her to ride sidesaddle, accounting for some of their leisurely pace. Worse, the sensation of chain-mail pressing against her reminded her of Andret. It was a feeling a part of her wanted badly to explore. It was yet another feeling that had to be balanced against her duty to Alamut, strategic planning, spiritual responsibilities and an ever-present hunger for blood.

Increasingly pummeled by the divisions in her own mind, she thought, *I have become too many people.*

After a lengthy silence, Sir Hugh suddenly asked, "When and how did He come to you, Amala?"

Of late, he'd taken to speaking with her in the presence of his fellows as though they were alone, or the other Templars mere extensions of his will. They were for the most part his loyal childer, it was true, but speaking in front of them still made Amala uneasy.

Not now! Don't demand I speak of Jesus as Lord now! Allah forgive me.

She leaned out a bit and allowed her round green eyes to focus on his face. "It took many years. I was raised Muslim. To accept Him meant turning against my family, my father, my mother, my brother and sisters," she said, parsing her words.

"I am come to turn brother against brother..." Hugh quoted. "But there *was* a moment, wasn't there? After which the world itself, though familiar, clearly was no longer the same?"

"Was there such a moment for you?" she asked.

He nodded briskly. "Many. Each time I close my eyes and hear her voice, the cosmos is shattered and rebuilt anew. But we've all heard me tell of that."

Light laughter sprang from the knights at their master's self-effacement. It occurred to Amala that Sir Hugh was, of late, carrying himself more like a prince than a Templar, and his men behaved ever more like the members of his court.

"So this night," Sir Hugh said, crushing all hope Amala had of avoiding the question, "I ask that we hear from you."

Amala closed her eyes, gritted her teeth, and conjured, from a sad mating between memory and imagination, what she knew they wanted to hear. "A monk stayed behind after a lost battle, to help a wounded man. The two successfully hid from our soldiers, but when the old men and boys from my village scoured the battlefield for any arms and supplies the army failed to salvage, they came upon them. To prove themselves to Allah, they said, they threw small stones and sticks, until by and by they killed the wounded one. They took the monk prisoner, since the toothless old men thought he might be worth some sort of ransom.

"He was kept in a small, lightless hole," she continued. "I was taught that God wanted no man to suffer like that, so I sneaked food to him at night. Sometimes we talked. Days later, unable to agree on what amount to ask for, or from whom, the villagers just decided to kill him." She shifted slightly. "I think if there was a single moment that altered my course, it was when I saw his peaceful smile as his head rolled freely from his neck. He did not believe, in any way, that he was coming to an end, and thought only he would soon see God."

The knights nodded in heartfelt appreciation. Amala crumbled inside. What was she thinking? How could she have thus offered infidels any comfort? The story's gist was true enough, but the details had been shifted. The monk had been no Christian, but a Muslim scribe. Amala and the man's killers had been the Christians in that tale. Gritting her teeth at having so abused the memory, she wondered at what point precisely *taqiyya* evolved into sin, at what point, precisely, the person became the mask.

They'd just reached the crest of a small hill, and now, beyond some slight patches of wood, the high walls of Constantinople were visible, scorched and damaged from the siege. Hugh slipped from his horse, went to his knees and prayed. The other Templars did the same, leaving Amala to cross herself awkwardly and kneel, adding further to her discomfort.

The next night, they reached the great estate. Though not owned, *per se*, by the powerful Lasombra merchant Gabriella of Genoa, she had made catspaws of the noble family that dwelled there, and occupied it completely when she needed a haven away from the city. A mere few miles from the city walls, it provided an incomplete sanctuary from the war. Incomplete, because the deep tracks of siege engines insulted the fertile fields, and the road was tramped to mud by the foot- and hoofprints of an army. Soon, though, they also rode by untouched groves of olive trees and other farmlands, tended in the day by the peasants, then followed an untouched road that wound along the path of a small river where the wheel of an old broken mill still creaked.

A stone wall and iron gate surrounded the central grounds. There, peacocks slept unmolested, the prized rainbow spectacle of the males' feathers folded beneath their bodies for the night. The main house was nestled between tall, old-growth trees that competed in height with the lofty roof. White and green marble frescoes fit seamlessly into the smooth, ivory-colored walls. Though the centuries-old home's central form was square, with the open-air atria typical of Roman construction no doubt nestled within, a series of smaller rooms, with their own fine ceramic roofs, jutted out at regular intervals.

Amala watched Hugh as he took in the surroundings, trying to guess why his gaze had focused on the tall tower that dominated the house's southern side. It was clearly a more recent addition, though efforts had been made to match the original structure in both color and style. It provided both a view of the estate and the distant merchant ports of Galata. What was his interest?

Should an army gather here, it would be the perfect spot from which to oversee them, she realized. *The river Maritsa near Adrianople is too shallow for ships at any rate. Sir Hugh's crusade will have to be launched through other ports. In Constantinople. He imagines this his base.*

"All of you, dismount and prepare to greet our hostess," Hugh said as he leapt off his horse. As all obeyed, he pulled off his right glove and walked up to the oaken doors, which, though beautiful, looked strong enough to hold off an army. He lifted its large brass ring and pounded three times.

Pulled inward by two servants, the doors opened. In the center of a large hall, flanked by ghoulish lords and ladies, stood Gabriella of Genoa. Though in her thirties at the time of her Embrace, her skin had lost but a shade of the beautiful ruddy complexion people of her homeland were known for. Her face, though not pretty in a standard sense, was well formed and tended, and her black eyes radiated keen understanding. She'd taken to wearing Byzantine dress, topped with a heavily jeweled and decorated purple and gold stole, made from the finest silk brocades. Its gold patterns glittered in the light of the lamps her servants held. Bell-shaped sleeves hung loosely at her wrist as she touched her fingers to her forehead in greeting.

"Sir Hugh of Clairvaux, thank you for making the journey to see me," she said. "Especially when so many come instead to you."

Hugh stepped up, took her hand, and bowed deeply. "It is I who thank you, Bishop, for agreeing to make time to hear my request."

Gabriella gave him a formal smile as he rose. "It pleases me that you present yourself this way and use my Lasombra title. I'd feared the Templar in you might take offense at our use of church nomenclature. It is well known to us how many of Caine's children you have already drawn to your side, and how many more teeter on the brink, both prince and elder, fearfully withholding support for your valiant efforts until they are better able to discern which way the winds blow. I daresay with my favor you could draw quite a number from within Constantinople's walls as well. And we also both know that, without my support, you and your men will be walking toward Jerusalem."

"Quite so, Bishop," Hugh answered. "But if that's what it takes, that is what we shall do, as the first crusaders did."

"Tsk, tsk. Let's hope it doesn't come to that," she said in a pleasant tone.

Gabriella waved them all inside. "My servants will take you to your quarters. The rooms have been appointed in appropriate Templar style, with, of course, the exception of the presence of fresh blood, which I trust you will enjoy. So much of it has been wasted on the ground these days. We'll speak again shortly, in private, Sir Hugh."

She whirled, her clothing lagging only slightly behind her form. Perpetually flanked by her ladies, as if they were somehow attached, she walked off along a row of marble colonnades. Hugh and his knights were led up the wide staircase to the second floor where the bed chambers were.

Amala was led away from the men by a single servant, to another wing. As she traveled the corridors, she noted the number of statues, mosaics and paintings that filled the halls. Some were still unpacked, wrapped in protective wood frames; others were displayed prominently.

One unusual mosaic depicted a bearded Arabic man. A fiery angel, with the features of the Toreador Michael seen in so much of the art of Greek Cainites, was forcing his hand into the man's chest.

Seeing her curiosity, the young Greek ghoul who led her explained, "When the crusaders breached the walls, the Bishop did what she could to bring at least some of the city's great treasures here to protect them. She is a hard woman, with a sharp mind for trade. I have never seen her betray a single emotion she did not wish known. Yet I know that nightly she openly weeps over the great works she was not able to preserve. Have you ever heard of any who possess such a love of beauty?"

Amala shook her head. "I have only such a love for God. What does this mosaic depict?"

The servant glanced at it, trying to recall. Her face relaxed as the story came to mind. "It shows the prophet Muhammad, based on the story of how the angels cleaned a single black spot from his heart and made it perfect. It's one of the bishop's favorites. It was commissioned by Michael as an overture to the Muslims who lived among us."

At once, Amala wanted to explode, but managed to contain herself. "Such images are prohibited by Muslim law," she managed to say, calmly enough. Inside, she wanted to kill the ghoul, Gabriella, Hugh, all the Templars and then herself.

The servant shrugged. "Yes. I understand they were quite upset. Michael had it carefully hidden to prevent them from destroying it completely. Perhaps that's why it survived the sacking."

"Take me to my room now, please," Amala said.

The Greek nodded, led her down the hall and opened the door to a large chamber. Inside was a lush bed, a tall open window leading out onto a balcony, an armoire, a table with a wash basin, fresh linen, a goblet, and a pitcher, which her nose told her contained the promised blood. Intricate tapestries hanging from the wall and ceiling gave the room a more colorful appearance than the stone halls. It was, in its way, as elegantly appointed as some of the wealthier homes in Egypt.

"We assumed you were no Templar," the woman explained, noting Amala's surprise, "and therefore had not taken their harsh vows. Will this do?"

"It will," Amala said, then managed to add, "Thank you."

The servant entered, poured some blood from the pitcher into the goblet and handed it to Amala. "Is there anything else you require?"

"No," Amala said, sipping the liquid, her hunger delighted to find it still warm. She was desperate for something to soothe her, and lost herself in the repast far more than was usual.

The Greek servant, perhaps one of the very nobles who had once owned this house, stood in the doorway, curiously watching her feed.

"I would like to be alone."

The wraith-like figure bowed and exited.

Amala made certain the door was shut and noted the time by the moon's position. Then she clasped her hands, faced southeast toward Mecca and, as she bowed her head below her heart, gratefully intoned, "*Allahu akbar*," thus beginning her *isha*, or evening prayer. It was her first in many a night.

But even the joy of supplication was short-lived. A desire to destroy the graven image that depicted the Prophet welled within her, and, try as she might, she could find no convincing argument against the impulse. To do so would clearly put her in danger, but having so recently raped a memory for the sake of her disguise, she feared more for the state of her soul. With that abomination mounted ten yards down the hall, it felt as though, by leaving it intact, she had slipped to the far side of sin.

Hurting in her heart, Amala went through the ritual motions, hoping they might free her. Despite her best efforts to focus, her mind continued to stray, and her longings, though formless, were heeding the call of her frustration, rising ever closer to the surface of her mind. Unable to take comfort in the divine, she forced her thoughts to the sticky strands of the infidel web she yet tried to maneuver through, hoping analysis and strategy might take the place of prayer in calming the Beast within her.

Should Gabriella agree to supply the ships Hugh would ask for, a network of support would tumble into place. Within weeks, Amala calculated, the number of his followers would swell to as many as two thousand. The body of the army would of course be thralls and ghouls, but the Cainites among them could number as many as two hundred. Should he then manage to establish even a small hold in the lands of Egypt, even on some remote coastline, how quickly could he become a rallying point for others? The Setites there, serpent-worshipping foes of Islam and the Assamites, would be greatly heartened. In mortal courts, a daring and successful raid by a Templar force could inspire others to action—especially with the right vampiric whispers supporting it.

And what then?

Here I am, an Assamite warrior, and rather than plunging my teeth into their necks, I tell them tales of my conversion to Christianity. Here I am, a Muslim woman, passing before a graven image of the Prophet, unable to raise either hand or word against it. How much more will I risk for the soul of a dog who reminds me of a dead woman's lover?

When the words and motions of her prayer ended, rather than the smallest sparkle of communion, she felt hollow, abandoned, not by Allah, but by her own machinations. She walked over to the balcony where the great night beckoned, wild and free, but then turned her back even on it. A huge sadness welled up in her alongside the Beast. Perhaps this was the emptiness that led elders to choose torpid slumber over action.

In case it was, rather than giving in, she scanned the great house's high walls, focusing on windows and openings, trying to guess exactly where Hugh would be meeting with Gabriella. After briefly testing the wall's strength, she managed the climb down in two leaps, the way a mountain lion might scale the ragged rock walls of its well-known home.

Equally cat-like in her quiet, she crept along the flat base of the house, examining the source of any dim lights that shone from within. In a high-roofed sitting room, cramped with the presence of a dozen crates, she spotted her targets.

Sir Hugh stood by a roaring hearth, his mailed limbs and white-mantled body glowing orange from the flames, giving him the aspect of a ruddy demon from hell. Bishop Gabriella, still wearing the fine gown she'd greeted them in, sat in the center of a soft couch large enough to sit three comfortably. As Amala crept closer, she could hear their conversation.

"How will you distinguish those who seek to fight with you? By clan? By religion? What means will you use to see into their hearts?" Gabriella asked, with an almost royal tone.

"Any Cainite who seeks to serve the will of the Queen of Heaven and her purposes, as revealed through me, is welcome," Hugh answered, though clearly even he knew it was not the proper response.

Gabriella shook her head. "And if our kings were the wisest men in the world, earth would be a paradise and there would be no need for heaven. What of those who don't share your lofty aesthetic? Shall we make Cairo what Constantinople is today? And if not, how will you sort such pillagers out? And, in fact, does any army succeed without them?" she asked.

Hugh put both hands up against the hearth's dark gray mantelpiece, lighting his whole face with the glow from the fire. "Bishop, I saw with my own eyes a great bronze statue of Zeus, four hundred years old, pulled down from his seat on Olympus with tawdry ropes so badly made they barely held together long enough to complete their cruel task. I watched as his masterfully poured head was lopped off by repeated blows from a crude, cheap sword, cared for by neither maker nor owner, then tossed into the flames for smelting. I saw the finely carved locks of his great beard collapse into molten rivers. All the while, I wished I could assault the vile creatures that did this, drag them screaming out from behind the Lord's name, to face His wrath and mine."

When he began, he'd managed to achieve a hypnotic eloquence to his voice, but by the end he was so caught in the memory of his rage, he was snarling, baring his fangs. Gabriella could not help but pull back at the sight of him.

Amala, watching, felt her own rage stir in sympathy and pulled herself back. Even righteous anger—especially righteous anger—could easily lead to a frenzied, destructive rage.

Hugh glanced at Gabriella and realized he was no longer quite forming words. He pulled back and managed a far calmer smile. "My hand was stayed only because part of me still knew that if I acted, my quest to save other such items from these crude and barbaric hands would be forfeit," he concluded. "I certainly wouldn't tolerate such behavior among my own."

With that, Amala's sympathy for the Templar grew. She fought much the same battle to hew to her ideals and remain in control. The bishop, apparently moved as well, drifted off and focused on something in her own memory.

"They put some mortal whore on the patriarchal throne in the Church of Hagia Sophia, did you know? Had her singing bawdy tunes of fornication, while they scooped anything made of gold into their filthy sacks. There, in the same halls where emperors were crowned. Once I could not step near that sacred building, now I come and go as I please through its desecrated carcass..." her voice trailed off.

"Well, at least Templars do not destroy what they steal," she said at last. "But who would have thought we'd live to see a time when that was considered a sign of ethics?"

Unwilling or unable to disagree, Hugh said nothing.

Stiffening, she regained control of herself, and fully broke whatever spell Hugh's earlier words had cast on her. "I'm a merchant, Sir Hugh. I seek trade and the power behind it, that I may extend my influence and better my position. Even now, I would see Constantinople used as the resource it is, not trampled underfoot en route to the unobtainable goal of quenching desire itself."

"My goals are not unobtainable," Sir Hugh responded.

"No, but they *are* terribly unlikely, dear knight," she said.

"Bishop Gabriella," Hugh interrupted, "in 1099 when the crusaders first saw Jerusalem, they were but thirteen thousand men, with no scaling ladders to climb its walls, scant food and no water. Thirsty, hungry, dying, they clung to their faith and a miracle occurred. A fleet of ships— some of them Genoese—filled with carpenters and supplies arrived. They built the ladders they needed and within a month, the city was theirs!"

"I know my history," Gabriella said. "And I advise you not interrupt again, especially since I may indeed help you."

"Even if you do not believe our holy endeavor can succeed?" Hugh looked at her sternly. "You seek to use the Queen of Heaven's words for your own advantage, to distract your rivals perhaps?"

"Do not lecture me about my own motivations. I do what I must to protect my interests and preserve what I have built here." She nodded slightly, indicating the estate that remained pristine near a city looted and burned. "In any event, I have always found it strange to hear of divine inspiration from one of ours. The only question is whether it's worth the money it will take to give you your ships and supplies to gain only a possible victory in Egypt. You are strong, you are smart, and it seems the right sort of thing enrages you, but I will need something more, Sir Hugh, to prove that there is a chance your army will do more than simply sink in the ocean once they leave the Golden Horn."

"What do you suggest, Lady? My best men are here by my side. If there is some artifact you wish to retrieve from the city, it would be our honor to do so," Hugh said.

She shook her head. "No, don't tempt me. Even I realize Templars can fight. It must be done outside Constantinople and it must be done with the people you've been training. Perhaps you can test your mettle against one of the Latin or Greek armies floating about the countryside these days. Whatever it is, I do not offer specifics, and I will give you three weeks to do it, no less."

"The task pleases me," Hugh said. "It will provide focus for our cause. Very well." She was expecting a bow, but instead the knight continued talking. "But please tell me, something, Bishop, and then I will take my leave."

"If I can, Sir Hugh."

"The Queen of Heaven has said to me that you lost much when the Greeks of the city rioted and attacked the Latins in their midst some years ago. Was it the death of your Lillian that destroyed your faith?"

For the first time in the conversation, her composure failed. Her eyes flashed with animal hatred and the shadows themselves seemed to momentarily darken around her. She lowered her gaze to the floor, fighting to rein in the Beast, before speaking again. "Who told you that?"

"The Queen, of course." Hugh's voice was calm, as if Gabriella was somehow foolish for even asking.

"Prove your abilities, Templar." Gabriella stood up brusquely and her servants leapt to assist her. "And leave the past to me."

The meeting over, Hugh bowed. Gabriella was gone before he raised his eyes anew.

Outside, Amala too wondered how Hugh had known about Gabriella's past. Might he have more spies in the city than she gave him credit for? She had difficulty believing his trances granted him such details, but what if she were wrong? Could he derive such facts from the Prophet's words? It was said all history was contained in the Qur'an, encoded. Could Sir Hugh be unraveling the secrets of the ages?

Within the room, as if summoned by Amala's thoughts, a familiar contagion inflamed the lone knight. Sweating blood, the only liquid sustainable in his body, Hugh went to his knees. Amala still had difficulty believing in the trances as a source of information, but there was little other possibility. Seeing him so vulnerable, she realized at once it could not be him unraveling those truths, but someone else doing it for him. He was smart, but not that smart. Strong, but not that strong. Seeing him as a pawn reminded her all the more of poor Andret. And with that thought, the marvelous distraction that the meeting had provided collapsed like the wall that had blocked her path to Adrianople. A rush of strange feelings, some remembered, some new, came at her and she grew afraid she was falling in love. If that was even possible for an unliving thing.

Inside, Hugh's shoulders twitched forward and back. His eyes rolled up into his head and he tumbled to the ground, like a hanged man cut free from the post. She noticed at once that the spasms were stronger than usual, and wondered if it had to do with their proximity to Constantinople, where the great change in the Ventrue had first occurred. In any event, she found herself trying to open the window, to get to him, to offer what comfort she could.

His mouth opened and closed as his unliving lungs forced air through his vocal chords. By and by the motions formed words: "He, God, is one. God is He on whom all depend. He begets not, nor is He begotten and none is like Him. Idolatry is worse than carnage. Angels do not enter a house which has either a dog or a picture in it. Fight against them until idolatry is no more and God's religion reigns supreme."

Regardless of their source or intent, Amala felt the words burn her, as if the sounds themselves were judging her, accusing her, ripping all reason from her mind and causing the festering guilt within her to rupture. *The mosaic! He is speaking to me about the image of the Prophet!*

"When the sky is rent asunder; when the stars scatter and the oceans roll together; when the graves are hurled about; each soul shall know what it has done and what it has failed to do."

Then the pent-up rage fanned through her being unmolested. Yes, she had failed, clearly she had failed. But what to do?

She sped back to her room and the hallway beyond. Leaping panther-like on the mosaic, Amala yanked the vile abomination free from the wall and smashed it, shattering the face of Muhammad and the grotesque figure of Michael. Plaster and broken tiles covered the floor. Her hands were scratched and bleeding. Leaning against the spot where the image of the Prophet had been hanging, she sobbed.

Among all the twisted questions that tangled in her mind, a simple heartfelt truth would not be shaken: *Allah spoke to me through Sir Hugh, and I obeyed.*

She had gone too far to turn back. She had fallen in love with Sir Hugh and now believed the Prophet spoke through him, though how or why she could not say. She had to bring him to God. She would do anything, sacrifice herself to save him, from Christ, from his Ventrue masters, from his "blessed queen" herself, whatever she turned out to be, and bring him, and thereby herself, to God. It was only this admission that allowed her fractured psyche to reassemble, and slowly regain control.

Returning by and by to her surroundings, Amala looked down at the debris at her feet and realized that she, the

162   Assamite

only Arabic woman in the house, the only person who was admittedly a former Muslim, would be the clearest person to blame. Her newfound conviction would then be for naught, as she would either be caught, or have to flee.

Thinking numbly that there was yet time and yet hope, she secured a linen from her chamber and cleaned up the shattered mosaic as best she could. Could its disappearance be overlooked? Perhaps. She could bury it or toss it in the river. With the linen slung sack-like over her shoulder, she again made the climb down from her balcony. The power of her blood let her avoid making any sound at all.

But this time she was not the only interloper among the sleeping peacocks. By a grove of olive trees, the stocky, bear-like figure she'd seen weeks back outside the Templar camp, the one she'd been following when the Greek refugees surrounded her, stood. Who was this stranger, then, haunting Sir Hugh? Whatever his work here, he was leaving. Fully healed now, she could cover the distance between them in seconds, but they were too close to the house. If he managed to signal someone, the Templars would come running and she'd have to explain both the sack and the plaster dust on her clothes.

Instead she slowly followed the figure, deciding to wait until some distance had been placed between them and the estate, carrying the sack with her, with the thought of using his trail to displace blame. For his part, once they cleared the estate, the intruder ambled along, almost leisurely at times, so she knew he suspected nothing. After a mile, she reasoned they were far enough away, and planned how best to immobilize him for questioning.

She was just about to leap on him when Fajr emerged from the shadows that had been hiding him, fading into visibility. He was muttering something, his words swallowed up by Amala's ability.

She gave him a stern look, but it was too late. The bear-like figure caught a glimpse of the movement, turned to confirm he was being followed, and bolted. Amala was dumbstruck and allowed sound to flow back into the area.

"Oh! You were following him?" Fajr said. "I'm so sorry. I get so distracted sometimes I completely forget where I am."

Amala glared at him then pointed at the fleeing figure. They both went after him in a trot. "Once you have told me whatever it is that's so important, you will find that creature and learn what it is he wants with Sir Hugh," she barked as they ran.

"Of course, Amala, I'm so terribly…"

"Speak quickly! What do you want?"

"Sihr has deigned to reappear," the vizier said, trying his best to comply. "So, you see, he is not Licinius's prisoner. He's simply been, well… meditating, alone. I'll let him explain that to you."

The dark figure had reached the side of a hill.

"The news then is good, and you have someone to catch up with," Amala said, nodding toward the distant man as she slowed.

Fajr glanced at the small shadow as it made its way up the hill's side. Once he reached the top, he would be out of sight, and Fajr hated following trails. He waved Amala to keep up with him.

"There's more, perhaps not so good," Fajr said. "Sihr is making plans and wants your permission to carry them out. He wishes to free the Assamite prisoner from Licinius's captivity."

Amala looked sharply away for an instant. "Let him."

"What? The danger!"

"Let him! Help him if you can! I've thought long about our captured fellow. Let him," she said, then, nodding toward the figure as it was about to dive over the top of the hill, added, "Now go."

Curtly bowing, Fajr sped up and once more melted into the night.

Why didn't I go with him? Amala wondered as she slowed.

The answer clattered beside her. She still had this stupid sack she had to dispose of, and once Sir Hugh's visions were at an end he would seek her. Fajr's questioning mind was better suited at interrogations anyway, and she was comfortable he would prevail.

There was a small river nearby. Adjusting a few of the signs her quarry had left inadvertently, marking his direction, Amala made it look as though he had stopped by the river. There she disposed of the majority of the mosaic. Carefully following his trail back towards the estate, she left a few clear bits and pieces along the way. If he were caught by the Templars and not Fajr, she would surely be undone, but this painfully clear trail, visible to even the lowliest footmen, let alone Gondemar or Hugh, might well swerve suspicion away from her and buy her yet more time.

Her own safety briefly secured, the thought that the intruder was more interested in the Templar than herself came back. Unbidden concern for the knight's safety welled in her chest. She raced back to the window of the room where he lay, to ensure he was all right. It was only when she realized how relieved she was to see him vaguely stirring on the floor, that she again became deeply depressed at the thought of the trap her heart was laying for her.

Chapter Fifteen

Cursing inwardly, Fajr slipped down the hillside, doing his best to move from shadow to shadow as the ebon figure on the trail below picked up speed. Unlike Amala and Sihr, Fajr needed the advantage of such natural camouflage to remain unseen by his quarry. The man displayed great strength and agility as he raced, which gave him away as a Cainite. And now it looked like the man would reach Constantinople before he felt comfortable enough to slow down again.

Then all at once, having come upon some strange sight that demanded attention even at the threat of imminent death, the figure halted and staggered back, suddenly afraid, but unable to tear his gaze away.

Fajr raced up to see what could have caused the sudden change in plans.

Among the leaves, against a boulder, dragged along from some distance given the old marks in the dirt, were several corpses.

Now why would that stop a Cainite? Fajr wondered. And he came so close to the man that, had Fajr been easily visible, they could have been confused for two friends walking together.

Fajr could see that the corpses' faces were rotted and torn, the skin more blackened and frayed than mere age and rotting would have left them. Nevertheless, from their mantles and swords Fajr was able to recognize them as the missing men from the Templar camps. Ghouls, obviously drained to the last by a Cainite. They'd never made it to the Templar masters to whom they wished to betray Sir Hugh, as Sihr had described.

There was no chance this was the sorcerer's work. Something horribly vile, something diseased had perpetrated these killings. The evidence was plain to the vizier and his unwary companion in a form both repulsive yet morbidly fascinating.

A family of rats had feasted on the bodies, but they now lay, two and three together, nearby, writhing on the ground, unable to move much at all, their skins infected with pus-filled sores. Their small squeals almost made him pity them. Wondering if this could be a blood disease that then might somehow infect

Assamite

Cainites, he stepped back. How horrid it would be for him, who prided himself on existing unseen among mortals, to become a carrier of such a dreadful sickness. He would be forced into isolation, becoming some sort of nomad like Sihr.

Recalling his prey, Fajr looked up to see that the man was on the move again, now disappearing beyond yet another hill. At first Fajr thought he would simply follow the trail again, but once he reached the other side, after a few yards, it grew cold.

Fajr was perplexed. His senses were keen and he could spot those hiding in shadows and nooks with ease. If his quarry was able to vanish more thoroughly, to fade utterly from sight like Amala, why hadn't he done so earlier? Had Fajr been seen?

He looked around. He was close to Constantinople now, very close. So close that an entrance or two to the tunnels that crisscrossed her bowels might well be nearby, an easy exit for his quarry. He stamped at the ground, hoping to hear if it was hollow, but couldn't tell for certain.

But yes, it made sense. That's why the bodies had been abandoned here. Couldn't bring those things easily into the tunnels, after all.

The new information set the vizier's mind to work. Whatever killed the Templars was protecting Sir Hugh. Clearly it was not a god or saint, then. Powerful, and with strange purpose, it was very possibly also what guided his visions. If so, it must be a creature of great knowledge. It also carried plague, it seemed, and probably dwelt in Constantinople.

But what was it? An elder? Some new monster? How could it be found, tracked?

This Cainite he'd followed was clearly not the force behind Sir Hugh, or else why step back shocked from the corpses? Perhaps he was not so much interested in Sir Hugh as in whatever this creature was. Perhaps he also knew more of the puzzle pieces.

Fajr grabbed his papers and began scribbling. He didn't stop until it was nearly dawn.

Chapter Sixteen

June 20, 1204

The situation was had changed since their last meeting, and Cassius took it upon himself to politely order the Templar about as much as possible. "I'm afraid my words are meant for Sir Hugh alone," he said, the lesser of the knights. "By order of Prince Licinius."

Gondemar threw his hands up in the air. "Sir Hugh, this lickspittle has made nothing but requests since his arrival and he has yet to impart a single word of this great message the prince has for us. First, he must be given proper quarters, then he must feed, then he must be allowed to pick a bauble for the prince, then he must be rested, and now he must be alone with you? How much more are we to bear?"

Amala, trying to remain as unobtrusive as possible in the hopes that she was in fact not meant to leave, wished she'd been able to say much the same.

Sir Hugh turned to the tall thin man. "A good question. These men are my arms and legs, this woman all but shares my very soul. I do not dismiss them lightly."

"Nevertheless," Cassius said plainly.

"Will this be your last request?" Sir Hugh said. "I mean, of course, before I hear this news of great import?"

Cassius frowned a bit. He'd wanted to see if he could get yet another trinket out of Sir Hugh when they were alone. But the information was indeed important, and he had already had much fun.

"It will be," he said.

"Very well," Hugh said, and waved his fellows from the room. When Amala hesitated, he looked her in the eye and said, "It won't be long. I promise."

Sir Hugh rose and closed the huge oak doors behind them as they left. Then he pivoted, blocking the door, which Cassius noted at once was the only exit.

"Is this about the captured Assamite?" Hugh said.

"It is."

Hugh, holding onto the great door's latch with his hands, leaned forward and let his gaze burn into Cassius's eyes. "Then speak quickly."

"I must speak it as the prince bade me," Cassius protested.

"Oh yes, but you must speak it now." Hugh squeezed the latch tighter.

"Very well. We had heard the stories that the Saracens do not succumb to torture, but of course we tried anyway, it being the prince's preferred method. Indeed, they are as legend has them, this one at least, and even the removal of most of his limbs, though clearly painful, prompted not a single useful crumb of information. This took many, many nights, and we all contributed our best ideas to the process, but eventually the prince decided on a new tack."

"Go on," Hugh nodded, still impatient.

"Yes, well, the prince thought to make him love him, offering him only his own vitae for three nights in a row," Cassius said.

"The blood oath," Hugh nodded.

"But sadly, this failed as well, or at least did not have its intended effect. The creature was as rebellious as ever, even spitting blood in his face," Cassius said.

"Well, Assamites may well have already all taken blood oaths as part of their training," Hugh said. "Go on."

Cassius grinned, "Nevertheless, it did open a new path for us."

"How so?"

"We happened to notice, well, I happened to notice, that when the prince fed him, he became savage. Even the smallest amount of Cainite blood provoked a feeding lust the likes of which I have rarely seen. We had to add several straps, just to keep him from pulling himself completely to pieces."

"Really?"

"It was quite amazing to see. You are surely familiar with the lust one sees in ghouls long-deprived of their master's blood?" Cassius waved his hand dismissively. "With so many bonded sergeants at hand, I'm sure you are. Well it was very much like that blood-hunger, only fired with the rage our kind know so well."

Hugh broke eye contact for a second, his strategic mind at work. "Perhaps some of the Saracens, having fed so long upon Cainite vitae, become addicted to it."

"My thinking exactly." Cassius smiled. "So, once we discovered this fellow's particular predilection, we were able to use it against him, offering him the longed-for substance a mere drop at a time. Then withholding for hours, then giving him just another drop. He crumbled in a few nights, and soon spoke freely of everything. A pity we hadn't discovered his weakness earlier. He might have kept his limbs," Cassius said, shrugging.

"And what, at long last, did he speak of?" Hugh said.

"Many things, but I think the thing of greatest interest to you was the location of an Assamite stronghold hidden near Byzantium itself. Part of an order within their clan called, of all things, the Web of Knives," Cassius revealed at last. "I've brought some maps that the prince prepared."

Sir Hugh let go of the latch at once and rushed forward. His face burst into a wide grin. He grabbed Cassius with both arms and gave him a massive, powerful hug.

"Oh great fortune! What better intelligence could fall into my hands at this time! Thank the prince! Thank him! And thank you, good Cassius, for telling me this tale! Now I have a target for my army, and a way to give Lady Gabriella the worthy proof she seeks! What great fortune!" Hugh bellowed.

"Oh yes," Cassius said, smiling broadly. He was well aware of the despatches between Gabriella and Licinius that had decided, behind the Templar's back, just what Hugh's mission should be. "Quite a coincidence. Most fortuitous!"

After that, the seneschal, satisfied for any slight the Templar had caused him in front of the refugees, was more than happy to present the maps.

Hugh called Gondemar back in and they cleared the nearest table to examine the drawings. The first was a wide view of the terrain, showing the stronghold situated in a mountainous pass some fifty miles due west of Constantinople proper.

"It is a training facility, called Yesayel biet, or the Leaking House," Cassius reported. "It is run by a single elder. It is one of several training centers, apparently, but its proximity would indicate it a likely source for those who attacked you."

"The design is formidable. See how it is protected by mountain on two sides, and this river runs right by it?" Hugh said.

"Through it, Sir Hugh," Cassius corrected as he pointed towards the second drawing, which indicated the fortress's size and the fact that the river did indeed run down from the high ground, through the fort's arched center, and then down to the valley below. Any entrance or exit was completely submerged.

"Then it is not simply formidable, it is brilliant," Hugh said, nodding. "A human assault on such a structure would be impossible, a Cainite attack nearly so. Even troops that required no air would be greatly slowed by such an underwater entry, easily slaughtered as they came up."

He drummed his fingers on the table, thinking. "Gondemar, from among the refugees, how many bowmen can we have ready, how soon?"

"Just bowmen?" Gondemar asked.

"Yes, our own men will serve as cavalry and men-at-arms," Hugh said. "The Muslims have used showers of arrows to great advantage against us, forcing us into heavy armor for protection. I think it's high time we returned the favor."

Gondemar shrugged. "Perhaps two hundred total—mostly ghouls and thralls, with, say, thirty Cainites. But what good would a rain of arrows do when, as you say, the water makes the fortress impregnable?"

Hugh grinned widely, showing his pointed teeth. The Beast in him was tickled. "Have you dealt with Greek fire yet, Gondemar?"

"Of course," the aide-de-camp said, but could not suppress a shudder. Relatively little could do serious harm to a vampire's body, but fire could and it caused an instinctive fear in all blood-drinkers, no matter how stoic. "A terrible, flammable substance. It burns across every surface: stone, earth, wood, flesh, even—"

"Even water," Hugh finished. He indicated a point at the river above the fortress. "Imagine what it would be like if we managed to pour barrels of the stuff into the river here, and then, after it had floated within the fortress, ignited it?" he said.

Gondemar laughed with delight. "And then our archers would rain down on whatever managed to flee! Even the Saracen gift of stealth would be near-useless in a torrent of arrows!" The seneschal shifted uncomfortably. "But the flames would destroy whatever was inside. What of gathering intelligence? Or plunder?"

"We have had quite enough plunder, I think," Hugh said. "I understand your concerns, and I wish there was another way. Nevertheless, our goal is Egypt and this is war. Sacrifices must be made."

He turned to Gondemar. "Go back to the camps and bring me the most prominent Greeks among our volunteers, any with military background, and treat them with more than due respect. Greek fire is their most preciously guarded secret and we must make it clear we do not require that they reveal it, only that they make it for us, to be used in a terribly worthy cause. And prepare the others for a lengthy march."

Gondemar pivoted, full of purpose, and did exactly as he was instructed.

Chapter Seventeen

July 10, 1204

To be alone is to have no need for language, that hideous scar on the mind that severs it from the body.

To be alone is to hear the song of your own soul in harmony with God.

To be alone is to taste, with the tongue, the solid continuum of God's plans.

To be alone is to be equal to the stars.

Sensing his master's desire, the great horse, upon reaching the ridge, stopped.

Sihr Haddad turned and looked back at the solid black clouds of smoke rising from the mountain's center, trying to listen. The sound of falling timbers and stones were muffled by the distant cheers of Sir Hugh's strange new army.

To be alone is to be nothing, Sihr concluded.

A rustling among the branches behind him turned his attention away from the conflagration and towards the path he had just left. Fajr and Amala, each on their own steed, now faded in from the shadows.

"You leave quite a trail," Fajr said. "Have you grown incautious in your solitude?"

Sihr shook his head. "I was hoping to lead some of the Christians away, but they are all too fascinated by their pretty fire."

Amala rode up next to Sihr and regarded the scene with a deep sadness. "Alamut has no great love for the Web, but they are still of the blood of Haqim. This is a terrible day for us all," she said.

As if fumbling for an excuse, Fajr spoke quickly, "Of course we knew the attack was coming, we just didn't know where the stronghold was. Hugh kept the information from

Amala for her own protection, lest she try to follow. The maps and plans remained most carefully hidden, despite my best efforts at liberating them. We gleaned the preparations, the strategies, even risked exposure by capturing and torturing a Templar man-at-arms. Unfortunately, he knew as little as we."

Amala, strangely sad and distant, nodded, confirming his story. "In the end, all we could do was follow the army. By then, it was too late."

"We did block a path and send half their supply of Greek fire tumbling into the ravine," Fajr said, shrugging. "And we procured this lovely horse for myself."

"This was only half?" Sihr said. "Then they never meant to try to pry any secrets from the place."

She nodded numbly again. "No. They wanted only to destroy it, as a bauble for Sir Hugh to present to Gabriella."

"How much time did you have here, Sihr?" Fajr asked.

"Two nights," the sorcerer answered sadly.

"Two nights?!" Amala said aghast. "Two nights, and you could do nothing to prepare a defense, or aid an evacuation?"

"They did not trust me. They would not believe me. I was too… other," the sorcerer said.

***

It was the night the army prepared to leave on its journey into the mountains, when the guard on Prince Licinius's star prisoner was finally relaxed enough to allow Sihr to penetrate the tunnels where they held him. Sihr had found the location a week earlier, but all the activity about it made acting impossible.

Sneaking up near them was no problem, even for the tall, lanky Sihr. The stone floor, slick with water, provided only a small challenge for his approach. Still, there were two powerful armed men situated outside the small chamber in the tunnels. Angry at his own ambivalence and inactivity, the sorcerer determined he would dispatch them by the most painful method possible.

First, he concentrated on the blood in his system and the unique gifts he owed Haqim. He thought of the way, in the heat of battle or in the middle of sorcerous effort, the blood became fiery and all external sounds faded. With practiced ease, he pushed that hot sensation out into the world and felt all sound in the chamber die. *Now,* he thought, *you two can scream all you want.*

Next he moved his hands and fingers in a rapid dance, and a thick green ball of fire formed in his hands, growing rapidly in size until he could contain it no longer. He released it in the direction of his targets. With a rush, it sped across the short distance, and erupted on one of the guards in a full inferno, instantly covering him in flames from head to foot.

Sihr watched with delight as the fiery creature, shrieking soundlessly, fell into the grip of apoplectic terror. The sorcerer mouthed a few words and swept his hands together in a clap. The burning guard suddenly flew through the air as if picked up by the hand of God. He slammed right into his fellow crusader, setting him alight as well.

The stories of Ventrue hardiness were true, it seemed, up to a point. Indeed, both guards struggled and writhed far longer than Sihr expected. One even managed to stand and take a few steps toward Sihr. But in the end, as it always did, fire won out over undead flesh.

Sihr paid their ashes no mind and entered the chamber.

Seeing the limbless, toothless creature filled Sihr's heart with pity. It had barely enough muscle left to writhe on the slab where it was chained. The deep dark skin and the weapons and clothing piled haphazardly in the corner identified him at once to the ancient sorcerer as an Assamite. Sihr's first thought was to crush its head and be done with it. He'd done the same for desert animals similarly wounded.

Sihr stepped over it and stared into the creature's eyes. Recognizing their kinship, tears of thin blood welled in its eyes. Sihr swallowed up the silence of his fiery blood anew and spoke. "May the peace of Allah be with you."

"An ooh," the prisoner said.

"Did you tell them Alamut's location?" Sihr asked.

Without fear, it shook its head, no.

"That much is good," Sihr said. "But what did you tell them?"

"…'eb on 'ives," it muttered. "Yesayel biet."

After a slow, painful conversation, Sihr was able to determine it had given away the location of the stronghold where it was trained. After learning what he could of its location and its occupants, Sihr closed the thing's eyes and drained what little remained of its blood, leaving it to a well-deserved final death.

The army had already left. Finding Fajr or Amala, who probably dogged it, would cost time. If he rode alone, he might reach Yesayel biet in time to warn them. Sihr rode furiously through the night, as the flat forests of poplars gave way to hilly terrain with older growth. Catching up, then passing the army, he rode as far into the pre-dawn twilight as he could before the sun forced him to take cover. It was two more such nights before the hills gave way to rocky slopes and mountains and he found the thick, fast-flowing river that flowed through Yesayel biet.

By the middle of the third night, he had a full night on the army, maybe two. At last he came to the clearing the dead warrior had described, and scanned the mountainside for his destination. Though the night was cloudless and well lit, it was only when he followed the thick river's twisting path up into the mountains that he finally saw the fortress. If there were a construction by man that Sihr could abide, then this fortress was it. Half-carved from the mountain rock itself, what stones there were in it that had been transported for the construction had been carefully selected to match the natural colors. Windows at first glance appeared as mere caves, turrets as outcroppings, shielded from sight all the more by the gush of glacial waters that crashed and frothed from its arched center.

At first glance, Sihr wondered how he would gain entrance at all, but as he circled closer, his steed was able to find near-hidden trails that led up along the rushing river. From here it looked as though the river drowned the only entrance, save for the high slits reserved for crossbow and arrow perches.

Sihr could quiet the horse, but not obfuscate it completely, and so was a bit surprised to find no guard or ghoul to greet him as he approached. He surmised that if the fortress was so impregnable, the inhabitants, perhaps wisely, preferred to attack and defend from within its walls.

The steed could take him no further. Clearly the only way to gain entrance was to dive beneath the rushing water and pull oneself along whatever handholds might be found there. With regret, Sihr decided he would have to leave his charger behind. With a quick slash of his dagger, he split his palm open and let the horse lap at the wound a few moments, the way other steeds might lick at an offered bit of sugar. Then Sihr chucked him on the chin and nodded towards a spot far below where the rushing waters pooled. Soundless, the horse nodded and began the trek down.

Sihr looked up at the structure one last time, trying to spy any observers. Taking them by surprise would be unwise, and it was far more likely they were already waiting to spring a trap on him. Holding his arms aloft so his thick, faded burgundy robes looped below his wrists, he shouted in Arabic, "Fellow Children of Haqim! I am here to bring you important information! Do not mistake me for a foe!"

With no answer forthcoming, Sihr concluded he was either not heard or that those inside had no wish to answer. In his haste to arrive, Sihr had gone three nights without feeding, and the black other that shared his body and darkened his skin now crawled about restlessly, waiting for an opening that might bring it appeasement. It welled as impatience as he half-dove, half-climbed into the water.

The rush of freezing liquid was indeed formidable, and he fell ten feet before catching his hands on the rocks that lay beneath. The lack of air was not an issue, but the sheer force of water perpetually threatened to hurl him from his precarious perch to the pool far, far, below. After making some progress upward, through sheer dint of unliving strength and will, Sihr found a set of carved hand- and footholds that eased and sped his journey.

After what felt like fifty feet, the footholds ended and he saw, through rising bubbles, a carved underwater passage that split the river into upper and lower halves. With little effort, he slipped into the passage. Here the flow was dampened and he moved about more easily. Above his head he could make out the surface and a large chamber above it. Candles and oil lights, blurred by the water, lit a dim great hall.

Arms spread to show he had no weapons, Sihr surfaced. He soon felt many hands on him, yanking him onto the floor, pressing him down with their feet and the tips of drawn swords.

Fight! the fuming Beast in him raged, but knowing that an aggressive display now would destroy his purpose, he held back. Instead, in a moment when the kicking and prodding stopped for an instant, he spat out, "Yesayel biet."

The reaction was quick. Sihr was at once pulled to standing. Arms held tightly behind him by two barrel-chested, thick-armed men, Sihr was turned swiftly about to face a gaunt, black-bearded man nearly his own size. Sihr pulled against his captors, instantly impressed by the strength their training here had achieved.

The bearded man held his hands clasped behind him, and bobbed briefly towards the sorcerer. "You should not know that name," he said.

"And yet I do, because one of your own was captured and tortured by Prince Licinius and he has given away the location of this place," Sihr said.

"Oh? Your skin is dark, but you do not appear to be a warrior. Who are you?"

"Sihr Haddad. A blood sorcerer. As we speak, a small army of Latins and Greeks advances here. A day away, perhaps two."

The bearded man laughed. The others laughed with him. "Latins *and* Greeks, is it?"

"Your intelligence fails you if you do not know of Sir Hugh of Clairvaux and his crusade," Sihr said.

"Of course we know of his sad efforts and the peasants he entertains. But let me put forth another theory regarding your presence here. For nearly a hundred years the Web of Knives has sought its own counsel, not that of Alamut. Why should I not surmise that now that Alamut covets our secrets and sends its agent here to learn them?" The bearded man leaned forward so that his nose nearly touched Sihr's. "But, I promise you, even if you survive, you will not even learn our names."

Sihr nearly lurched forward to bite off the offending nose. "You fool! How did I even know to come here?"

The bearded man shrugged. "As you say, you're a sorcerer. Powerful spells might pull the information even from the mind of one of our own."

"I…" Sihr shook his head violently to and fro, a wild stallion trying to pull free. "I understand, I do. I've walked the Bedouin path apart from Alamut for many years, but the clan is not your enemy. You have admirers in the Mountain. Is not Thetmes the Egyptian part of the Web?"

"Yes, certainly."

"Well, the entire clan holds him up as a great warrior! Even I have heard tales of his prowess and service to Haqim. But there is no time for this. You will learn soon enough the truth of my words. What harm is there in organizing a defense, or in simply planning an escape? Once revealed, your hidden training ground is no longer of any use. Still, we might hold them off, even beat them, and then discuss how best to secrete your knowledge elsewhere. How many of you are there? I count ten in this room."

After some slight hesitation, the bearded one narrowed his eyes dramatically and said, "There are many others. Hidden in the shadows of this place."

Sihr knew at once it was a lie, and could contain his rage no longer. It was like dealing with a score of Fajrs, only with stronger bodies and smaller minds. "There's no one here but the ten of you!" Sihr bellowed, trying again to pull free from the two men who held him fast.

The tone of utter conviction coupled with the deep timbre of the voice made it impossible to argue otherwise. Sihr guessed that in the mad rush following the fall of Constantinople, thinking themselves the least focus of attention in a war between Latin and Greek, the elder and trained warriors here had fanned out on missions the nature of which he could only guess at, leaving behind this small force.

"How many of you are vampires? Two? Three?" Sihr growled. "With so few of you, what makes this place a fortress can turn it into a tomb! You must abandon Yesayel biet at once!" He pulled so strongly, he tore his own arm from the socket. At a nod from the bearded leader, Sihr was shoved once more to the ground. He yelled and snarled as the pain riled the Beast within him.

"The only thing we will be abandoning is this conversation," the bearded one said. "Dawn approaches. If your mighty force appears, we will continue our conversation tomorrow night."

Aghast and confused, Sihr Haddad was tossed into a small, damp cell, driven to take small sustenance from the fat water rats that nested there. Somewhat strengthened by the blood, he forced his arm and shoulder into the stone wall, until the arm snapped back into place.

Uncertain what to do next, he thought of ways to escape by using his magic and wondered if he could defeat all ten of them, then drag them out to safety one at a time. Still, it was a formidable place, this fortress, and perhaps even just ten men could hold off an army from here. Perhaps if the fool who was left in charge had half a brain and sent out a scouting party, Sihr might yet be vindicated in time. Eventually, as thin squares of sunlight fell on the floor outside his cell, he drifted off into a restless sleep.

Over the course of the day, the squares shifted with the moving sun, then finally dimmed. Sihr Haddad woke to a half-whispered conversation.

"What is it? It floats on the water?"

"Inhale. The smell is strange."

Sihr stood and pulled himself towards the small barred window of his cell. The two burly men who had restrained him, and were since set to guard him, stood by the open canal of water that flowed from one end of the fortress to another. Something slick on the surface had attracted their attention. The shorter one bent down and scooped some onto his hand.

"Not algae. Too thick," he said, sniffing at it. "The smell is familiar."

His fellow grabbed a torch and brought it closer to the goo-covered hand.

"Careful," Sihr warned, not quite knowing why. But they laughed at him.

In an instant, the heat from the torch set the viscous substance, and the man's hand, aflame. He let out a mad, bestial whine. His hand a veritable torch, he raced about, slamming his burning appendage into the walls in an insane effort to put it out. The other guard dropped the torch and pulled back in terror at his victim's fate, backpedaling and raising his hands to shield his face. He made no move to help and Sihr realized that he was a Cainite, for though fire was an anathema to all that lived, only the undead knew such an utter dread of flames that even a small exposure could lead to such unreasoning terror. Footfalls filled the halls as the others raced to see what was going on.

Above and beyond that sound, above even the constant roar of the rushing river, Sihr heard a higher-pitched rush that was sweeping closer and closer.

Terror gripped him as he guessed what was going on. Sihr clasped his hands together in a brief ritual, then lifted the air in front of him as if he were withdrawing the timber from an invisible door. At once, in response, the heavy timber blocking his door rose and then dropped to the floor. At the sound of the clattering wood, all eyes in the room turned towards the cell.

Sihr jumped out, the fear of flame welling in his breast. *Ignore them! Ignore them all! Just run!* the Beast cried inside him. Unwilling to argue, he headed straight for the waters of the canal. Briefly, against the urging of the Beast, he tried to pull one of the warriors in with him, but the warrior, mistaking his action for an attack, pulled away. The rush of air was deafening now, forcing the Cainites to turn curiously in the direction of the fortress's rear wall. There was nothing further Sihr could do for them except die horribly, and that was something he was not willing to do.

As his feet left the stone floor, he caught, in the corner of his eye, a rush of fiery orange and red as it exploded from the far end of the fortress. Sihr thought at first he would not make it, but his body slipped below the water just before the canal's surface became a sheet of flame. From the submerged corridor below, he looked up and saw only fire. He thought he heard muffled screams, but couldn't be sure.

Swimming out from the corridor, he let the rushing river carry him out from the fortress. Arrows hissed through the water on all sides of him, but luckily, none found their mark as he tumbled helplessly to the pool a hundred yards below. There, though he managed to use the shadows to remain unseen, another rain of arrows met him. This time, a few caught him in the abdomen and shoulder.

Sihr cursed to himself as he realized most of the attacking force was composed of archers. He found his steed, waiting dutifully behind a tree, and wept to see that two arrows had hit it as well. Sihr's own vitae in the animal's system kept the wounds from being life-threatening as of yet, but a few more hits and the charger would be done for. Though it would have been far safer to abandon the horse and hide himself, Sihr was unwilling to let anything else die. He rode until he was finally out of range.

***

"A terrible burden to bear, Sihr Haddad," Amala said softly as he finished the tale. "I am sorry we could not have been with you."

Sihr's eyes opened wide at that, and he reared, as if his were the horse's head. "But you would have been if I had kept more closely in touch?" he said accusingly. "Do you think it more appropriate to blame me, or those fools who failed to heed my ample warning?"

"I am not without guilt in this," Amala snapped back. "Were it not for me, Sir Hugh might already be dead. Don't you think I know that? I suggest only that we must take what lessons we can from these mistakes, lest we spend our lives in repetition. Isn't this why you sought to reconnect with Alamut, with your fellow Children of Haqim?"

Sihr shook his head. "Of that I am no longer certain." He raised his long arm towards the round flame against the mountainside, now almost a ball. "Look at civilization, how easily it burns. I am glad, I tell you, glad in my heart that your ridiculous, gaudy, insulting Constantinople fell. I am only sorry the wilderness will not return to claim it. They are all scars on God's creation—your buildings, your books, your minds—and were it up to me, they would all fade like moonlight beneath the rising shadows of night. I will have no more part of this."

Without any discernible command from Sihr, his black horse turned and prepared to ride away.

He really means to leave us, Amala thought. *I can't allow that. I will need his power and his perspective to survive this myself.*

Rather than a personal plea which she was certain would fail, she tried to remind him of his responsibilities: "Sihr, your vow to the elders at Alamut, your visions…"

"Alamut is a city, different only in size. And here among you city-dwellers, where sacred baubles are traded like seashells and visions are as common as gossip, I can no longer even tell the value of my own insights. I will return to the desert. You will not miss me."

He turned away again.

"Three weeks," Amala said.

The horse stopped. "What?"

"You still believe in your own blood sorcery, don't you?" she said, riding up to him, trying to block his path with her own horse.

"Perhaps."

"In three weeks, it will be Thw al-Hijjah, early fall, the beginning of the Latin's August. That's when your augury said it would be the best time for the three of us to try to destroy Sir Hugh?"

"Yes..."

"Without you, we might fail."

As if an extension of the sorcerer's psyche, Sihr's horse hesitated and turned about. The sorcerer leaned forward, to find Amala's eyes with his own. "And you would see him truly dead on that day?" he asked. "Despite your feelings that he should be saved?"

Amala paused, but the sight of the burning stronghold steeled her resolve. "Because of them, Sihr, because of them. In three weeks, we will either know what is behind his visions, or we will finish him."

Chapter Eighteen

July 15, 1204

Rows of torches lit the lush garden, and a rapturous Sir Hugh watched the reflection of their yellow and orange lights flicker on the black liquid waters of the Bosporus. A massive military victory was behind him. Though Gabriella had yet to speak on it, he was now utterly convinced this water would soon take him and his followers into the very heart of God. He strolled the ornate parks of Galata, enjoying the few flowers that had survived the crusading soldiers of three months past. Enveloped this night by a rare peace, he let his eyes dance lazily along docks, imagining what these same quays would look like when they bore the ships he would fill with his army. Though he needed no air, he inhaled, letting his nostrils fill with the familiar scent of brine above the flowers' perfumes.

His gaze traveled up to the walls of the great city on the opposite bank, its towers and domes looking as grand and natural as the stars that twinkled above them. It was so plainly unlike the dying behemoth he'd seen on the eve of his great awakening. He wondered how they could possibly be the same place.

But, as the Blessed Queen assured him, appearances were deceptive. He knew even now, within the stolen palaces and grand homes, misguided mortals played bloody games, vying for what could only be a brief authority. Ever since Baldwin had been crowned emperor, the peace between him and his partner Boniface had been strained. More to the point, perhaps, in the catacombs, desecrated churches, tombs and more desolate homes, the Greek Cainites who remained in the city still wrestled with how to reorganize themselves, how to regain the reins that had slipped from their hands. And the Latin factions had moved in and were making their presence felt.

Sir Hugh thought both groups were blind, serving neither God nor their own best advantage. Believing in the vain constructs that took the space in their souls meant for ideals, they served not truth, but seeming—not God, but the prettiest of his angels, Satan.

Those who resisted Hugh baffled him deeply. Where else could Cainite and mortal co-exist symbiotically if not in the kingdom of heaven? Even the great city Constantinople, with all its finely rendered paeans to the longing of humanity, was as empty a reflection of the kingdom as the light that glittered on the water was of the torches above it. To be sure, there was a great resemblance to the undiscerning eye, but, just as surely, only one could burn.

A pang hit him as he recalled the lack of response to the letter he'd written to Alexander, the prince of Paris, and his sire's sire. The silence confused and deeply saddened him, more so even than the unfulfilled promises of Sir Abelard of the Order of the Bitter Ashes, who had spoken to him as a brother in his cause. And Appeles, long gone now. Hugh reasoned sadly he would have to accept that they too, like so many markers on his journey, would fall aside and vanish, ghostlike beneath the moon.

A shadow passing in front of one of the torches reminded him that Amala was here. She'd been very silent and moody of late, deep in her own thoughts. He knew she would be disappointed in his failure to confide his military plans to her, but as Gondemar had suggested, it was best to keep her in the dark lest she fall prey to some Assamite kidnappers.

Fearing for Amala made him realize how much his affection had grown for her. At times, with Gondemar and the others so frightfully obedient that their very humanity seemed ready to fade, hers was the only true voice. He wanted to tell her so much. But where to begin? And how much would the Blessed Mother allow him? She knew of Amala, and approved of their bond, but hinted at some dark fate for the girl that made Hugh tremble.

"Amala, I must tell you," he called to her, "for I trust that you, as my own heart, will not think me mad. The Queen of Heaven now speaks against the Church's rule. She speaks against imagery and idolatry. She speaks against language itself, communicating instead in colored fire. She wishes to take me beyond such fragile things. Beyond the Holy Trinity. Beyond the Order. Beyond all the trappings of human belief, to a place where she says I will feel as desolate and alone as God did when His spirit hovered over the water and He felt an aching need to create the illusion of the world. But, she also said, I must not then be weak as He was."

Amala was clearly disturbed, almost angry. "How can any man be stronger than God? Your words make me afraid for you."

"They are not mine, but the Queen's."

Staring, Amala circled him to see his face more clearly, drawing closer as she moved.

"She says I am to break the bonds I have sworn to uphold, to put aside the rules I have used to guide me. That, as her servant, I am to have whatever I want most dearly," Hugh said. He looked up and again gazed into her green eyes. She came near enough to touch.

"And what is it you want most dearly?" she asked softly.

Hugh kept his eyes locked on hers, trying to fold her into the aura of his being. "I have defeated the Assamites. I will claim Egypt, and one night, the Holy Land. Yet sometimes what I want is only to know the will of God and thereby destroy all desire. Sometimes, the only thing I can imagine desiring is *you*."

Her eyes flared, then she turned away, feeling a sudden flush of shame.

"I see. And what rules exactly are you to break?" Amala asked stiffly.

"Any," Hugh said, raising his hand to touch her hair. "All."

Thin blood dripped down his canines and Hugh felt desire echo through him. Coupling was rarely a concern for Cainites—its pleasures faded with the Embrace and the resulting, never-ending blood lust. But with Amala, it could be more. A symbol to be cherished as deeply as any work of art. For Hugh, it would symbolize both his departure from the Knights Templar and their vows of chastity, and his union with this woman who took his every third thought. She was the last thing he loved, aside from God.

Hugh moved forward to kiss her. He felt her ready to yield to his arms.

An abrupt, purposely loud cough made them both whirl from one another, in the direction of a man who'd been watching from nearby. Anger at the interruption gripped Hugh's face, until he recognized the Templar cross on the intruder's white mantle.

Did Appeles betray me to the Order, then? Hugh thought. The knight barely noticed as Amala quietly put several yards between herself and both men.

The blond knight, nearly as tall as Hugh, with flecks of white in his beard, nodded in greeting. When he spoke, his Latin had the accent of a German. "Good evening, brother. My house is here negotiating with the new Latin emperor for several sizable holdings in the region, in exchange for funding the Order provided. I am surprised, but delighted to see a brother here on this lovely night. Might I ask your name, good sir?"

"I am Hugh of Clairvaux," Hugh said stiffly. "Might I ask yours?"

The German's eyes widened. "Brother Hugh!" he laughed. "Then I am honored! I have heard wonderful tales of your adventures, the relics you've rescued, the intelligence you have gathered! I am Igolt, of the house of Wolfram."

Hugh warmed quickly. "And who among us has not heard of the valor of Igolt of Wolfram, who with ten men held the castle at Vadum Iacob for four days against hundreds of Saracens, until reinforcements could arrive!"

"It was only three days, and, of course, only through the virtue of His will, but I am glad to be known by it." Igolt shrugged humbly. "So, Brother Hugh, I expected you'd be older. You must come to our camp in the morning, share the truth of some of your exploits and enjoy our humble community."

"Yes," was all Hugh could think to say. Sir Geoffrey had always acted as an intermediary for Hugh with the Templar masters, receiving the orders and passing them on. This was the first truly mortal Templar Hugh had seen in a great while. Excuses would have to be made. Later, after they had made a base in Egypt, things would be different; but for now, attention from the Order was most unwelcome. At least it meant that Appeles, whatever his fate, had not thus betrayed him.

"This is good country, much more lush, naturally, than the deserts I've grown accustomed too, is closer in some ways to the black forests of my ancestral home," Igolt said. "But God's Holy Land is certainly not without beauty."

"I hope to see it again soon!" Hugh said.

Feeling camaraderie, Igolt stepped closer with an open smile. Hugh planned to return the gesture, but was suddenly gripped by a deep, cascading fear that sucked away in equal draughts his balance, his beliefs and his control. No longer certain where, or even exactly who he was, Hugh stumbled backwards and nearly fell. At first he mistook it for vertigo, but then he realized he was, at any moment and out of nowhere, about to lose himself to rage and hunger. It was a sensation he'd not experienced since first entering the Church of the Apostles. But that had not been this intense.

What is this? Some new state of sin? The Blessed Queen bade me to take what I want! The monstrous black island of pained want that shared his form surfaced at once, telling him to shred whatever was nearest, then run as quickly as possible. *No! I am Sir Hugh of Clairvaux, of the Templar....*

Suddenly he realized the source of this abyss was his fellow knight, Igolt. In the German's kind gaze, he saw the reproach of Christ for every innocent whose blood had fed him. In his steely eyes, he saw the glory of a man who fought for God against unbelievers and devils—devils like the one inside him. Looking at Sir Igolt, Hugh saw the chosen of God and knew he was rejected.

A sense of pained, animal betrayal washed over him, forcing him to question everything at once. *How could he be more holy than I? How quickly can I get away? Where can I be safe?*

"Brother Hugh? Are you all right? There are many odd diseases about," Igolt said, full of concern as he rushed closer to help. "You must be careful of your health. My own doctor is not far, let me take you to him."

Igolt reached out and grasped Hugh by the elbow, seeking to steady him. Unfortunately, his touch only worsened matters. Hugh swooned, thick pockets of beet-red sweat swarming to the surface of his cheeks. It was a struggle to respond at all.

Igolt, horrified by the blood welling to Hugh's face, drew his sword and waved it about at the air. "There is evil here! Praised be His name, and let Him protect His poor servants!"

"Amala," Hugh coughed. "Help me."

***

Amala, hoping to remain unnoticed until she decided what to do, almost cursed out loud. Though the distance from Igolt was helping her, Amala felt deeply threatened as well. The sensation was similar to one she'd felt upon approaching Mecca in her first years as a vampire.

The woman's presence newly pointed out to him, Igolt whirled toward her, the tip of his blade pointed at her chest. "You! I saw you in near-embrace with this chaste knight, about to pull him to Lucifer's realms! Do you now bewitch him with foul magic?"

Amala shook her head desperately as she backed away, hoping to appear helpless, a mad fear of this Christian's gaze welling within her. Igolt advanced, convinced he had found the source of the evil he sensed. Amala looked this way and that, for either a weapon or an exit route. Panic welled in her breast and it felt as though the very boundaries of her soul were being breached with each step he took. The best she could do was to keep her wits about her enough to continue moving back, keeping the knight at bay.

If she timed it properly, she could leap for the low-hanging branch of the tree she'd positioned herself under, wrap her legs around the knight's neck and snap it before his presence overcame her. The problem would be explaining her sudden fighting prowess to Sir Hugh, if he were still awake.

As it turned out, there was no need for her concern. Just when Igolt was about to lunge, his face twisted in pain. He pivoted away in a movement that resembled the spin of a poorly trained street dancer, and Amala saw the handle of a thrown dagger protruding from his shoulder. It had pierced his mail and was buried in his flesh nearly up to the hilt.

Beyond him, Amala saw that Hugh had risen, his arm still outstretched from the impressive throw. She realized that drawing the devout knight away had lessened his effect on Hugh, allowing him to recover partly. But it was more than that, as she quickly saw. The Ventrue was not only on his feet, he was utterly enraged, offended that this man should exist at all.

"Leave her alone!" he shrieked, red-faced, fangs bared.

Igolt's eyes grew wide. His thick lips curled in disgust. "You too, then, despite the holy sigil you carry and the great name you go by, are a devil? What then became of Sir Hugh? Did you and your vile whore slay him? Oh, his noble name shall be avenged! Come forward, monster and taste my steel!"

***

Torn between his beliefs and his raging hungers, Hugh's pitiful mind reeled. Part of him was yet aware that this knight was righteous. His very being vibrated with the fact. How then could Brother Igolt's instincts be so deceived?

"I am no monster! I *am* Hugh of Clairvaux!" Hugh shouted back. It was meant as a simple explanation of the truth, but his quavering voice revealed he was so deeply shaken he could no longer quite state what that truth was.

Igolt grinned at his foe's fear.

Hugh caught a glimpse of the truth in Igolt's deep blue eyes, an odd reflection of his own. The flash of a possibility permeated his mind, that perhaps he *was* the devil, or at least the devil's child. Quickly as it came, Hugh rallied all his internal resources to bury the thought in as dark and deep a recess of his being as he could find.

Drawing his sword, he screamed, "In the name of the Lord Jesus and His blessed mother Mary! What are you but flesh and bone? While I bear His mark and have been touched by the Blessed Queen's very hand!"

"How dare you even speak those holy names, gargoyle? You are a devil and I'll see you back to hell!" Igolt bellowed, bringing bits of phlegm to his lower lip as he circled to the left.

"Come then, let us walk the path together!" Hugh cried and charged forward.

***

Amala watched, dumbfounded as the two armored men utterly abandoned any sensible strategy and hurled themselves toward one another as if they were great mountain rams preparing to butt horns. She could only imagine that, with each step Hugh took towards the knight, yet another layer of his identity was being burned away. The pain would show him he was no Templar, no Christian, and that whatever spoke to him had lied. What, she wondered, would be left of him?

But Sir Hugh neither stopped nor hesitated. He used his sword as a pikeman would his spear, held firmly against his torso. Igolt's nature might cause Hugh pain or even drive him into madness, but it could not stop the Cainite's terrible momentum.

Hugh's aim was as true as Igolt's faith. His weight enabled the blade's tip to glide through the human's chain mail, into his breastbone, where it pierced his noble heart.

Amala opened her mouth as the two Templars slumped to the ground in a bloody heap, Igolt dead, Hugh unconscious.

Hugh's performance, his cunning and massive strength, made her finally realize that, should her ultimate task lead them into combat, she could hardly be certain of victory. Amala glanced around, equally amazed that no night watch had rushed forward at the battle cries and clash of arms. Perhaps now the city was used to screams in the night, wisely preferring to remain inside where it was warm and safe.

She stepped up to the two prone figures. As a precaution, she pulled the dagger from the human Templar's back, in case she needed a weapon to finish him. But it was unnecessary. She could tell by the heft of his body and the lack of discomfort in his presence that Igolt's spirit had fled to whatever reward awaited it, leaving only cooling flesh and pooling blood in its wake. Hugh's prone back was to her. She concealed the dagger in the folds of her tunic and knelt beside him. As she rolled him forward, she could see pained tears of blood streaming down his face.

This was quite a revelation for you, my love, she thought, musing on how quickly his fortunes had changed. One minute he was reveling in the destruction of an Assamite stronghold, prepared to take on the world; now he looked as though he would surrender to torpid slumber.

Allah works in mysterious ways, she thought. *Perhaps this will give us our chance to discuss Him.*

Though still delirious, Hugh sobbed, his frame shaking with each pained groan. He rolled back and forth, as if trying to stand but unable to. Full of pity, Amala bent down over him, her hand in a slightly awkward pose.

"Amala!" Hugh moaned loudly. "Amala!"

Chapter Nineteen

Watching from his hiding place in the shadows of a nearby archway, Fajr almost missed Amala's hand-signal. He was just too preoccupied with her other actions. She was playing a very dangerous game with this Templar, and he feared she was playing it with her own unstable heart. *What are you thinking?*

When he caught the signal, a quick sign for "follow," he snapped his attention back to matters at hand. *Follow? But you're just staying there,* he thought and looked around, his keen senses cutting through the play of shadows.

There. Another observer, hidden deeper in the garden. The thick gruff figure he'd followed from Gabriella's estate a month before was standing in a shadowed alcove in front of a small abandoned potter's shop, just across from the entrance to the garden. Amala must have seen him when she approached Hugh.

Though there was barely a shade's difference between the shadows and the cloth of his cloak and tunic, Fajr's unnaturally keen eyes made him out quite clearly this time. His head hung slightly forward from his shoulders, enhancing his resemblance to an upright bear, save for the long hair that hung over his forehead. His beard was neatly clipped and his legs surprisingly fat, given the speed of which Fajr knew him capable.

Seemingly satisfied that Amala was tending to Hugh, the mystery man soon walked off down the main street that followed the docks. Fajr, close behind, thought he was begging to be followed. He wouldn't escape this time.

A quarter mile away, in a small alley formed by two warehouses, the man pulled open a grate in the street and made his way into the sewer. Once there, he lit a torch, and, feeling about the wall for a particular spot, tripped a lever that opened a small door to the miles of tunnels that lay beneath the great city. Glancing up and down the sewer again, to make quite certain he'd not been followed, he cheerfully trotted down the stone steps.

Just as his foot was about to hit the ground, something heavy hurled itself into his back and sent him sprawling to the damp floor.

"Ack!" He managed nothing else before Fajr flipped him over, pulled him to half-standing and pressed a long thin dagger to a spot on his neck behind his chin.

The man glanced down at the blade and grinned. "I think you're making quite a mistake here, good fellow."

"No, no, no," Fajr assured him, smiling back enough to show his own teeth. "I know from your speed at our last encounter that you are Cainite, and now you know I am as well."

"Then the little dagger is still pointed at the base of my throat because—?" he asked with genuine curiosity.

"To keep you in check while we talk, of course," Fajr shrugged.

"I'm disappointed you would think such a little thing could stop me," he answered, then made ready to move. Fajr shoved him back with a strength that put the lie to his seeming frailty.

"Oh, don't be," he said, shaking his head. "They taught us this maneuver very early in our training, but it is still my favorite. The blade is long enough to reach through your neck and up into the center of your brain, where I would swish it around a bit, like making eggs. The blood-poison on my blade will leave permanent scars. You would survive, I'm sure, but your behavior would be more like that of a goat's than a man's. A Cainite goat, if that pleases you more."

Fajr was far exaggerating the potency of the poison he could draw from his blood, but he had yet to meet a Cainite who did not respect the possibility that he told the truth. For his part, the figure now looked upon the blade with some fear. His skin, Fajr noted, was extremely fair, almost as white as a true corpse's—a stark contrast to Fajr's own darkly hued flesh.

"You know," Fajr continued, "your deep voice reminds me of an associate, but do not think this protects you, since I would often like to stab him and scramble his brains a bit, and you may well give me the opportunity to do so by proxy. Now, it is my turn for questions and I have so many. Who are you?"

"Markus Musa Giovanni," the man said, managing to retain a tone of dignity.

"A Cappadocian, yes?" Members of that clan of Cainites were known for their pallor and something about the name Giovanni tickled a memory of a rumor having to do with them. No specifics came to mind, but it was worth the gamble to gain information. "A death worshipper?"

Markus nodded.

Fajr closed his mouth and smiled mischievously. "I have always found your so-called Clan of Death terribly interesting. But where are my manners? Thank you, friend Markus, for showing me the entrance to these delightful tunnels," Fajr said. "I am astounded I could have lived here so long without knowing them better. It almost makes me think perhaps you drew me here for your own purposes. But tell me quickly, why are you here in this fair city?"

"Curiosity about this place, about the Church of the Apostles, and what special treasures it might hold. I have a penchant for wanting to sate my curiosity, I'm afraid," Markus shrugged, trying to seem pleasant.

"That, I can certainly understand," Fajr nodded. "And, perhaps most pointedly, what is your interest in dogging the steps of Sir Hugh of Clairvaux?"

"Yes, that, well… he has a connection to this place."

"These tunnels?" Fajr said, his curiosity plainly piqued.

Markus grinned, feeling the balance of power shift slightly. "Not the tunnels exactly."

Noting his reaction, Fajr narrowed his eyes. "By Ar-Rahman, you should not play so with an old man's curiosity. It is difficult to tell when such games might get out of hand."

Markus looked away, but kept smiling. "I meant no disrespect. It simply occurred to me that you and I might not be at cross-purposes. Assuming, that is, that you're here to stop his mad crusade, and that you haven't done so yet out of concern that something might be behind him."

"Perhaps," Fajr muttered.

"Yes, well, then 'perhaps' there is something of interest I can show you in these tunnels. It's not too far off," Markus said.

Fajr, staring Markus in the eyes, could not contain his curiosity. He pulled back, releasing him. "Show me," he said.

Markus nodded, and did not try to flee. Instead, they lit torches and he led the old vizier through a network of tunnels that wound beneath the old city. After some time, Fajr glanced around and said, "We are near the Church of the Apostles, yes?"

Markus nodded. After a few more yards he came to a sudden halt, and pointed toward a shadow in the distance.

"Our destination. Now, don't stand too close, if you plan to continue to traffic with mortals," Markus warned. "I think whatever it is might be contagious."

Hesitating only briefly at Markus's words, Fajr inched forward, torch first, until its yellow glow fell on a grotesque, though somewhat familiar, sight. Half-eaten corpses wearing Templar mantles, their skin in texture and color like frayed charcoal, surrounded by sickly rats in the grip of some contagion. One of the bodies belonged to one of Sir Hugh's own ghouls, who'd gone missing only recently.

Fajr jumped back as one of the rats stumbled near him, squeaking as it forced its muzzle against the wall, unable to see. "I have seen this before. It is the work of the thing that guides Sir Hugh, is it not?"

"Yes."

"And what can you tell me of it?"

"My knowledge here was hard won," Markus answered. "See if you can figure it out."

Fajr felt the Beast rise in him and had a sudden urge to plunge his dagger deep into the Cappadocian's throat to see just how much damage he could do. But he held back, unable to quite resist the temptation to prove to the man, and to himself, that he could figure it out. He also guessed that Markus would be more inclined to share information this way.

"Let's see," the vizier began. "Sir Hugh's account and the presence of these corpses tell me that whatever the Templar encountered lairs in crypts near, or even within, the Church of the Apostles. Well-hidden crypts, I might add. Hugh must also be meeting regularly with this thing and sanctioning its feeding on his ghouls, for he hasn't raised an alarm about their disappearance."

"All true, as far as I can tell. But what of the creature's nature?"

He enjoys this game, Fajr realized. *If I play along, he'll tell me what I need to know.*

"It must be a Cainite," he said aloud, "to have drained the ghouls of their blood but leave their flesh. No natural predator would do so. But the flesh becomes diseased and virulently so, enough to infect scavengers of many sorts. The creature must be a carrier. The Nosferatu clan often uses these sorts of cisterns and passages, I have heard, and some carry sickness or leprosy, so one of their ilk makes for a strong candidate."

"A candidate only?"

"There are other possibilities." Fajr kept a conversational tone but focusing all his senses on Markus. His blood allowed him to do more than simply see better than most. With a little concentration, he could read the emotional states of those around him. Sometimes he caught glimpses of color or faint smells associated with emotions, but it was mostly a matter of becoming aware of all the subtle emotional cues the body provided: blinks, posture, tics.

"Assamites have been known to use blood-poison, after all," he began, but Markus didn't react. "Or some of the

Assamite

more exotic bloodlines, such as the damnable Baali," *nothing,* "or even your own clan's associates, the Lamia."

There. A wave of recognition and excitement washed over Markus so palpably, Fajr couldn't help but smile. "A Lamia? *That's* Hugh's Blessed Queen?"

Markus furrowed his brow, upset at having been outdone, but he relented. "Yes, a Lamia. What do you know of them?"

"Not a great deal. They've served as guardians for your clan, I believe; they have blood-altering abilities." Fajr picked at his memories. There was something else relevant there. "They revere Lilith, the first wife of Adam, yes?"

"Their Blessed Mother," Markus smiled. "Perhaps you also know of their dark ability to influence dreams and the will. This one has gotten a step or two ahead of her sisters in that particular realm. Sir Hugh speaks of the mother of the world?"

"The Queen of Heaven," Fajr corrected.

"Whatever. I believe it would serve both of our interests that this Lamia be removed. Seeing as how I am not given to much success in battle, it occurred to me that perhaps you and your… fellows might want to take on that little task," Markus said, falling just short of using the word *Assamite.* "What do you say?"

Fajr shook his head. "I must know all. What does a scholar of death want in the Church of the Apostles?"

Markus eyed him, letting just a bit of his intellect shine through, hoping it might make him look a bit fearsome. "As you say, we are scholars of death. You can probably guess what a scholar might want in a tomb. Information. But that is all I'll say."

Fajr pondered his position and their relative strength, wondering if he could in fact pry the remaining secret from the Cainite, but ultimately deciding not to try. The information he carried with him now, warming his mind as fresh vitae would warm his belly, was too vital to be lost in a foolish battle.

Stefan Petrucha   199

"Very well, friend Markus, tell me where this Lamia is, *exactly*."

***

The mists around Gabriella's estate were thick this evening, and all thoughts were on Sir Hugh, who remained barely conscious. The rumormongers said he was slipping into torpor, the depthless sleep that could claim elders for years—even centuries. So it was no surprise when Amala excused herself from the prayers for his recovery, to enjoy a walk in the misty air.

At an appointed spot past the estate's wall, she did not have to wait long before the flanks and sides of a great black steed formed from the wet shadows, Sihr soon visible astride it. Though remaining in the area as agreed, he'd been increasingly distant since their return from the battlefield, and even now presented himself unwillingly, preferring to stay half in shadow, so he could flee at a whim.

"Does he recover?" he finally asked.

"Not yet," Amala answered, thinking it wisest to keep her own answers short.

"A third option. If he falls to torpor, the crusade will be at an end," Sihr said.

"There's still time," Amala said. "His soul is at a crossroads. His paths have betrayed him. His visions, too. All that he will have left will be the word of Allah."

"Do you love him?" Sihr asked.

"What?" The question shook her deeply and she answered sharply. "What do you mean?"

"I mean, simply, how can you not love something you are trying to save?" Sihr asked. "And how can you destroy that which you love?"

"Regardless of my feelings, I am willing to see him slain," Amala answered, though the uncertainty in her voice was clear.

"Then you would finish him even if he fell into torpor?"

"You said yourself the crusade would then be at an end!"

"I misspoke," Sihr whispered, clearly taunting her. "It is clear we must destroy him completely."

"Why?" Amala shot back. "Do you try to drive me mad?"

"I only try to discover if you already are," Sihr shrugged. "Gondemar could take over, and use his body as some sort of relic. They must all be eliminated."

"No!" she blurted in spite of herself, trying to sort out her thoughts.

"Because you're in love with him," Sihr concluded. "Because you've gone mad. I noticed it back at Yesayel biet. Now it has festered to the surface. You're grasping at the childish memories of your days under the sun, returning to your Christian ways."

"Stop trying to confuse me!" she yelled at him. "I would never betray my vows to Allah and Alamut!"

"Haven't you done so already?" Sihr asked, goading her.

"How? When?"

"By falling in love with an infidel. We're supposed to kill them," Sihr said.

Amala's eyes narrowed. "I have been in this conversation before. It did not end well centuries ago, and it will not end well now. Take back your accusations, sorcerer."

"Why?" Sihr said.

Amala drew her blade. Sihr chuckled. "I could kill you before you even reached me."

"Let's see your sorcery then," Amala said, rushing forward. Sihr's horse moved likewise towards Amala, to meet her halfway.

"Wait!" Fajr shrieked as he arrived on the scene, diving between the two of them. He rolled on the dirt, rose between them and spoke quickly. "You fools can play this out later in whatever manner you prefer. For now, I will not let you sully the great knowledge I have uncovered. We three finally have something else to fight. Something quite solid, for a change."

Chapter Twenty

In Constantinople, city of cities, the hungry mortal frenzy for gold and power had long since given way to a more practiced, thoughtful rape, with packages wrapped in earnest, ships carefully loaded, and cargo dutifully logged. Bloated merchant ships from a dozen docks, hulls stuffed with treasure, set sail on the Bosporus, back to the Mediterranean, then west to Venice. It was all quite civilized.

In the early evening streets, tired crusaders and monks—along with some daring Greek nobles, merchants and workers—now moved about with relative impunity. There were those Latins who had yet to take their fill, who still scoured the ruins of some buildings and homes in search of what baubles remained. Despite them, for the most part, the echoes of urban life peeked out like the first green shoots of spring.

Amala squatted on the great wall, at long last again in battle garb, hovering above the body of the watchman she'd slain with a single scimitar stroke. It'd be ten minutes before his replacement came up the steps. If she and her fellows were still visible by then, she would either have to kill him quickly as well, or deal with an alarm. She quickly signaled Sihr and Fajr, who climbed as quickly as they could and joined her. Fajr, of course, had a question, but she shushed him.

Amala scanned the low roofs. With the help of Fajr, who knew these streets well, she plotted a course toward the great Church of the Holy Apostles. All five domes of the massive structure, laid out in a typical Greek-cross shape, were visible just west of the massive Aqueduct of Valens. There was still no guessing the Lamia's purpose, or why Sir Hugh so often quoted the Qur'an. Amala knew that even if the creature, in an unlikely fit of generosity, decided to explain all freely, they might never understand. Lamia could be inscrutable, that much she knew from her studies. Hence, in combat, which was as much about second-guessing the opponent as it was about personal skill or strength, they made particularly deadly foes. But better a tangible foe, no matter how inscrutable, than an ephemeral saint. Whatever the result, Amala felt in her bones that the weak point in this wall had been at last revealed.

Unified now in their goal of the moment, all disagreements had been put aside. Sihr and Fajr even shared a strong desire to raid the creature's lair. The arcane knowledge coveted and accumulated with care by any Lamia, particularly if she turned out to be an elder, was a prize indeed. Fajr's hunger at what might lie below the Church did not surprise Amala, but the potential for hidden sorcerous knowledge had even distracted Sihr from his deep contempt for her and the city.

Clinging to the ample darkness, she raced along the wall, then leapt into a cool, inviting nothing. Air rushed around her, invigorating her body, until her feet found the warehouse roof she'd targeted. It was a precious delight to be active again after so much deliberation, and so far away from the concerns of her divided heart. Looking back over her shoulder, she saw that, though Fajr had briefly sprawled to his knees, and Sihr bobbed as he ran, like a black giraffe, both followed easily enough. Less concerned now with her fellows, legs pumping with an even, staccato rhythm, she made her way, leaping from one rooftop to the next. Taking the tunnels had been an option, but Fajr warned they were full of traps and hidden dangers. The streets, too, would have been fair game to the Assamites, given their gifts for stealth, but this, for Amala, was the fastest, and admittedly most stimulating path. Sihr, too, had been happy to stay above the confines of city streets for as long as possible.

Attacking the distance bit by bit, with an efficiency bordering on the mechanical, the trio worked closer to their goal, until finally they stood opposite the gates to the ancient Church of the

Holy Apostles. It was a quiet night, to be sure, not many souls about, but the great church was uniquely lifeless.

"How can this be? Surely such a structure deserves some sort of protection," Amala said.

"Look," Fajr said, having been here more recently. He stepped closer and pointed toward the edge of the enormous main entrance. "The door half hangs. The surrounding stone is marked by torch-burns, its wood chipped by swords. No one is here because there is nothing within left to protect. It has been completely sacked."

With little to impeded their entrance, they walked up to the doors. Before stepping in, Amala paused to look at an illuminated verse that adorned the central doorway's lunette. The delicate Greek letters, so carefully painted, were, in their way, not unlike the *suras* from the Qur'an that adorned the walls of mosques. Amala feared they might still exact some toll, but as they stepped within, the three Children of Haqim felt only their own caution. The church had been completely desecrated.

Sihr, however, found himself uncomfortable simply at being once again indoors. He continued forward with a heavy, hesitant foot, his sole happening upon the small stone head of the Apostle Peter that once belonged to the articulated automaton. Not recognizing it was ever part of a larger piece, nor likely to care even if he did, Sihr gruffly ground his foot against the floor, dislodging its debris with disdain.

Their ultimate destination already revealed to Fajr by Markus, they quickly passed the twelve caskets that the Roman Emperor Constantine intended for the Apostles. Once, many had been the home of sacred bone fragments, locks of hair, or even mummified body parts, but now those precious relics were in the hands of Latins, be they crusader, Venetian merchant or Templar. Without knowing what the others thought, the three Muslims all took comfort in knowing that the Prophet's bones had been laid to rest in Medina, where they remained as yet undisturbed.

In the western arm, along the hall that ended in an atrium, they found the iron ring Markus had described, lodged in the stony face of Michael. Slowly, carefully, lest it spring some sort of trap, Amala twisted, then pulled. As promised, there was a scraping of stone as the wall opened, revealing a thin spiral staircase leading down.

"Markus Giovanni must desire whatever's down there very badly for him to be so open with us," Amala mused.

"Then of course," Fajr said, rubbing his hands together with excitement, "we must do our best to find it first."

Sihr moved to strike flint and steel against a small torch, but Amala stayed his hand. "Not yet," she said. Sihr nodded his understanding. With the ability to move silently, in the dark, they might catch the Lamia completely off guard.

Upon reaching the square room at the bottom, however, their unnatural silence met only its natural counterpart. The darkness, however, was interrupted by a weird green pall that emanated from thick speckles on the flat wall and the colonnades, shedding a thin, sickly light on the scene. Fajr scratched at the stuff and seemed satisfied with what he found—Amala guessed it some sort of fungus, but she couldn't be sure.

With the strange glow and the practiced instincts of jungle cats guiding them, the trio stalked from room to room, weapons drawn. Amala was hungry for the slightest movement, but the blackness was insulted only by the occasional blotch of fungus, and square patches of dim moonlight projected on the floor from a few narrow air ducts in the ceiling.

After two hours, having carefully covered the interlocking maze of rooms thrice, they came to a rest in the large, rectangular room at the labyrinth's center. Here, the rear wall had four alcoves. In each stood a life-size statue of the first four emperors' wives, locked in prayer for the dead, their serene white faces tilted heavenward. A fifth, taller figure, a shade whiter than the others, stood in the center of them, not in an alcove, but on a small pedestal.

"It would seem perhaps that the Lamia, if one was ever here, has fled," Fajr whispered, once they agreed by hand signal to allow sound to return to the chamber.

Sihr straightened, his head close to the ceiling, but did not sheathe his blade. "Or perhaps your source lied to save his neck? Could there be some other purpose for which he stalked Sir Hugh?"

"I do not believe so," Fajr said. "He took great pains to be sure I would understand where to find the entrance."

"Well, that door was hidden well enough," Amala pointed out. "Let's check again. This time, keep an eye out for any hidden switch or lever that might open yet another chamber."

While Amala and Fajr looked along the smooth walls and ceiling, Sihr felt more comfortable examining the statues, since they reminded him less of the prison that surrounded him.

"You know, the Lamia have a type of blood-poison, not unlike our own," Fajr said as his gaze darted about looking for an sign of unevenness. "I understand it affects the soul as much as the body. Something to keep in mind if we ever find her."

Sihr found himself quickly frustrated with the statues.

Peh, I can barely recognize a working door. What then would be the sign of a secret passage? he thought. Then he took a step back.

"Why isn't this statue in an alcove like the others?" Sihr asked aloud, his bass voice vibrating off the walls. Fajr and Amala stopped to look at it. Noticing their attention, he thought perhaps he had found something. He stepped closely toward it, bent slightly down and ran his hand along its face. He was surprised to find it supple.

"What do you want here!?!" it shrieked, its black and white eyes suddenly wide open. With a rush of dry air, a stony palm jutted out into the sorcerer's chest, sending Sihr careening into the opposite wall, like a tree trunk suddenly toppled in a storm. Amala and Fajr turned to face it with their blades, but by then it had somehow crawled up onto the high ceiling, where it hung like an insect.

"By Allah, look at its eyes! They do not focus! The creature is mad!" Fajr said as he rushed to help Sihr to his feet.

"No, no, no!" the thing screeched. "To *live* at all, in any way, is madness. I am closer now to sanity than nearly any creature in this world. So very close, a mere breath may push me over into the beloved dark, snuffed as a candle's flame. Do you come to snuff Lorah out, little Assamites? To bring me to the blessed mother Lilith, my pretty Child of Haqim?"

"What we do with you remains to be seen," Amala called up to her, trying to sound commanding. "You know of the Templar Hugh of Clairvaux?"

The Lamia smiled as she took in Amala's features, weighing her worth as if a judgmental mother sizing up her son's first love. She shook her head and mockingly pouted. "You're here too soon, Amala. Hugh was not to bring you to me yet. You were to be his final sacrifice to me. Oh well."

"What do you want of him? Why do you invade his dreams?" Sihr asked, not really expecting an answer.

"Want?" the Lamia spat, turning towards the sorcerer, the word itself offensive to her. "Why, I but *want* him not to *want*. I *want* us all to *want* no longer. To end this badly written shadow-play and restore ourselves to the truth, to the Blessed Queen. To Lilith," she said, staring in a way that made her resemble a horrid white fish packed in ice and waiting to die.

Amala poked her sword up toward the ceiling. "Oh? And is she in Egypt these days?"

The Lamia closed her eyes, then released her grip. She fell in front of Amala, at the last second righting herself so they stood face to face. At once, the Lamia snatched her arms back towards her body, a sudden movement that Amala mistook for an attack.

All reflex, the Assamite swung her scimitar laterally. Seeing the swing, the Lamia lurched to the side, but the blade caught her hand, neatly slicing off two fingers. There was no blood. It felt to Amala as though she'd sundered a bag of dry oats rather than flesh and cartilage. The severed digits tumbled to the ground at Fajr's feet.

The Lamia hissed and made a lunge toward the vizier. Amala's blade held her back.

"Give me my fingers!" Lorah shrieked.

Amala and Sihr blocked her view of Fajr. Fajr quietly scooped up the fingers.

"In the desert, we trade, demoness. What will you give us for them?" Sihr said.

The Lamia stared at him aghast for a moment, then said, "I will answer a question for each."

"Why should we believe you?" Amala said, following the sorcerer's bizarre lead. "I say we just burn them!"

The fear in her eyes seemed sincere. "No! I want to see them! I want to touch them! Because they are dead and they are mine! What could matter more to a creature such as I?"

"Give her one finger, Fajr," Amala said. "We'll see how it goes."

Gingerly, Fajr tossed the smaller of the two pieces to the ground in front of the creature. Lorah snatched it up as though it were the last drop of blood in the world. She looked at it, held it this way and that in the dim light, marveling that it had once been part and parcel of what she called her self. Her strange examination done, she rolled the finger in the palm of one hand and looked back at the Assamites.

"Ask," she said.

"Why does Sir Hugh quote the Qur'an?" Amala said, staring into the Lamia's dull, glassy eyes.

"Because it is so unique and so holy," Lorah said in a clearly mocking tone. She twisted her face into a mask of terrible fear, one an actor might wear on a stage, then lowered her hands to the floor in false supplication as she spoke:

"Seeing your great form with many faces, many eyes, many arms, many thighs and feet, and many terrible tusks and stomachs, O Mighty Armed, the worlds are terrified and so am I."

Amala's brow furrowed, and Sihr seemed offended, but Fajr was amazed. He repeated the words to himself faster and faster, trying to recall their source. "The Bhagavad Gita," he sputtered out at last. "She quotes the holy book of the Hindus. Why? Why do you quote the holy book of the Hindus?"

Lorah did not answer. Instead, falling languorously back into the wall behind her as if making love to it, she sighed and pressed her palms backwards against its surface. In this impossible position, she climbed vertically, all the while still facing them with her wide, hideous grin.

> "We are what we think.
> All that we are arises
> With our thoughts.
> With our thoughts,
> We make our world."

Again the vizier repeated the words, faster and faster, this time ultimately stamping his foot in rhythm, as if that would kick the source from his brain.

"Siddhartha Gautama," the vizier responded at last, unable to keep from grinning. "I'm certain of it. Also called the Buddha. One of the elders at our school had traveled the East. He taught us of him. It is as though this creature somehow has access to all the holy books in the world."

"That would explain how she could whisper such things to Hugh," Sihr said.

"But not why," Amala said.

From her perch on the ceiling, flicking a tongue that resembled a small, black, legless lizard, the Lamia purred, "The heaven and earth would like to kiss."

Fajr shrugged, disappointed. "That one's easy. The Talmud."

Her back still to the ceiling, Lorah glared down at them. "Any and all."

A falling stone again, this time she landed directly in front of Amala's blade. "For I have at my fingertips any and all," she said.

"She does not answer," Sihr boomed, waiting word from Amala to attack. "This is all distraction."

The Lamia laughed, swinging her arms wide. "No, you fool, this *world* is distraction!"

"If you have access to all manner of holy word, you've told us how. My question was *why*?" Amala said sternly.

In a simultaneous movement, the Lamia curled her lips into a smile and raised her shoulders, "To disarm him, sweet Assamite. To disarm him and make him mine."

She took her finger and popped it into her mouth. As she chewed, Lorah cupped her remaining fingers as if around an invisible ball, then pivoted them on the wrist, describing opposing patterns in the air. "Beyond the crude enthrallment of a mere blood oath, the soul *must* be disarmed to be truly opened to the will of another. Just as the Sufis seek to disarm themselves to Allah by filling their minds with contradictions. For my Hugh, his heart was full of Christ. Islam was his Satan. For each Gospel quote he took to his heart, one from the Qur'an undid him. *I am Alpha and Omega, the first and the last* on the one side. *Muhammad was the seal of the prophets* on the other. Angel cannot be devil, devil not angel, yes? It is easy when you know the secret shape of things, as I do. The earth itself is written in the small of Lilith's back. There, in time, all things meet their opposite and die. All things are thus undone. Just as I can undo you. See?"

She swallowed and spun around, at first giggling childishly, then cackling like an old crone.

"Ana l-Haq! Ana l-Haq!"

Fajr was about to open his mouth, when Amala cut him off. "The words of Mansur al-Hallaj, yes, I know. The Sufi who begged for his own death because he felt life itself distracted him from Allah."

"And how long will you keep me thus separate from Lilith?" the Lamia begged. "Will you try to kill me soon, I hope?"

Amala shook her head. "We still have one more finger."

"And what would you ask for it?" the Lamia whispered.

"What's in Egypt that you wanted so badly you would try to send an entire crusade to fetch it?" Amala said.

In response, the Lamia snarled.

Though her torso didn't move, all four of the thing's limbs shot out to touch hidden switches on the wall behind her. Old stones ground quickly, shifting at the sudden lurch of unseen weights cascading along furrows deep beneath them. Whole walls turned, floors pivoted. At once, the floor plan of the crypts was different.

Staring at the four featureless walls she now faced alone, Amala cursed herself.

"Sihr! Fajr!" Amala called.

She heard the sorcerer bellow from somewhere off to her right.

"I am here, Amala, in a featureless cube," he said. "There is an air duct above, but that is all. I can't say I like it very much."

"Prepare what sorcery you have! Fajr! Where are you?" she cried.

A shaking voice beyond the wall ahead responded.

"I am here… with… with the Lamia," he answered.

Then Amala heard Lorah's loud dry laugh. Realizing the vizier was no match for the creature, Amala lunged forward, trying to force the edge of her blade into the spaces between the stones that made the wall, hoping she might somehow be able to pry one free. It was hopeless, so she tried the sides and the bottom of the wall proper. There was a small space between the floor and the wall that she managed to thrust her blade through. Perhaps if she could find the pivot on which the wall moved, she might yet pry it open.

"Sihr! Fajr! There is a gap in the bottom of these walls," Amala called.

Lorah heard as well. "Don't bother. There is no way through," she cried. "Unless, of course, you acquire the Mother's blessing and realize there are no walls at all. But then you must first abandon your Allah, your Haqim, and hope!"

Fajr and Lorah's voices fell quiet, to normal speech. With the thick stone muffling the sounds, Amala couldn't make out any words.

"Fajr, what is she saying?" Amala cried. There was no answer.

***

Beyond the wall, Lorah straightened, to stand upright. The motion came with a strange popping noise, as if her bones were snapping as she moved. On her feet, she stepped closer to Fajr's wrinkled face. She took her finger and gently stroked his upper lip, caressing the space between the bare flesh and the line of his white moustache.

"It will be her turn to have me soon enough," the Lamia whispered. "But you still have my finger, so let us take this moment for ourselves, vizier. You and I. My hungry heart, your hungry mind."

Her index finger found the single hair on his face that was still black, and used a cracked fingernail to gently lift it away from the others. "You're an old one," she said admiringly.

He looked into her wide, fishlike eyes, any fear he had quelled by fascination. "As are you," he said.

The Lamia shook her head. "Not so old as I look. But *you* were long-lived when you still breathed."

Fajr nodded. "Embraced at the age of seventy-two, because, as my sire said, my thirst for knowledge could not be appeased in a single lifetime."

"Did your sire give you a choice?" she said, trying to coo, but managing a sound more akin to a rodent's squeal. "You do not strike me as one who cares much for Cainite shadow games."

Fajr shrugged, unable to take his eyes off her. "The choice was purely theoretical, between the peace of death and the hunger of study, as he put it. Though I'd devoted my life to scholarship, I still wanted to know it all. It was a foregone conclusion."

Lorah nodded, smiling. "Yes. I could tell that about you, the way you hung on my words, anxious to tether them to some point in time, meeting my verbal caresses with your own. I know how hungry you are to know. Did you understand what I was saying?"

"Yes. For Hugh, the Qur'an represented the opposite of his Templar training. With each spiritual concept canceling the other out, he was left a blank slate upon which you could write," Fajr said.

She nodded her approval.

"Well then, vizier. You still have Lorah's finger. Is your question for me the same as hers would have been?" she said.

"Oh, I would ask so much more," Fajr said. "But that would still be my first question."

The Lamia smiled and nodded. Then she lowered her hand out of sight for a moment. Fajr tensed, fearing she would strike him. Instead, she smiled again and stroked his hair to calm him, as if he were a lap dog startled by his mistress's sudden move. Instead of a weapon, she held something else before him, a small stone shard, more yellow and white than gray, irregularly shaped, but longer than wide, almost the size of her finger. As it floated before his eyes, poised between skeletal thumb and index finger, he could see writing carved into it, a single word in an ancient tongue.

As if drawing herself ever closer to death, her shoulders heaved to suck in the breath she needed for speech. "Do you know Chaldean?" she hissed out.

Fajr nodded.

"And what does it say?"

He scrunched his eyes to better focus and read, aloud, "Lilith."

"Yes. The Dark Mother. It was with this, her very name, that she taught me all," the Lamia explained. "And made me so much more than my sisters."

"Really? This stone? What has it to do with Hugh, and with Egypt?" Fajr asked, his mind all at once the usual jumble of questions. "Where did you get it? What is it?"

"You are a man of learning," she taunted, "surely you have heard of the Sargon Codex?"

"I thought it only rumor and conjecture." A thrill of possibility coursed down Fajr's spine. "Then it exists? In Egypt somewhere? Is that a piece of the codex? How did you come by it?"

She held it out to him as if it were the kiss of a woman, or a bowl of warm vitae.

"No need to ask me. Ask Her yourself. All you have to do is hold Her. Hold Her a moment and you will see the last hour. Hold Her longer, the last year. Hold Her longer still and you will see everything that has occurred since this false creation first ruptured the silence with its infernal wails, and you will have all the knowledge there is to be had," she explained. "Oh my. Isn't that what you always wanted?"

"Then this is how you knew so many things. This is the source of your strange powers, from the influence over Sir Hugh to your ability to walk these walls. This is how you were able to manipulate events," he muttered. "And now you want me to hold it."

Mesmerized, Fajr reached out to take the stone in his hands. But there was one more question to be asked and he hesitated. "Why? Why do you give this to me?"

Lorah smiled, trying to make her features seem as pleasant as possible and failing abysmally. "To disarm and destroy you," she said plainly. "Because She loves you and you love Her. Because I know you won't be able to let Her go in time to save yourself."

214

Assamite

"Save myself?" Fajr said, curiosity welling in his chest as his hand fluttered just an inch over the stone's rough broken edges.

"Why do you hesitate? Don't you want to know Her as I have? At any cost?" she asked.

"Yes," Fajr said. Then he snatched the shard from her hand, as if convinced she meant to pull it away at the last possible moment. But she did not. And She, it, was his.

She was like ice against his palm, only rougher. A chill from the shard quickly worked its way beneath the skin of his hand, stiffening his curled fingers. Up his arm it crept, moving deeply along his shoulders and neck, then directly into his brain, from the base. As if it were a cup and She the ocean, the tingling filled that intellectual organ. At first he felt Her as mere words, a cacophony of voices, but then Lorah faded from view and the scraping of Amala's sword against the rock grew distant and muffled.

Fajr's brain flooded with a torrent of whole images, not merely visual, but complete in all the senses, touch, smell and the ineffable perceptions of the skin. It was as she said, all things, moving backwards. At first he saw the conversation they had just had. Then the shifting walls. The journey through the city. The months among the Templars. Then, as if the eidetic flow were a boulder rushing uncontrollably faster and faster down a steep hill, the images came in a deluge, one atop the other with no distinction possible among or in between. The Fourth Crusade that crushed his home. The tide of Islam beating against the eastern empire. His life, her life, all lives. The rise of Salah ad-Din, of the Fatimid dynasty, the Abbasid, the Umayyad and all the caliphs therein. Then came the life of the Prophet himself, spinning backwards to the first men who walked the earth. Species rose and fell. Strange beasts that now lived only in dream raced in hordes on unknowable terrain. Volcanoes sucked the earth back into the globe's fiery depths, oceans claimed the land, until finally there was only the blackness before creation.

Fajr let out a pained whine, as if a babe betrayed by its mother, and crumpled to the ground, the blackness of torpor replacing the images in his mind. Lorah knelt over him to feed.

"Fajr!" Amala shouted, having heard his sad cry through the wall.

"He no longer has concern with names, or objects, or places, Assamite. Not even his own," the Lamia shouted back once she had drunk her fill. She tossed her remaining severed finger in her mouth and chewed it down. Next, she took the shard from Fajr's desiccated hand and slipped it once more beneath her white robe. She kicked the vizier's drained, doll-like form out of her way and pressed a few more of the stones on the wall. With another rush of pulleys and shifting walls, Lorah, Fajr's blood lending some color to her lips, stood facing the enraged Amala.

"Fajr!" she cried again.

The Lamia shook her head. "You shouldn't mourn when people get what they want. It's quite selfish, you know? Ah, but that's been your problem all along, hasn't it? I mean, look at your best friend. Look what you wound up doing to her just because she wanted what you could not condone."

Amala was no longer interested in hearing what the creature knew or why. With nearly untenable speed, Amala's scimitar sliced through the air toward the ghostly pale figure. Lorah saw it coming. With a sigh of pleasure and the crunch of a collar bone, she cocked her head to the side, as if she were the skeleton of some great bird of prey. For a moment it seemed as though she really would allow the Assamite to end her there and then with a single blow, but as the blade reached the edges of her body, she ducked so quickly there was no visible movement. It was as though one moment she was there, about to be decapitated, and the next she was a full foot lower.

But Amala, able to move just as quickly, caught the tip of her shoulder with her blade, neatly slicing off what should have been a half-inch of skin and muscle. Instead again, there was no blood, and the Lamia's body, to the touch of her blade, felt more like air than earthly substance.

Amala whirled, ready to strike again. Lorah was waiting. Open mouthed, she lunged. There were barely any gums in her gaping maw, her fangs and teeth held in place only by the bone of her jaw. Her whole head resembled a skull wrapped in thin paper, made oily by the recent influx of vitae. As she came forward, Amala could see the Lamia's mouth fill with a black bile that her tongue quickly lapped up about her lips and incisors. It was the blood-poison Fajr had spoken of.

"Kiss me!" Lorah said, flying at her.

Amala tried to block her by pressing her hands out and up into the shoulders of the creature's hurtling form. Expecting the airy texture her sword had found, she was astounded to find the Lamia now as heavy, solid and strong as stone. The Lamia's shocking weight pushed Amala backwards. She'd almost avoided the dripping teeth completely, but Lorah fell forward, raking her incisors across Amala's chest, slicing her leather armor and some skin beneath.

Though she could see, between the torn flaps of her armor, that the wound was little more than a scratch, it felt as though the gash had opened a burning hole in her undead flesh. Amala fought the pain to stay in control, gritting her teeth as she rolled and stood, the wavering edge of her blade trying to hold back the gloating Lamia.

As Lorah moved about with breathtaking quickness, Amala realized she would never be able to strike her by following her movements. Before the wound, she barely matched the thing's quickness; now Amala was at a distinct disadvantage. The Assamite instead tried to second-guess her, apparently slicing randomly at thin air. It was a dangerous tactic: The Lamia could just as easily seize the advantage if Amala left herself open, but at the dizzying pace both moved, it might take her a moment to realize what Amala was up to.

After two misses, Amala got lucky. Her blade slashed lengthwise across the creature's abdomen. This time a few thick black drops welled on the parted surface of the Lamia's skin. Lorah staggered back but then, ignoring her wound, she drew her long arms to either side of her and shivered, sending flecks of dried skin into the air around her like dust. A pained wheezing ensued as the Lamia drew in as much of the tomb's fetid air as her lungs could hold. Paper-thin lids closed over fishlike, languid eyes as she concentrated and drew her morbid essence into the air trapped within her lungs.

Thinking the Lamia was reeling from the scimitar gash, Amala decided to press her advantage. Blade above her head, held by a crooked right arm, she jumped forward, hoping to deliver, if not a deathblow, then at least a second grievous wound.

Rather than dodging, the Lamia came forward, grabbed the blade and drew the scimitar into her shoulder. It shredded bone and burst from her dried back. At the same moment, she craned her neck, bringing her face inches from Amala's, whereupon she exhaled a noxious dark green cloud that completely enveloped the warrior's head.

Coughing and gagging, Amala tried to pull her blade free, but the Lamia twisted to the side with it still inside her, yanking it from the Assamite's suddenly feeble grasp. In moments, Amala was on her knees, heaving and gasping. The noxious fumes had worked their way deeply into her lungs. Organs that had long ago ceased to draw in air for sustenance, now accepted toxic humors as if they were made to do so. A strange numbness spread over Amala's skin, and from there into her muscles.

She shook her head and tried to stand. Her well-honed, hard-earned fighting mind, a myriad of defensive and offensive patterns, reflexive body movements, and an exhaustive catalogue of images and sounds to watch for while facing an opponent, found itself suddenly shoved from her consciousness. Instead, from the most forgotten corners of her being, a

218   Assamite

wellspring of denied dread and untended remorse burst to the surface and dominated her. Amala sank to the floor, her arms feeling almost too weak to hold her torso up.

Meanwhile, the giddy Lorah strutted about the rectangular room as if about to introduce a comedy play to an audience of admirers.

"Sometimes I envy the kine, living as they do so much closer to death, and the truth, than we. So much closer, every moment, but so few can see it! So few!" she said.

Then Lorah lay down on her long lean belly, rubbing the lengthy wound into the stone floor as she wiggled toward the prone Amala. "Do you think it's because it blocks the entirety of their vision? Do you think it looms so large they can see nothing else and so think it not there at all?"

Amala could no longer move, let alone answer. The crackling sense of an imminent, pointless doom, following an equally pointless existence, rippled throughout her being. She had been so wrong for so long, about everything—unworthy of her family, unworthy of Haqim, unworthy even of Allah, He who would accept any faithful of heart. She should have killed the stupid knight at once and been done with it, rather than languish in proud possibilities, along with the memories of her fellow murderess.

Andret! Sweet, innocent Andret! And Amala! The real, living Amala, the one who had walked in the day centuries ago, who had lived and loved with a ferocity and faith she could not even recall. What had she done to them both? What had she done to that simple love those long centuries ago? All useless now. The foggy, growing fingers of torpor, the unliving coma that afflicted many Cainites, slowly wrapped their way about her being, entirely unopposed.

Lorah, lively now, ran her hands along her torso, peeling dried skin with her nails as she went. "Oh, to feel the flesh stripped away, the bone crushed, the breath choked out, to become the nothing floating amidst all nothings, free of the irritation of sight and sound, no more to be distracted by touch or even thought. What greater heaven than oblivion?"

Smiling as a lover might upon waking to find the object of affection nearby, Lorah stared deeply into Amala's eyes. "But even then, oh gently, oh so gently, must one move, lest some small slip be made and the World, by accident, be made to see again."

After a silence, as if recalling she still had form, the creature smiled, then stretched her long, desiccated form over her hapless foe, leaning down to whisper in her ear. The Lamia's voice was a sharp hiss now, like that of a desert viper that had acquired the ability to speak, but barely.

"A story, a story. We have to tell you. It's the only way to shatter the last illusion. Recall the wise king Solomon, Muslim, how when two women came to him, both claiming to be mother of the same child, he offered to split it in half?" As if slightly uncomfortable, she twisted her left shoulder, and, after a loud crack of bone, emitted a satisfied sigh.

"Well, many years later during a siege of Samaria, a city of Palestine, there was no water, and there was no food. The king went walking in the evening air and heard a woman weeping." Her eyes went theatrically wide. "'Why do you weep?' the king asked."

The Lamia's face scrunched into a wicked pout. "This woman here has said to me, 'Give up your son; we will eat him today , and eat my son tomorrow.' So we cooked my son and ate him. The next day, I said to her, 'Give up your son for us to eat,' but she has hidden her son!"

The Assamite warrior whimpered as the words penetrated her heart. Her identity had become an unbearable source of pain. Now her psyche lapped up the story as if it were her own. She was the hungry mother, the eaten child. She was the child who dared live and the mother who hid him.

The Lamia nodded. "That is the world, Assamite. That is the answer your god gives to prayers: Eat, eat, eat!"

"Allah is merciful," Amala somehow managed to whisper.

Lorah rose up, shocked that the warrior could speak at all. "Allah is a thief and a liar!" she shrieked. "Your precious Qur'an is little more than a copy of a copy of a copy, a warped echo of the truth, like the very firmament itself! Your false creator, Ialdabaoth, was cast off as a miscarriage, because it had no soul. Confusing itself with true gods, it made this misshapen world!"

Amala couldn't quite see what happened next. The world that existed outside her despair had been reduced to a dim flashing of light and dark shapes, but it looked as though Lorah had removed a small object from the folds of her robe and was now rubbing and rolling it along her body. "I have found Her! She lives hidden in all things, but now especially in me. Yes, you will see Her first, but I will join you soon enough!"

Then, for Amala, even the light and dark started to melt together, and she felt herself entering torpor. With Lorah above her thus, it would quickly mean her destruction, but she somehow couldn't bring herself to care.

Chapter Twenty-One

It had taken many nights back in the fold of the Queen of Heaven's visions to restore some sense of calm to the mind of Sir Hugh of Clairvaux. On several occasions, Gondemar feared his sire had been lost to torpor, or something even worse, only to have Sir Hugh impossibly rise from his sickbed and battle demons only he could see. Now he emerged more determined than ever, as though his experience with the Templar Igolt had revealed whatever was weakest in him and hence allowed it to be burned away. Though yet unsteady, Sir Hugh knew he must take advantage of the tide of rising support for him since the sack of Yesayel biet, and that in some instances, such as this, his personal presence was required. Wavering only slightly at the door to the great mansion in the heart of Constantinople, he composed himself and indicated that Gondemar should knock.

Ghouls pulled the doors open. Hugh's gaze pushed past them and locked on their host.

Lanzo von Sachsen rose from the central couch to greet his guests, his heavy wolf-hide cape swirling easily about him. A brawny figure, his blonde hair cut short, his sharp face clean-shaven, von Sachsen looked all too accustomed to the comforts of his luxurious cape's weight and the luxuries that surrounded him in this fine manse.

As the Templars stepped inside, Hugh noted the rare tapestries covering the walls, the thick skins lining the cold floors, and the bolts of rare silk piled about the great room. Near the couch, an eight-foot-tall box dominated the space, ornately inscribed with a complex symmetric design more appropriate to Arabia than Constantinople. Though candles and lanterns littered the space, the arched ceilings and even the far walls were out of the reach of small lights, and so remained dully hidden in black. Were it not for the stale motionless air, one might believe one were still outdoors.

"Welcome!" von Sachsen boomed in a meaty German accent. "My deep, deep congratulation on your defeat of the Assamites!"

As he walked the room's long length to meet his guests, the servant ghouls that pooled about barely shifted, as if able to make only slight, slow, mechanical movements.

"It is so good to see a true Christian warrior, Sir Hugh, what with so many posing dogs sniffing about," he said. "A warrior willing to act while others stuff their gullets!" Never letting his attention waver from his guests, von Sachsen roughly shoved aside a wan servant who dared not move quickly enough, sending him and his tray sprawling to the ground.

Hugh watched the show with some amusement and even noticed a slight smile on Gondemar's face at the man's theatrical brusqueness.

"I am proud, proud to know that Ventrue blood flows in both our veins," von Sachsen said, grasping Sir Hugh by both shoulders with his strong hands.

"And I…" Sir Hugh began.

Before he could continue, the German took that to be the entirety of his response. Von Sachsen whirled to Hugh's side, wrapped an arm about the Templar's shoulder, and walked him toward the large box.

"I am particularly delighted that the Greeks find you so appealing. The small differences between our churches have always mattered little to me, especially when our true enemies are so clear." He pointedly furrowed his brow to indicate how seriously he took brotherhood among all servants of Christ.

"Yes," Hugh managed to eke out.

Von Sachsen shook his head. "Though these Greeks build their city homes too large for my tastes! And this one, which we acquired when the current occupants uh… fled, is one of the smaller ones. Here! I've said so much to you already, and we've barely made it to our seats! But, hearing of your taste for fine things, I have a gift for you!"

Von Sachsen swept his hand up and down in front of the box. "One of my ships overtook an Egyptian trading vessel. If the captain was to be believed as he begged for his life, this grand device was intended for the caliph's palace!"

Hugh admired the fine woodwork and careful painting.

"It's—" he began, but von Sachsen cut him off again, this time with a boisterous laugh.

"But you don't even know what it is yet! Press the button on the left! Quickly, quickly!" he said, gesturing with the impatience of a man who'd never gotten used to waiting for anything.

As Hugh did, nothing happened. Von Sachsen rolled his eyes. "Ach! Push harder! You won't break it! Here…"

After a firm shove from the German's index finger, the button clicked. Hugh heard a series of small pulleys, followed by the sound of liquid pouring from one container to another. Chuckling, von Sachsen firmly used both hands to position Hugh in front of the cabinet. After a few more moments, the door popped open. Hugh, startled, stepped back, as a life-size mechanical servant, wearing a headband and dressed in fine silks, rolled forward on wheels. It presented a goblet full of blood and dutifully bowed its head. Hugh, marveling at its craftsmanship, did nothing. Von Sachsen nudged him with his elbow.

"Take it! Take the cup!"

Hugh did, whereupon the servant straightened and rolled back into place. The door, on a spring-hinge, shut as it did. Von Sachsen smiled and nodded, imitating the automaton's gesture.

"Marvelous," Hugh said, this time planning to speak just the one word, lest his host cut him off again.

"It was intended for wine, but of course I couldn't resist substituting something of more substance," von Sachsen said. "I'll have it delivered to you. Consider it a small trophy for your great conquest."

Hesitant to voice his thanks, Hugh tipped the goblet toward the German in a silent toast. He was moving to take a sip, when his nostrils caught the scent of something odd. Von Sachsen nodded.

"There are spices in it that my people use to keep it from congealing. I've found it helps prevent the mechanism clogging. You may like it, you may not, but there it is. In time, you get used to it," he said.

Hugh put the goblet back up toward his lips, but von Sachsen took it from him. "Here, this is silly, I will give you something fresher."

"The automaton is magnificent," Hugh said truthfully. He had never seen its like.

"I knew you would appreciate it. You know, I've had to keep myself several times from destroying it!"

Hugh's brow furrowed, "But why?"

Von Sachsen shrugged. "It annoys me no end that the Saracens' skills might exceed our own."

Smiling again, he led the Templar deeper into the room. After practically pushing Sir Hugh into a large seat, von Sachsen fell back into his couch and waved his arms for Gondemar and the men to join.

"Sit, sit! Eat! Drink! All of you! In Jesus's name, the body must be maintained and honed so that it can fight both the battles within and without!" A chained and gagged Saracen, obviously a prisoner, was shoved forth within reach of von Sachsen. "As I promised, something fresher. In fact, this fellow was on the ship!"

Yanking the well-muscled body across his wide lap, he pulled the man's neck to the side and buried his face in it. At first the victim's face contorted with pain, but soon the devilish pleasure of the Cainite's feeding overtook his features. After a moment, von Sachsen pulled back from his meal, warm blood dripping from his teeth, and offered the open neck to Hugh.

"I heard of your run-in with your mortal brother-knight. A sad business that, but it was necessary. You are worth a hundred, perhaps a thousand kine, on any night, and especially in this campaign you lead. Why let their sad misunderstandings about our nature undo our righteous destiny, eh? Once, I loathed the darkness and what I had become, before I felt the true extent of the power that had been granted me. What a boon to live so long, to fight forever in His name. Is that not so, Sir Hugh?"

"It is so," Hugh answered, smiling back. He bent forward to accept von Sachsen's gift. Seeing this, Gondemar and the other knights likewise accepted the meals brought before them. Gondemar made sure not to drink too quickly or too much lest his senses be dulled, in case his sire needed him.

Serious again, von Sachsen raised his hand to cover half his mouth and spoke in a hushed voice. "The whispers of your admirers are full of it, but I want to hear it from your own lips. It is true Egypt is your goal?" He finally gave Hugh a silence in which to speak.

Hugh nodded. "In the name of the Blessed Queen who guides me, I will not rest until we are there."

"Good! Wonderful!" von Sachsen bellowed, his laughter echoing off the high ceiling and distant walls. "I know there are those who argue we play into the hands of those damned serpents, the Setites, but I say why not use your enemies to destroy one another? What is it the Arabs say? The enemy of my enemy is my friend? Well, perhaps that's going too far in this case, but once we're in Egypt, the Setites will rise against the Assamites and the Muslims, and then, once the larger threat is removed, we united Christians can carve out *their* forked tongues."

Hugh smiled and nodded as von Sachsen chuckled. He was quite pleased to be in this man's affirming presence. This jovial nobleman, a fellow Ventrue, appeared on the verge of joining the new crusade himself. All that remained was Gabriella's ships. Sir Hugh wondered what, since the destruction of Yesayel biet had provided the worthy proof she asked for, the merchant had yet to ponder? Von Sachsen's voice, brooking no split in any attention paid it, quickly yanked Hugh back into the room.

"I have long been a proponent of such an action. Perhaps we would not be here in these streets, in this borrowed home, but in Cairo, had not my efforts been undermined by the foolish intervention of the cursed serpent worshippers. As you may have heard, two concealed themselves as my aides when the mortal crusaders gathered in Venice two years ago. One was murdered by Assamites. A female assassin was involved, I'm told," von Sachsen said.

Hugh's brow furrowed. "Not long ago, two made an attempt on my own life."

"Hah, they are difficult foes. And dogged, most dogged. Another reason one must always be careful, especially now that you have so boldly wounded them. You must always think," he said, tapping the side of his head with his thick index finger, "to move only when the time is right and not before."

Hugh met his gaze. "You wish me to delay the crusade?"

"Ah. I'm afraid you and I share the weakness of being easily read by our faces," von Sachsen said pleasantly, flashing his hand before his own expression. "Our minds do not easily hold our hearts at bay. I'd hoped to introduce this matter more subtly. No matter. You are, I know, a man who appreciates, in addition to art, direct talk.

"Bringing our holy might to bear on Egypt has long been my greatest wish," the German continued, "but things have changed. Byzantium is at a crossroads and the mortals are splitting up her carcass. The situation is, if anything, worse among the Cainites gathered here. Pillaged as she has been, Constantinople is still one of Christendom's great cities, and she still has no Cainite prince. That Venetian Lasombra Alfonzo seeks to make a claim, but the Tzimisce, Toreador and Gangrel factions resent him, and the majority of his own clan turn their back because of his wicked adherence to the vile Cainite Heresy. There is no stability. So, I am now forced to consider, what good would it be to take Egypt, but lose Byzantium because it was so quickly left in disarray? There, I have laid it out for you plainly enough."

"And how do you see the situation here stabilized to our best interest?" Hugh asked.

"You mock me gently. I appreciate that. But who better than *I* to sit on the throne? Think what it would mean to have a Ventrue on the throne of Constantinople! I have the strength, I have the will, I have the resources and the manpower behind me."

"What then do you lack?" Hugh asked.

"Ah," he grinned, this time showing some teeth. "Perhaps nothing. Perhaps only the support of a younger Ventrue who has, not only the Holy Mother, but both Greek and Latin behind him. In addition, I am a vassal of Lord Hardestadt, while you, ultimately, are vassal and grandchilde of Alexander of Paris. To have support from two of the most potent Ventrue elders in Europe would clearly solidify my position here. Let me speak even more plainly. If you delay your departure and help me secure the throne, I can promise you a thousand trained fighting men. And perhaps, by the time you reach Egypt's shores, I will even be in a position here to begin a second front to the east. In three years' time, perhaps we could meet in Baghdad."

Hugh was genuinely confused. "Sir, these decisions are not made by me, but by the Blessed Queen I serve."

"Ah..." Von Sachsen waved his hands in the air, attempting to conjure the appropriate phrasing. "Might then it be possible to... to consult with the Queen on the matter?"

Hugh stiffened. His eyes filled with anger and his voice came out with a snarling edge. "You do not understand. This is no ruse, no game, no trick from a street magician with which I enthrall these souls, for the sake of mere material power. My guidance comes directly from the Mother of God. Would you truly have me *question* her?"

The German recoiled slightly, then tensed. Hugh expected von Sachsen to lash out and the Beast within his soul rejoiced at the prospect of bloodletting. Instead the German regained his composure and spoke softly.

"No, no, good knight, I simply meant... we all *pray*, do we not? Perhaps not so much to receive the things we ask for, but to come to a greater understanding of why things must be as they are. I, a servant of Christ like yourself, ask only that you do the same for my poor sake, to express through your most special and sacred connection my concerns, that I might in turn be blessed to hear the response from the mother of my Lord, whatever it may be."

Hugh huffed, but was placated.

Chapter Twenty-Two

Sihr Haddad had heard enough to realize the battle against the demented Lamia was not going in Amala's favor. Unable to breach the featureless stone walls of the chamber he was trapped in, he glanced above at the long, narrow ventilation shaft and caught a glimpse of a single star, visible between the top grate's iron rungs, hanging in the night sky. This would be risky.

A year ago he would have simply conserved his energies until it was his turn for battle. Amala's defeat would be a reflection only on her abilities, after all. Now, his time among others had changed him. Regardless of his estimation of his own abilities, he could not allow another Child of Haqim to perish because of him.

Decades of sorcerous study under the cloudless night sky had taught him ways to tap into the stars' many secrets. As they looked down on all creation, he could look at them and see what they saw. In theory, if there was another ventilation shaft in the room where Amala and Lorah battled that provided an unobstructed view of the night sky, he should be able to peer into the next chamber and perhaps affect the events within. He wracked his brain trying to conjure an accurate image of that room's ceiling from memory, but could not.

With no other options, Sihr scratched patterns into the stone floor, pulling drops of blood from his own veins. As he did, he realized that, for the first time he could remember, he was nervous that he would not succeed. After all, he'd only used such sorcery in the wild, an environment he understood. Here, everything, even the air, felt corrupt and corrupting. What if he lacked the energy? Or a cloud should happen to pass? Or if there was no grate in the other room at all?

Rather than continue with half a mind, he took a moment to banish the concerns, lest distraction become a self-fulfilling prophecy. His mind as clear as he could make it, he fixed his eyes on the solitary star, called upon the power in his blood and chanted the ritual words. With a burst of ethereal wind, his mind felt suddenly free of his form. It rose faster and faster, though the shaft, up above the street, above the buildings, above the city. On and on he went, through cold black ether, racing towards the star.

Reaching the great white gem as it hung in Allah's firmament, Sihr's hand reached out and pressed the blessed light into his forehead. Then he turned and sped back down, a great black bodiless bird, finding anew the world, the city, the streets and the air shaft that led to the room where Amala and Lorah fought.

The reward for his effort, aside from the exhilarating flight of his soul, was extraordinary success. Though still chanting, though still in his body in the room nearby, he could now also see, hear and smell the rectangular room and square annex where Amala was fighting the Lamia. The situation was worse than he'd imagined. Amala was prone, nearly motionless, her eyelids fluttering shut. Lorah, meanwhile, had stretched out on top of her, preparing either a final attack, or worse, to feed.

Though drained from his effort, Sihr realized he could not hesitate. Once more he called upon his sorcerous abilities, this time the more practiced magic of moving objects through the sheer force of his will.

Lorah bared her fangs and was about to plunge them into Amala's vulnerable neck, but just before she thrust forward, Sihr guided the fallen scimitar back into Amala's hand, where it landed with a loud *thunk*. Then, moving Amala's body as a child might move a doll to make it seem alive, he caused Amala's sword-arm to rise and block the Lamia's descent. Lorah hesitated, greatly confused. She was even more confused when Amala's entire body, guided by the sorcerer, stood. With Lorah thus taken aback, Sihr had Amala's knee kick up, pushing the Lamia back.

The Lamia issued a sound somewhere between a cry a croak. "What is this?" she said, watching, hypnotized as Amala's body, eyes still closed, stood and assumed a battle stance.

In the next room, his mind crying for rest with each effort, Sihr realized he was little match for Lorah in physical combat. He hoped the sight of Amala somehow overcoming her powers might distract the Lamia enough to give him the time either to think of some other way of defeating her, or somehow rouse his companion from the edge of torpor.

"Are you even alive?" Lorah said, circling the Assamite. Her head moved up and down as she scanned Amala's leather-clad form.

"Or are you now some sort of toy?" she hissed, and lunged forward. Sweating blood and barely standing himself, Sihr was able to have Amala parry, and even slice toward the Lamia's arm. Recalling the blade's sharpness, Lorah backed off and circled again. Sihr moved Amala's body along, matching Lorah's movements.

Something had to happen quickly. His hands were beginning to shake from the strain, making Amala's form waver. Seeing this, Lorah bided her time, slowly circling.

Sihr was desperate for a new way to strike at his enemy before the strain of animating Amala took its toll. He wished he could simply open the secret doors, but the complex set of levers would take hours to figure out, and the mechanics of such things were not among Sihr's areas of expertise. He longed to evoke the greenish blood-flames that he'd used to reduce the guards in Adrianople to ash. But those could only be ignited with his own blood, and no matter how well he could project his senses through the night stars, he could not transport his physical shell.

Then he recalled the space between floor and wall Amala had discovered. It was possible he could use it to hurl flame into the next room, but given the crack's thin size, there would almost surely be a backlash, one that could send the fires back at him. The thought made him shake with fear and Amala's animated form shudder in response, but he recalled the mad, obsessed bravery of Fajr as the vizier plucked Hugh's letter from the campfire. If the scrawny city-dweller could control himself in the face of fire, Sihr resolved he would do the same, and withstand the pain as long as he could.

In a sudden burst of energy and activity, Sihr caused Amala's form to pivot. The Lamia, anticipating an attack, did as Sihr had hoped, and reared back into the wall that separated him from her.

As he gyrated and flexed his hands to conjure the flame swiftly, Amala mechanically performed likewise, though to no effect.

As Lorah puzzled at this strange new dance, a sheet of green fire erupted from the base of the wall behind her, wrapping itself around her feet, then climbing up as high as her chest. She shrieked as wisps of smoke curled from the dry white cloths she wore. With a sudden whoosh, yellow flame licked out from her chest as her desiccated flesh fed the fire. She howled and stumbled forward, tearing into her own flesh, trying to remove the pain.

Back in his small room, the sheet of fire licked back, sprawling along the floor and kissing the edge of the sorcerer's burgundy robes. Though the flame itself did not touch him, it took all his remaining will to keep from fleeing in terror.

Allah! Please let me finish what I have begun! he wept inwardly as the tips of his robe smoked. He felt his fear welling, slowed by his will, but moving nonetheless, up through his throat and into his arms and legs. Images of the death of Yesayel biet flashed in his mind, with unbidden pictures of the mad agony those within must have suffered. But then he thought of Fajr and the campfire, of his vow to the elders at Alamut, of Amala, of the desert voices that called him here. Somehow, he briefly managed to hold on and force Amala into a final lunge. Her blade sliced halfway into Lorah's neck and the two tumbled down to the floor.

After that, Sihr could hold on no longer. His consciousness flew back from the room to his body. Then he fled into the corner of the room furthest from the fading flame, and rolled his massive form into a small ball. Shivering, convinced he had failed, he fell into darkness.

***

Lorah, her head half-off, still writhed beside the motionless Amala, shrieking. As the flames continued to eat at her, she managed to curl her lips into a mad grin, welcoming the final death she believed was the only certain way to rejoin the Dark Mother.

"Ialdabaoth, I have thwarted you! Your pained whispers flee my form and I am free. Lilith, my mother, my love, I am waiting."

So saying, the Lamia pressed the stone shard into the thin skin of her own palm, hoping either somehow to become one with it, or at least to conceal it within her dying flesh.

Amala, through her near-torpor, felt the flames that attacked Lorah licking against her own open wounds. She opened her eyes and howled, deep in the grip of the mad, red fear of destroying flame. More in an animal effort to get away from the pain than anything else, she tripped forward, applying the final needed pressure to her scimitar. With a pop, the blade set the Lamia's head free. At once the ancient creature's form shriveled into a mix of smoking dust and fragmented bone, uncounted years doing their long-delayed work in a matter of seconds. Amala backed away from the last flames in a panicked crawl until the stone wall stopped her. It was several minutes after the fire had died before she returned to herself.

As she tried to piece together what had happened, she failed to notice, among the bones of the creature's hand, the stone shard, its color only a shade of difference from the rest of the smoky remains. Her tired mind, still pulling free of both the deathly depression of torpor and the animal fear that had brought her out of it, forced itself to other matters.

It took a few minutes to find all the secret levers Lorah had manipulated. During the process, Amala started once, thinking one of the tall simulacra had moved. Rather than risk an encounter with a second daughter of Lilith, no matter how remote the chance, she found a large stone and methodically crushed the head of each statue.

After another ten minutes of guessing, she happened upon the combination of levers that restored the crypts' original floor-plan. Then she stumbled more than raced about, calling Sihr's name.

When Amala found him, in a heap, sweating precious blood, shivering and near death, she guessed what had happened. The sorcerer had allowed the mission to be accomplished, and saved her life at risk to himself. Leaning down beside him, she pulled open his heavy eyelids and saw he was still conscious, but terribly weak. She looked into his dark pupils until they seemed to recognize her, then met his recognition with her own steely gaze.

"Old one, was that the first time you risked your life for another of your clan?" she asked curiously.

Sihr nodded.

She pulled the Bedouin sorcerer to a sitting position, half-wrapped him in a blanket from her backpack, since it was too small to cover all of him, and stared once more into his black desert eyes.

"Thank you," she said plainly.

"You're welcome," Sihr replied faintly. Then he surrendered to slumber.

Chapter Twenty-Three

The moment Lorah died, the careful threads she'd sewn into the mind of Sir Hugh of Clairvaux slipped from her dying fingers.

Falling at once to his knees, Hugh felt within himself for the Queen of Heaven, but she was gone.

He felt within himself for Jesus, the son of God and the salvation of all mankind, but He was gone.

He felt within himself for his own soul, searching deep and hard through his being, and just as he was about to give up, something vile, black and full of bile welled up from deep within him to devour his questing mind. Thus eaten, the searching stopped.

Robbed even of that, numbness flooded Sir Hugh. It was not a strange numbness; his body had felt it for decades, ever since his Embrace, but now it wasn't simply his body that was becoming numb. Sir Hugh of Clairvaux's soul was becoming a corpse.

Von Sachsen watched with great concern as the Templar's body shivered. Hugh made a motion as if to rise, but instead crashed to the floor. The German was familiar with the strange rites and physical manifestations that sometimes accompanied communion and now thought Hugh was acceding to his request, that at any moment he might hear from this Templar whatever it was Hugh imagined to be the voice of God. The expectation was given more weight when Gondemar and Hugh's other men did absolutely nothing as their master writhed on the floor.

Then the spasms became more violent. His spirit shredded, Hugh's powerful limbs flailed in all directions. A wooden table within the sweep of his arms was shattered into kindling. Tormented, Hugh gritted and ground his teeth, then growled. Then, instead of the usual rush of divine words, a sickly brownish foam poured from his throat.

Seeing this, Gondemar's expression changed quickly. He knelt beside Hugh and pulled his eyes open. He turned briefly to the other men and made a small swipe against his chin. Recognizing the signal, but a little surprised it would ever be used, they moved to carry Sir Hugh from the room. Remembering where they were, Gondemar spun and bowed to von Sachsen. The German Ventrue looked at him, then eyed the crusting blood on the Saracen's neck.

"Is it poison? I choose my meals with care, but these are dangerous times, in a dangerous place," he said.

"No, most noble sir. I do not believe it is, but I will know more once I have my medical tools," Gondemar said. "Sir Hugh, or myself will contact you as soon as his condition is known. My apologies."

Von Sachsen nodded, but said nothing. Taking this for understanding, Gondemar whirled and helped his men carry Hugh out into the night.

Once certain he was alone, Lanzo von Sachsen mused on the meeting's ambiguous ending. What did it mean? At best, that Hugh's crusade would be delayed. At worst, that it would not. At least, if the crusade did go ahead, a potential rival to the throne of Constantinople would be eliminated. But then, he wondered if it had even dawned on this strange Templar that he himself might be a likely candidate for the city's throne? Von Sachsen had been about to take more sustenance from the Saracen, but decided against it. Ordering his servants to remove the remains, he rose, planning to acquire something even more fresh, by his own efforts.

Outside, Hugh continued to shake and lash out. The three knights strapped him to the back of a horse and rode quickly back to the estate that had become their base of operations. There they tried to bring him to his bed chamber in the tower quarters, but Hugh was intent on fighting them, punching, scratching and pulling. By now, he was moving with increasing weakness, as if suddenly rendered a child. By the time they reached the tower room, the fit had subsided. And when he finally felt his bed beneath him, he seemed to regain some awareness of his surroundings.

Gondemar pored over his sire's body, looking for marks, wounds, discoloration, a strange smell, anything at all that might give some slight indication of what was happening to him. Just as the seneschal was running out of ideas, Hugh looked up, noticed Gondemar's bloodied lip, and felt ashamed.

"Gondemar! I've struck you. I am so horribly sorry," Hugh hoarsely whispered.

Gondemar wiped the blood away and shook his head. "You have so often put your blade between myself and death, I only wish I could now so stand between you and whatever tries your soul," he answered. And in truth, despite his examinations, he had no idea what that was.

"I know, and I thank you, friend, but some places we must all go alone," Hugh answered. He dwelled on the final word "alone" as if it had suddenly acquired a new, more desperate resonance. "Send Amala to me."

Gondemar nodded and closed the door behind him.

Chapter Twenty-Four

July 25, 1204

Amala stood with her back to the closed oak door of the tower room, full of mixed apprehension and pity as Sir Hugh of Clairvaux stormed about, more beast than man. He was on the verge of frenzied rage, in which case she could easily become a convenient target, but his pain was so palpable, she never entertained the thought of leaving him. Gondemar had been so relieved to find her, so sick with worry over Sir Hugh, that he'd never even questioned where she'd been. Indeed, Hugh's seizure and half-conscious state the night before were as nothing compared to the raging fury with which he'd woken this dusk.

"I have lost her!" he snarled.

The rough wooden stool he had carried with him ever since joining the Order cracked in two as it hit the floor.

"I look inward and see nothing!"

His sacred Templar blade tore across the tower room's meager distance and sliced through the center of one of the bed's four thick posts.

"Nothing!"

The mosaic of mother, child and archangel, over which the artisan had labored for months, slammed into the wall. The carefully colored tiles shattered like thin glass, then fell into an unrecognizable heap.

Sir Hugh of Clairvaux, on the verge of succeeding in what was only hours before his heart's sole desire, staggered about his tower bedchamber, tears of blood streaming from his eyes.

"My heart is as black as the deepest night. My soul, the ocean before God brought forth the world," he said.

He turned towards the large boxed automaton that von Sachsen had had dutifully delivered, and was about to turn his rage on its intricate mechanisms, when he suddenly recalled the little bowing statue of the Apostle Peter at the Church of the Holy Apostles and how angry its destruction had made him then.

Have I now become like Sir Nudd, then? he thought, horrified.

His wavering eyes happened on the shattered mosaic, and it filled him with even more grief. He turned from the sight to lock eyes with Amala. She instinctively braced for an attack, but did not move.

"You must," she said evenly, "somehow… calm yourself."

"Why?" he snarled. "Lest Satan claim me? Well, let the Beast have me then!"

As if suddenly aware of what he was saying, and what he had tried to stand for these many decades, he muttered, more sadly, "Let the Beast have me…."

Hugh stumbled toward her, fell to his knees and buried his head in her bosom, wiping the blood from his eyes on her gown. Though taken aback by the sudden physical contact, she ran her fingers gently through the locks of his curly hair, trying to feel the source of his mind's pain.

"I have cleaved with heart and soul to one inconstant phantom after another! First Christ, then the Templar rule, then the mark of Caine, and now the Blessed Queen! All prove false, all prove distant," he moaned.

A shaky silence followed as he swallowed the blood pooling in his mouth. He pulled his head up slowly, apologetically, and looked up into her round green eyes.

"Or was it not any of *them*? Was it *me* all along who failed? Am I, as that good knight I slew said, in truth nothing more than an unholy monster? Amala, please, you know me, you have seen and heard all there is to see and hear of me. I beg you, tell me what is true, tell me what is real!"

The Lamia's answers to her questions under the Church of the Apostles had forced Amala to abandon the notion that Allah was communing with Hugh, and the thought of converting him had fled with it. But looking at him now, so tired, so open, so full of pleading, she wondered if she didn't at least owe him, in the name of the feelings they shared, her own version of the truth. Knowing he was on the brink, perhaps of true sanity, perhaps of true madness, she cupped his great head in her small hands and tried to find the right words.

"You sought to wrap your mind around that which is greater than the mind can comprehend. Whatever a mortal or a Cainite can do or conceive, God is greater," she whispered.

"Yes," Hugh said, half-shaking, half-nodding. "*Allahu akbar.*"

"*Allahu akbar,*" she whispered back. "God is greater."

It was the beginning of the *salat*, the prayer to Allah. She looked toward the balcony. The moon was high in the sky, indicating that the time was nearly mid-evening, the time when a million Muslims across the world would be turning toward Mecca. And Sir Hugh, kneeling before her, had already muttered the first few words.

Could it all be coincidence? *Must* it all be coincidence? Could the words Lorah had planted to disarm him have taken seed of their own accord? And why not? How could even a vile thing like the dead Lamia drain the Prophet's words of their meaning to the soul? As if in answer, a story came to mind: the tale of the holy man Sahl ibn Abdallah, who instructed one of his students to say "Allah, Allah!" over and over, without stopping. After a while, he said it even in his sleep. Then the teacher told the student to be silent and think on the word, until his whole being was absorbed by God. One day a stone tumbled onto the student's head and, in the blood that had fallen from the wound, the words "Allah, Allah!" were seen written.

The Prophet's word was divine in and of itself, no matter who spoke it, whether it came from the caliph or a croaking toad. And they spoke not only to Hugh, but to her as well, to all. She had only to fully believe that herself to make the attempt worthwhile.

"And he is merciful," she said, looking down at Hugh. Again, Hugh nodded and repeated, "And he is merciful."

Gently she pulled him to standing. As if in love, or some blissful form of abject slavery, he rose to his feet. She turned and stood next to him. Feeling her soft form beside him, he moved to embrace her.

"No," she said, turning him gently in the other direction. "We must face Mecca."

Hugh resisted at first, then turned. As Amala raised her hands to her ears, palms out, the posture called *qiyam*, Sir Hugh did likewise.

"*Allahu akbar*," she said again.

"*Allahu akbar*," he repeated. And as she recited, he said, now in tandem with her:

> *Praise and glory be to you, O Allah. Blessed be Your Name, exalted be Your Majesty and Glory. There is no God but You.*
> *I seek Allah's shelter from Satan, the condemned.*
> *In the Name of Allah, the Beneficent, the Merciful.*
> *Praise be to Allah, the Cherisher and Sustainer of the Worlds;*
> *Most Gracious, Most Merciful; Master of the Day of Judgment*
> *Thee do we worship, and Thine aid we seek,*
> *Show us the straight way,*
> *the way of those on whom Thou hast bestowed Thy Grace,*
> *Those whose portion is not wrath,*
> *And who go not astray.*

Bowing forward, they said, "*Allahu akbar*" once again.

Then, fully aware of what he was doing, Hugh once again welcomed the sensation of the divine into his heart. Slowly, piece by piece, Amala helping Hugh with each word and gesture, they went through the evening prayer to Allah.

"Amen."

"Amin."

When it was over, they were both as exhausted as if they'd made love a thousand times. Facing him, she pushed the locks from his forehead and kissed his tired brow. As she helped him lie back on his bed, the gray haze in his eyes lifted. Some warm blood, left in a goblet by Gondemar, restored even more calm, and some quiet strength to his form.

"I want to be far from here, away from the false shadows that grip Europe," Hugh said, looking about. "Just you and I."

"That can be done," she said softly. "Arrangements can be made. Come with me tonight."

"No,. There are things I must do here first, alone. But please, you go, and make our plans."

"No. You're yet tired, confused," Amala protested.

"Tired, yes," Hugh said. "But not confused. It will be all right. I promise."

He raised his hand and rubbed his fingers against her cheek. She closed her eyes until his hand withdrew.

"Before you go," he said. "A gift."

As she watched, he got up, stumbled toward a small chest and opened it. With a solemn expression, he withdrew a perfect white silk gown, yet another treasure he'd kept from Geoffrey and the Templars.

"When I saw it," he said, holding it out to her, "I couldn't see how beautiful it was, because I kept thinking how much more beautiful it would be on you."

Seeing her hesitation, Hugh pleaded with his eyes. "They shall enter the garden of Eden, where they shall be decked with pearls and bracelets of gold, and arrayed in robes of silk," he quoted from the Qur'an.

She stepped closer and stroked the fine fabric, feeling some subtle new danger to her soul.

"Before we go to this strange new world, Amala, will you give yourself to me? It may not be the same as in our breathing days, but for me it would mean so much."

"And then we will pray to Allah?"

Hugh nodded. "Of course."

"Then, yes," she answered with a smile. "The preparations will take some time, but I will return soon with news."

Stefan Petrucha   243

"I will make your excuses to our hosts. They will not realize it, but I will also be saying my farewells," Hugh answered.

He watched her go, then lay back down on his expensive bed, rolled onto his back and stared at the stones that formed the ceiling.

He had lied to her. There was nothing else here for him to do, but he wanted badly to be alone, to sort through all that had happened one last time, to entertain his doubts and meet his fears.

He knew all about the Muslims. Having fought them for years it was only appropriate this be his latest transformation. Yet still he wanted, always wanted, something more. In Islam, he remembered, there were two levels to paradise. The first was an endless satiating of all the mortal instincts. But the second was the greater prize, *ridwa*, a merging with God. And wasn't that, after all, what he truly longed for? Wasn't that the desire to which each threshold brought him? A few seconds of balance, with no sense of distinction between himself and God, before he inevitably teetered off in one direction or another. Was not the true goal then not any single ritual or religion, but to somehow find and remain in that blessed equanimity? Not just to hear or feel His will, but to *become* Him, now and forever?

He pressed his hands down and felt the feather mattress beneath him, vaguely recalling his oath of poverty. Time would take it, seize its form, make it rot. Angry at its impermanence, he squeezed the material tightly in his hands, and wondered how real anything that could die was.

How real any of this was.

How real any of it had ever been.

Where was the key, the core, the door that would melt all such boundaries?

Where was the kingdom?

Was it in the crushed plaster head of Peter on the floor of the Church of the Apostles, or in the mind that had designed it? In him, was it not in the Order he cleaved to, no matter what its name? Wasn't that what separated him from the Beast he struggled so often against, and tonight, a mere hour ago, had almost given in to? Wasn't that what could be brought into the world, through fighting, through designing, through Being? Order?

He remembered at once the Greek priest's family, who had lived protected with him for so long, sheep in the midst of hungry wolves. Now they were a symbol of order kept sanctified from chaos by the force of His will. Well, not the Lord's will exactly. Hugh's will. Hugh had kept his word, and they lived. His oath. His order.

Didn't that prove something, at least?

Chapter Twenty-Five

July 27, 1204

On the very grounds of Bishop Gabriella's estate, in the abandoned mill, Sihr lay back on the bed of leaves Amala had made for him. Barely able to move his eyes, he let them rest with a view of the long wooden shaft that spun slowly in the center of the cracked millstone. Outside, the relentless river still moved the great waterwheel's paddles, heedless of anyone's designs. Once, such a machine, reeking as it did of civilization and the city, would have annoyed him no end. No longer.

A new, calmer awareness had taken him since the Lamia's destruction, and the sorcerer felt as though he were finally beginning to see the more subtle connections between himself and others. For instance, without having to turn his head, recognizing some strange aura that was uniquely her, he knew Amala had returned. Wordless, she stepped closer, then gently propped him up into a seated position, and helped him drink from a fresh bowl of blood. It was good, strong vitae and his body shivered with pleasure.

"Sir Hugh's?" Sihr asked through narrowed eyes.

Amala shook her head. "No. One of Hugh's Templars who took part in the raid on Yesayel biet. Dead now, a small bit of vengeance for you. They are so excited and busy with their preparations it may be days before he's missed."

"Then you've met with Sir Hugh?"

"Yes. Two days ago. I've spent much of the time since trying to figure out how to tell you about it."

Sihr waited, expecting more. Amala set the bowl aside and looked down at him.

"Do you believe in the mercy of Allah?"

"I do," Sihr said.

Amala hesitated, then began. "With Lorah dead, Sir Hugh had a crisis of faith. He abandoned his vows to the Templars and his crusade, and joined me in praying to Allah."

"What?" Sihr said, then he started to laugh weakly. "If only all the Christians would so simply see the truth!"

"It's true. I'm making arrangements to take him out of the country. You may return to Alamut, while I take him to the Hijazi Ventrue in Arabia. I still await word to see if he would be welcome."

"As I said, you are in love with him," Sihr stated plainly.

"Yes."

Dizzied by his returning strength, he looked to Amala and asked, "And our mission?"

"Without Hugh, the immediate threat to the Islamic lands is ended. Aside from the fact that we might now learn much from him, word of his new faith would chill the hearts of our enemies. Our mission is thus complete," she explained. "You may return to Alamut and tell them you have completed your obligation to me."

"How long do you anticipate these arrangements will take?" Sihr asked.

"A week. Assuming all goes well, I should be ready to spirit him away in less than ten days," Amala guessed. There were ways to speed messages to the clan, but their deliberation would yet take time.

Sihr lightly laughed.

"What is it?" Amala asked.

"That will be Thw al-Hijjah, the beginning of August. The time my augury said would be the best to kill him. But it seems he does die then, after a fashion. I remain at your disposal until then. For whatever purpose."

Amala smiled. "Is it good we waited, Sihr?"

"Perhaps. Licinius might have hunted Assamites more vigorously if Hugh were dead, and Lorah would still be free to find another vessel to act out her plans," the sorcerer ventured.

"But Fajr might still be with us," she said.

Sihr shook his head. "That one, though I miss him, always lived on borrowed time. At least he died in righteous combat. And what else can we really ask? Perhaps it is like your wall." He chuckled. "Perhaps it is all like the wall."

"I'm surprised you agree so readily," Amala said.

Sihr shrugged. "For the first time in many weeks, I think I may not only complete my return to Alamut, but that, despite my transgressions, it may prove worthwhile."

Amala shook her head, apologetically. "Sihr Haddad, your transgressions are nothing compared to mine. Particularly the ones you know nothing of."

"More so than falling in love with our target? Then I should be delighted to hear tell of them," Sihr said.

"Someday you will," Amala answered. "I owe you that much."

Sihr managed to lift the bowl himself this time, and took a long hard drink.

***

By the next night, despite the lack of news, Amala could no longer stay away from Sir Hugh, and decided to tell him of her nascent plans. As she raced through the great hall, a few servants paused, and two visiting nobles followed her with odd gazes. Her excitement had bred recklessness. She was traveling far too quickly, far too assuredly for what she professed to be. Quickly, she twisted her legs and crashed to the floor, tearing her clothes and drawing blood as her left calf scraped stone. Those who'd been watching with suspicion now laughed, comforted by their imagined superiority. She meekly gathered herself and proceeded, with considerably less haste, up the tower stairs.

Why do nobles gather here tonight? she wondered. Sir Hugh would doubtless tell her. It could be a simple meeting called by Gabriella. The estate was yet a pleasant respite from the city. Recalling her image, Amala was relieved to note that Lucita of Aragon was not yet among those who milled about.

248   Assamite

Her speech prepared by the time she reached the top stairs, she wondered about his response to the specifics of her plans. What would he say? How would he say it? Could such a thing really be? Would he care to be among Ventrue at all? Would he accept having to be disguised for the journey? The blur of changes and false identities brought another thought to her mind. Hugh knew she was Muslim, but had he guessed she was a Child of Haqim? In his fragile state, she would have to ease him into the full truth as gently as possible, lest his soul bolt from her and Allah like some frightened rabbit.

She paused at the door and lowered her head, subsuming herself once more into his humble servant. Then she knocked.

"Yes?" his voice came from within. There was an odd quiver to it, as if he were somehow afraid.

"It is Amala, my love," she said, unable to conceal her excitement. "I wanted to tell you how the things we spoke of are proceeding."

"Amala! Come in!" Hugh answered. His voice brightened, though there was still clearly some sadness at its edge. She was comforted to hear him sound so strong.

She pushed open the door. Her smile vanished.

Scattered about the room, as if they were playthings that had mysteriously earned the contempt of the spoiled noble child that owned them, were various pieces of human bodies, sheared, torn and otherwise rent into sections no larger than a hand. It took her a few moments, but then she recognized, from the features of the halved and quartered faces, that this collection of meat was once the family Hugh had proudly rescued when he strode into the refugee camp a mere few months ago.

Hugh sat in the pile's midst, rubbing his bloodied hands, unable to decide whether to clean or taste them. He turned to her, crazed, first smiling, then ashamed, eager to explain.

"Oh, Amala, after the Queen of Heaven left me, I became myself the sole harbinger of order, and I just didn't know anymore what was real and what was dream, and I had to… I had to understand, I had to know. I had to… to look inside…."

The horror on her face evident, he was suddenly embarrassed.

"But it's all right now," he said. "I've figured it out. Really. And there's been some most wonderful news. Gabriella has agreed to give me the ships. The crusade will proceed. Who needs, after all, the mere Queen of Heaven, when they have me, the King?"

He wiped his hands on his thighs and stood.

"Shall we pray now to Allah?" he asked.

Chapter Twenty-Six

August 3, 1204
Thw al-Hijjah

Most of the peacocks that inhabited the grassy garden fled for their lives when the arrivals began. Among the rare birds that remained, some smartly occupied those nooks and crannies whose small size provided protection from the mass of nocturnal interlopers. But a few, their tiny avian brains unable to adapt to the sudden change in their placid environment, stood dumbly about until, in all their graceful beauty, they were trampled roughly underfoot, or grabbed by gruff, bored hands and torn to pieces.

A dark throng now inhabited the flat acre beneath the main building's tall tower, a short ungainly forest that shuffled and spoke. They milled, murmured, checked and re-checked their weapons, their armor and the costumes that covered them and their supplies. The majority of the crowd were, of course, ghouls and thralls, and some of the thralls had yet to guess their masters' nature. They only knew they would be following a great leader across the sea to attack Muslims. In the end, that was all many needed to know.

The exact number of true Cainites was known only to the commanders. They fed on what sustenance they had brought and whispered to one another about what life would be like on the sea, or how best to slay a Setite or Assamite. Sir Gondemar and his Templars did their best to keep things in some sort of order, but the mounting excitement would not abate.

On this night, Greek and Latin, Toreador and Malkavian, all alike gathered in the darkness to join, or at least watch, what many felt would be a historic event. Others thought, and a few dared whisper, that even should this new crusade fail to change the boundaries drawn by mapmakers and historians, at least it would be a welcome respite from the devastation and confusion that had riddled their existence in recent months.

Farther back from the tower's base, in considerably more comfort, those of greater power and distinction were also on hand: the Greek Ventrue Nicepherus and his gaggle of Byzantine stalwarts, the German von Sachsen, the Lasombra Bishop Gabriella, Lucita of Aragon and Prince Licinius of Adrianople, and more. Even the Bishop Alfonzo, though Gabriella's longstanding rival, had sent a representative as well as a modest group of armed ghouls to take part in the journey, lest he be found either too enthusiastic or too disrespectful, and undermine his own efforts at gaining position.

Inside the tower, Sir Hugh mounted the staircase and quickly trod the gray stone steps up into the top room, each footfall reminding him of the powerful heart that had once beat within his chest. Tonight, he found the carved rock strangely light to the touch of his boots. The floors of this decorated place had always felt less substantive than the camp's muddy earth, but this was different. It all felt too easily pushed away.

Then he realized the stones weren't different—he was. There was a new buoyancy to his steps, as though, even fully clad in armor, he were carried up the stairs as he had been through events, by vast, unseen, angelic wings. At last he was free, free of false visions, free of oaths, free of a banal sense of order, free to follow his own unfettered will as the whole of the law. Having realized at last that order was what fragmented the unified world, including sundering man from God, he would now devote himself to the destruction of all such distinctions.

And if that meant no further line to be drawn between himself and the Beast, so much the better. He hadn't had much trouble from his darker longings since he adopted his latest path, and trusted he had found a way to render them, in fulfillment, meaningless.

He had been afraid at first that Amala would flee his light, but having vanished for a time, she came back to him, realized how right and righteous he was, and offered herself to him. At the top of the stairs, in the tower chamber now considered his, Amala waited to see him one last time before the great campaign began.

In the past, he'd held back from Amala, dreading the echoes of human love her soft presence inflamed in his breast, and how madly it distracted him from the divine. But that was over—and he meant to use his feelings for her to free himself.

He paused at the closed oak door and inhaled. Air was not necessary, but he wanted to fill his senses with the scene. Smelling the musty wood and sharp wrought iron, he tried to smell her very presence in the room beyond. The comforts here had been so easy to grow accustomed to, the past's austerity so simple to forget. The feel of silk against the skin, soft mattresses for the daily rest, the warmth of a controlled fire, the taste of seasoned flesh and blood, all these danced in his head, and, despite his past oaths, he made no effort to abandon them. He'd decided such privations were foolish. All orders, rules, disciplines, and misguided yearnings of lesser beings, had faded once and for all before a single internal command: *I can have no love other than love for God.*

The Queen of Heaven had once told him the world was an illusion, a vast, gangly, grotesque costume wrongly concealing the face of God. She'd said the only way to reach Him was to shred it forever. This was not merely to turn away from the wants and needs of the flesh, as the Templars sought, but to crush, rend and drive those longings from the very fabric of creation, to embrace and love, not life, but death, to reveal, naked and waiting, the dark mother hiding beneath. But now the Queen was gone. He'd seen her dust in his dreams, heard her scream in his heart. Hugh imagined that the myriad hells beyond existence were now all vying to play host to her black soul.

I can have no love other than love for God.

When Hugh's hands had caressed and then freed Biton and the rest of the Greek monk's terrified family, he knew at long last in his heart of hearts that she had been wrong. It was then, when, at long last, the distant tortured feelings that haunted him had died, and his disparate thoughts, the shards of belief and longing, melted into one. The false Queen had stolen so much, stolen, in fact, the back of his own mind. But that was over now.

I can have no love other than love for God.

He pulled his gloves off, tossed them on the floor, then pressed his hand against the door until it creaked, enjoying the rough surface that tickled his palms. The final conclusion was undeniable. In the Lord's words, it had been before him all along, but he had not seen it. The world was not an illusion, nor had it ever been a sad shadow of the kingdom to come, meant to test its poor denizens with sinful lusts. The world *was* the kingdom. The world *was* heaven—and Sir Hugh, a dozen illusions shed with each new thought, had finally arrived at true understanding: His will and God's will no longer had any distinction between them. Hunger was life.

I can have no love other than love for God.

He pushed, and felt with joy the creak of the opening door in his spine.

Amala was on the bed, her back to him, utterly submissive, wearing the promised white silk gown. She was there now just for him. Her skin seemed darker than he remembered—or was that the candle light?

He stepped closer, feeling the distance between them slowly die, but she did not move. She knew he was there, yes, but the anticipation, he imagined, was as delicious for her as for him.

254   Assamite

A foot from the bed, he removed his armor and wore only his cloth mantle—a final tribute to the Order that had helped him rise, but was helpless to let him fly. In a gesture not unlike prayer, he climbed on the bed and let his knees sink into the mattress near her buttocks.

There he knelt for a moment.

I can have no love other than love for God.

With neither hesitation nor impatience, he leaned forward and kissed her neck, for the first and last time, and thought that celibacy was a wall that only allowed the sin of lust to thrive.

I can have no love other than love for God.

He stroked her hair, for the first and last time, and felt that piety was a narrow focus that only served to limit the senses.

I can have no love other than love for God.

He let the strands of her black hair fall between his fingers a few at a time, for the first and last time, and felt that service to others was a shadow of service to the self.

He wrapped his arms around her breasts, pulled her to him tightly, and thought that a vow to poverty was a desecration of divine need.

I can have no love other than love for God.

Each rule, no rule. In nature no order was imposed. Instead it rose from the tiniest speck of dirt to the eternal celestial lights that ran their course in the sky's vault. All acted, not out of obedience to something outside themselves, not hewing to something that tore against their nature, but in love and utter harmony with what they were. They lived through a dance with their own hunger.

I can have no love other than love for God.

He had at last become submissive, not to the unholy Queen, or to the rules of the Order, or to his clan and sire, or even to Jesus or Allah. He had become at last submissive to the fire of his own desire, that which for so long he had tried so hard to repress, to tame, to subdue. And now, his true god, it raged free, the very need that gave him life, the very need that was the source of being itself.

I can have no love other than love for God.

He opened his mouth, saliva running down the space between his upper and lower lips, then gently ran just one incisor against Amala's cheek, slicing the skin oh so gently, as if it were some rare expensive paper. Then, as the beads of blood rose to the surface, he kissed them into his mouth. When that gentle wound sealed, he made another, and another, finally lifting the dress he had given her off and allowing his hands to fall between her legs.

It was symbolic yes, but even Creation itself was ritual.

***

Hours later, while the mass outside readied, caroused and connived expectantly, having had his dear Amala as completely as his unfettered imagination allowed, Sir Hugh sighed and lay back, whispering to her the words of the Qur'an:

"On that day the heavens shall become like molten brass, and the mountains like tufts of wool scattered in the wind. Friends will meet, but shall not speak to one another. To redeem himself from the torment of that day the sinner will gladly sacrifice his children, his wife, his brother, the kinsfolk who gave him shelter, and all the people of the earth, if then this might deliver him."

Complete, full of the dizzy love drinking her blood had brought him, Hugh of Clairvaux made ready to wrap his powerful hands around her head and snap her smooth, strong neck. Their coupling now complete, he meant to release her from a world that had no place for her, and to end forever the final distraction from his destiny.

The Queen of Heaven had wanted him to mount and then kill Amala in her name. It was to be his final sacrifice, to show he had no love greater than his love for God. Only now, it would be a sacrifice to himself as God.

I can have no love other than love for God.

Hands cupped about her beloved head, fingers tingling at the soft touch of her skin, he closed his eyes and let his mind linger along the spots on the backs of his hand where the curve of her hair touched him. Hoping the last thing she would feel would be his touch, he tensed his arms and prepared to snap her neck.

Chapter Twenty-Seven

Not until the very moment he twisted her head to the side did she truly accept that Sir Hugh of Clairvaux was not Andret, and she not the long-ago Amala who had loved him. She was a warrior, a servant of Allah and of Haqim. As a servant of Allah, in the name of those who sought salvation around the world, she had given him every possible opportunity to find the Prophet's light. As a servant of Haqim, in the name of those who had died on this mission and a million others, her remaining duty was clear.

Hugh was evidently surprised by how thick and strong her neck muscles were. Taking all due advantage of his hesitation, she ducked her lithe body down toward the floor, leaving only the ends of her shoulder-length hair in his hands. A grunt of confusion erupted in his throat, but before it could reach his mouth, her two feet shot up and slammed, rock-like, into the sides of his head. There was no sentimental hesitation on her part, as she had feared. It felt good to do this monster harm.

He winced, and she shifted her feet further back and locked them around his neck, forming a sturdy brace of muscle, flesh and bone. He raised his arms to pull her legs apart, but she pulled sharply forward. Steely leg muscles strained against the weight of his naked body, shifting him forward. Her hands shot up beneath his waist, hoisting him. She felt herself grin as his large form went aloft, hurled over her body. After a brief, impossible flight, the battle-hardened Templar sprawled forcibly on the stone floor, looking much like the doll she kept close at hand. His ceremonial armor was carefully piled atop a wooden chair against the wall. It tumbled as he slid into it, the full helmet bending slightly from his weight as it slid beneath him.

She watched as he watched the pieces of his armor hit the ground. There was no clatter.

Now do you know what I am? she thought.

"*Banu Haqim*," he mouthed, his voice stolen by her blood's ability to deaden all sound.

She was already rolling onto her feet.

Hugh brought his body, unscathed despite the stones' sharp surfaces, into a defensive crouch.

Black blood rose nearly effortlessly in the palms of her hands, pooling and dripping. Her own Beast was delighted at the free rein she gave it now. If she moved quickly, the battle would be hers. One touch to his skin could quickly put him at her mercy.

She sprang. But as she came at him, he grabbed a wooden chair and held it in front of him to ward her off. Unable to reach him she landed deftly a yard in front of him, then bobbed on the soles of her feet. With a series of feints, she tested his reflexes, judging on which side he moved more slowly, gauging how far his arms could extend the chair.

The thrill of combat rose in her breast. *It is good to shed some of the illusion I have carried so long,* she thought.

But then Hugh pushed forward, ramming the top of the chair into her chest. She grabbed at the wooden arms, but he twisted the chair to the side, forcing it past her arms. The hard wood connected with her head and sent her flying back toward the bed's base. It hadn't quite knocked her off her feet, but now the chair's sides were smeared with the viscous venom.

While she tried to regain her balance, he pressed forward, using the chair to lift her bodily off the ground, then heaving her onto the plush bed. She wriggled upward, trying to gain a seated position, but he hurled the chair into her forehead. The thick oak cracked as it hit, leaving a bloody gash and sending her tumbling back once more, momentarily stunned.

His hands free, Hugh lifted either side of the thick bedding. Clutching these tightly, he bent forward to grab the two opposite sides. All she could see were flashes of white and an occasional glimpse of gray stone.

Stefan Petrucha   259

With all four corners in his hands, he moved quickly to wrap her in it. Her arms and legs flailed, trying to poke out and smear him, so he shook the bedding violently, keeping her off balance.

Bits of Assamite blood-poison flicked this way and that, until the smallest drop splashed against his bare shoulder. As the liquid passed through his skin and dug into his veins, his mouth opened to scream, but no sound emerged. He shook the bundled bedding violently, until her hands collapsed within the ad hoc sac he'd formed. Then he swung it, and her, with his full strength into the wall. She felt her body crash into the stone and her bones break, all without a sound.

As quickly as the pleasure of combat had risen in her, it faded in the suffocating confines of the sheets and the pain of her wounds. *I have underestimated him terribly. It is just as likely I will die here. Perhaps more likely.*

He moved to lift the bedding, planning to swing again. A few more such blows would incapacitate her, but the drop of poison, though not enough to kill, made him weak. His arms were no longer strong enough to lift her, so he felt through the thick cloth and used it to wipe her hands and body clean of the venom as best he could. Then he dropped her in a bundle. She watched through an opening in the sheets as he staggered backward toward the balcony, realizing luck had saved her.

Within the cloth, she writhed, getting her bearings. At first she tried to unwrap herself, then simply shredded the sheets with a burst of bestial strength. Once free, she stared at her palms, angry but impressed that the Templar's notion had worked so well; there was no longer enough poison on her to kill him. Calling more from her veins would further weaken her and she needed the precious vitae in her veins to heal her wounds and to give her strength and speed enough to counter Hugh's next attack. Indeed, he was already reaching for the sword that lay among the chain mail and clothing he'd abandoned upon his entrance to the room.

She felt herself smile, and thought what a pity it would have been to simply poison him, but then cursed herself and dismissed such bravado as the growling of the Beast. The only way she would survive this would be to take any advantage luck and her skill could procure. She was grateful she'd avoided drinking any of his blood during their lovemaking, and a bit shocked that her own blood hadn't at the very least enhanced his sympathies for her.

Whatever dark corner of being he's found for himself is beyond the call of the blood, she reasoned. *But I have a surprise for him as well.*

She dove to the floor and whirled toward the bed. Sir Hugh moved forward, swinging at her back, only to find himself quickly leaping back from the silvery flash of a scimitar. He'd granted his lover free access to the tower chamber and she'd taken the liberty of concealing a favorite weapon.

Their battle now taking a new face, he smiled at her. She put her legs astride for better balance, and smiled back.

A flurry of swings and parries ensued, far faster than the human eye could perceive. The silver and white sparks that spit from the clashing blades threatened to set the bedding aflame.

She briefly imagined they might be at a standoff, her speed compensating for his power and skill. Then Hugh spun, avoiding one of her thrusts, and swung wide, sending the edge of his blade toward the top of her head. She easily moved out of the way, only to realize her head was not his target at all. With a swift chop, he lopped off one of the wooden bedposts, caught the splintered piece in his free hand, then hurled it toward her. As the sharp wooden missile careened toward her head, she quickly lifted her scimitar to block it, and nearly succeeded. The wood's hard end slammed into the right side of her forehead, jerking her head back. The room spun. Blood dripped into both eyes, blinding her.

Taking a precious moment to wipe her eyes clean, she saw, through the blur, that Hugh was heading for the door. He was now out of range of the tattered blanket of silence she was able to generate in her weakened state. He could flee, or call for help. The tower would swarm in a moment with his supporters.

It is over, she said bitterly to herself. *I have lost. Allah forgive me!*

But instead, he pulled the iron bolt across the door, locking it. At the crunch of metal against wood, he grinned and turned to face her, his blue eyes glittering with madness.

"I sought service, I sought union, I sought truth, but every path betrayed me, with slavery, dissonance and lies," he said. "Now I see that even you, my sweet Amala, even those ghostly crowds outside that await my word, these very walls, this very body, is all but a test, another surface to shred. My mind has been clouded, my feelings unclear, but I will shirk my duty no longer. I will face you, defeat you, and move beyond."

The Child of Haqim raised her blade. "You will not dismiss me so easily."

"You don't understand," Hugh said. She could hear the genuine sadness in his voice. "None were *easily* dismissed. In truth, I loved them all."

With that, Hugh barreled toward her, head down, preparing to crush her with his very body. In the fractions of a second before impact, she scanned his form and the tower room, hungry for anything at all that might help her. Recalling that during the furious clash of their blades his left arm had moved slightly more slowly than his right, she ducked toward his right side as he came, hoping that with some luck she might briefly gain position behind him.

Hugh altered his course enough to swing his left arm and drive his blade deep into her thigh. Then, from the momentum, he stumbled forward, unable to right himself for several steps.

She rolled forward in agony, but considered herself lucky. The same blow to her head would have ended the fight and her very existence. As it was, she spied an opening and swung her scimitar at his leg with all her strength. She cut deep into his skin and muscle, but his Ventrue blood made it like striking the heaviest of cedar. Against another foe, she might have amputated a limb—with him, she had to be contented with sending him stumbling to the stony ground.

She stood, but the wound in her thigh slowed her terribly, allowing her only to half-hobble toward him. Had she made it an inch or two closer, she might have been able to strike again, but Hugh was up already, his wound knitting itself closed.

Again their blades met in a silent rush of silvery flashes, each crashing blow met by an equally deft parry. The blood within her rushed to her thigh to close the wound. The Beast hungered as her reserves were depleted further and she wondered how long she could keep this up. Hugh swung his sword with his right hand, then used his left arm to slam into her wrist as her scimitar rose to block. Her fingers opened beneath his powerful blow, and the blade careened out of her hand, sailing end over end, slashing the mattress. Its energy spent, it tumbled sideways on the bed.

She looked into his eyes and saw that he was now lost somewhere between calculating man and savage beast. Hugh dropped his own weapon, grabbed both her wrists and pulled her close. His eyes wide and feral, he screamed silently at her, his hot dry breath mixed with red spittle. While she winced, he moved to plunge his sharp teeth into her neck.

I will not fall thus! she swore.

He twisted his head forward, and though it reopened the imperfectly healed wound in her thigh, she came up with her knee and delivered a series of quick, hard blows to his abdomen. She doubted she'd done any damage, but the impact pushed him back. Hugh became enraged, furious at being even briefly thwarted. He was losing even the ability to strategize.

She pushed him aside and leapt for her blade on the bed, but as she dived, he grabbed her feet in midair, pulling her to the floor. The two squirmed on the stone, clawing at one another. Hugh tried to pin her beneath his weight, while she desperately tried to reach the bed. Open mouthed, she plunged her teeth into his arm. He gritted his teeth and yanked his arm free of her jaws, but while he was diverted, she nearly managed to free herself. Just as she was about to slip away, Hugh reached down into the wound in her thigh and plunged his fingers in as deep as they could go.

The advantage his, Hugh rolled atop her, pressing either knee into her shoulders. She twisted this way and that, but each lurch only brought fresh agony from her wound. Panting, he reached for her scimitar. Holding the pointed tip in one hand, the curved hilt in the other, he pressed it down toward her, inches away from crushing her neck.

She could no longer maintain the aura of silence she'd used in their battle, and sound returned to her ears. She thought he would simply kill her. Instead he had something to say first.

"Do you like my friend, the Beast?" he said, smiling down at her. "You see, it's not so bad once you accept it. It makes everything so much easier. Knowing I will not long deny it whatever it desires, it more easily lets slip the reins. But you are not the Amala whose love I would have been pained to sacrifice to it. You are something else again, and I am tired of leaving mysteries behind. So, before I move on to the next world, sweet shade, though it's clear you owe me no such favor, will you tell me what you are?"

Well, why not tell him then? At least I die as myself, she thought.

The burden of a hundred lies finally gave way and the very features of the woman beneath him shifted and changed. Her head stretched slightly so it was no longer quite so round. Her eyes darkened from green to brown and squeezed from near-circles to almonds. Her whole form seemed to grow an inch or two—though Hugh felt no shifting under him—and her muscles tightened and gained definition. Her skin grew rough and darker. A small birthmark appeared on one cheek where none had been before.

Amala was gone, and there was now someone completely different beneath Sir Hugh's borrowed blade. "Who are you, demon?" he asked.

"I am Fatima bint Thetmes al-Faqadi, Child of Haqim and servant of God," she hissed. "I will yet be your death."

Though his grip on the sword did not waver, sadness took his features. "So devilish, you Assamites, so practiced in your lies. Do you even really know who you are anymore? Tell me, Fatima, was Amala, the woman I loved, just a mask? Did she ever live, if only in your heart? Was there ever on this earth such a person as Amala?"

Fatima narrowed her eyes, "Yes, but she loved a Christian crusader more than Allah, so I ran her through with his sword and watched her bleed to death by his corpse."

"Did you love her, Fatima, to know her so well you could become her?"

"Yes."

"What a world, then, what a world, to create something so lovely, only to have it destroyed by the likes of you. When you arrive in the land beyond, if you see Amala, bring her my greetings, and my love," he said.

He pressed forward on his blade, the Beast rising once more in his eyes.

Fatima closed her eyes and waited.

Chapter Twenty-Eight

"Hugh! Hugh! Hugh!" the throng chanted. They screeched, shouted, bellowed and called, building the sound louder and louder until they could swear it was shaking the old estate's very walls. The chant continued, beat after beat, and all who joined it were certain it would end with a signal to begin their world anew.

But the chanting had gone on too long, and the motionless stance of Sir Hugh was increasingly inappropriate. Surely he would say something now?

When the shouts continued and he did not, Gondemar felt a sudden sense of dread. Cursing, the seneschal raced for the main door to the estate. Not knowing what else to do, the knights at his side followed.

Picking up both fear and speed as he went, Gondemar stormed through the great hall and up the tower steps. Testing the door, he realized it was bolted from within, and at once threw his full weight against the oak. It gave a bit, then splintered when the two knights joined him. Amidst the shards of wood, Gondemar stumbled into the room. The furniture and bed were shredded; blood was everywhere. The crumpled bedding, darkly stained with what he instantly recognized as Assamite blood-poison, was heaped in a corner. His worst fears were confirmed. There had been an additional attack by the Assamites.

Yet there was Sir Hugh, standing on the balcony.

At first, Gondemar was relieved. But still, Hugh had not even responded to the sound of the crashing door. Was he under some spell?

Briefly afraid he might be chastised for interrupting some divine communion, Gondemar stepped up toward his sire and liege. The crowd's shouts deafening, he called, "Sir Hugh? Sir Hugh?" Realizing his words were lost in the roar of voices, he stepped closer and tapped him. When Sir Hugh still did not move, Gondemar grasped him on the shoulder and nudged him slightly.

Hugh's torso moved to the right. His head, severed neatly at the neck, teetered, then tumbled forward. It thudded on the balcony's ledge, rolled, then fell into the crowd. The rest of the body, now shorn from its careful balance, twirled slightly and collapsed to the ground.

Gondemar was stricken, aflame, and screamed his pain to the world. The roar of voices did not stop, but his great cry soon infected the sound. As the wave of awareness passed through the gathering, the crowd no longer spoke a single name, or in unison. The sound became shouting, in anger, in betrayal, in accusation. Von Sachsen's crusaders fell upon the stunned Greeks. Realizing what would come next, harried vampiric princes and dignitaries fled as quickly as they were able, amidst growing panic and cries for revenge. The sight of fresh blood drew many back against their wills, but even those who remained until the end would later deny they had been there at all.

Gondemar, no longer caring who in particular might be responsible, drew his sword, jumped up upon the balcony's ledge, and hurled himself into the crowd, whereupon he slashed at anything that moved. Hugh's Templars quickly followed suit, killing indiscriminately, leaving any sorting of right and wrong, foe and friend, to God.

What happened next could not be called a battle so much as a frenzied, massive surrender to the Beast. It was not until dawn threatened to destroy the many Cainites among them that the crush of violence quieted and the grand "army" trickled away to what comfort and protection remained.

For hours, Fatima al-Faqadi, once again wearing the features of the long-dead Amala, and Sihr Haddad watched from atop the abandoned mill a mile away, where the battle's details were a blur and the fresh blood so distant it did not call. Sihr marveled at the army's collapse just as he had at the tumbling pile of twigs, rocks and branches that blocked the road to Adrianople.

The final moments of her battle with Hugh had been quick and, Fatima did not deceive herself, lucky. Sir Hugh, fully in the grip of the Beast, had pressed forward with the scimitar, intending to sever her head. As he did, she wedged both of her hands up into the blade, blocking its downward movement with the bones of her hands. With terrific effort, she was able to generate just a bit more of the blood-poison. It was not enough to kill, but that was not its purpose. Biting the inside of her cheek, she spat the poisoned blood into his face. Blinded by the stinging venom, he staggered back, enraged and incautious as only an animal could be. She rose and spun so she would once again be engaging his slower left side, and this time made it past his flailing arm. As he growled and raked about with his hands, unseeing, she snapped her scimitar up in her bleeding hands, swallowed all pain, funneled as much blood as she could into her tight muscles, and ended Sir Hugh of Clairvaux with one herculean slice.

His body was young enough so that it did not crumble to dust and she thought, but could not be sure, that his lips were curled in a slight smile, thankful to have his trials in this world at an end. She wondered also if his eyes had seen any of what came next before the Final Death took him, and, indeed, if his soul saw anything now.

Once Hugh's strong Ventrue blood had given her back some strength, it was a simple matter to dress his corpse in his grand armor, then quietly, invisibly prop him, doll-like, before his eager worshippers. It was an idea she'd gotten from seeing the automaton von Sachsen had given him as a gift. The theatric effect was perfect. The resulting shock and anticipated riot not only made for a great display of her clan's power and prowess, it provided enough distraction for her and Sihr's exit to be most leisurely.

She assumed the three Assamite brothers who had moved against him were survivors from the destroyed Yesayel biet stronghold seeking vengeance. She regretted, among so much else to regret, that they could not somehow be warned. Also gnawing at her was the realization she'd never learned what the Lamia wanted so very badly in Egypt.

But now there were more immediate questions hanging in the air between her and Sihr. She had again approached him in her guise as Amala, to more easily explain what had transpired with Hugh, and to ensure they were a safe distance away. But now, the mission truly complete, she felt terrific guilt at deceiving the man who had saved her life.

Seeing the delight and appreciation in the sorcerer's eyes as he watched the near-army's debacle, she said quietly, "Sihr Haddad, your own success is twice what you think it is, because your mission was made doubly difficult by the facts I have concealed from you about myself."

"I do not understand," Sihr said. "Is this the transgression of which you spoke?"

She dropped her mask, restoring her true features.

"My name is not Amala. It is Fatima al-Faqadi," she said.

Sihr narrowed his eyes. "The childe of Thetmes the Egyptian? I would have felt more comfortable following your commands, had you told me. Why do so now?"

"Sir Hugh was driven mad by shadows. I want you to have something more than lies," she said. Then she told Sihr the story of her long-ago lover Amala and all the crusaders they had slain so many decades ago.

"When I first entered the clan and came to Alamut, a mark against me was the guilt I carried for Amala's death. How could I, the elders rightly guessed, fully serve any other purpose, Haqim's or Allah's, with such a weight wrapped around my soul? My sire, however, was convinced that, with the proper tutelage, I could overcome it. At his instruction, I carried Amala's doll with me, meditating on it, and her, nightly. I was to do so until an opportunity arose for me to become who she was, and thereby face my feelings. Since the clan saw fit to send me into Christian lands again last April, I saw an opportunity to give the dead Amala one last chance to prove her strategy of love," Fatima explained.

"And have you let her go?" Sihr asked. "Have you yet let her go?"

Fatima frowned. "I already knew I had been more concerned with Amala's betrayal of me than of Allah, but it took this journey to understand that she hadn't actually betrayed either of us. Knowing that, I am free to mourn her and my foolish deed of long ago. As to whether I have let her go or not…"

Wordless, she withdrew the doll from her backpack, and showed it to Sihr. He nodded.

"Perhaps it is fitting that, since we were both on such personal quests, that we only meet now, at their ends," Sihr mused.

Smiling at his graciousness, Fatima gently arranged the doll's straw hair before placing it back among her other few belongings. She briefly lamented the fact that she had never shared the story with Fajr, who doubtless would have been most satisfied to have yet another mystery revealed.

***

Exhausted, Kosmas Pangalos extricated himself from the carnage at last. He rested against the old mill's stone wall and tried to decide what to do next. Grateful he was able to hide under a cart for most of the riot, snarling and slashing from his hiding spot, he now thought it best to try to make it as far away as possible before dawn. He paused briefly and looked back at the scene. The Cainite rage had now turned on the manor itself. Flames had broken out within the estate. He thought he could make out Gabriella amidst the smoke as she frantically directed her servants to try to save the treasures within.

Stefan Petrucha   271

Turning away, the kettle-maker turned Cainite, Cainite turned crusader, hefted the too-long sword in his hand one more time, then tossed it to the ground in disgust. Though sorry to see Sir Hugh dead, losing the blade and the future it would have required of him made him feel light and free. It was, he felt, an adventure he'd gained more by missing out on. Worlds ended, worlds began, he mused. That much he'd seen himself. Sometimes, he guessed, they began again.

When the fighting finally died down, many in the remaining crowd whimpered and wailed about what to do next. Some were already turning back toward the road that led to the refugee camp, perhaps to await the return of the Nosferatu Malachite, or some new leader. But Kosmas Pangalos had no desire to repeat that part of his life. So, when he spotted a fat-necked female ghoul on a horse-drawn cart headed back toward the city, he decided instead to toddle off in that direction, back to the streets he knew so well. Surely they could not have changed all that much.

Could they?

Epilogue

The Present

"Beginning roughly the first week of August 1204, four months after conquering the greatest city in the world, Boniface's men battered the walls of Adrianople, putting that city under siege against the will of the new emperor, his former partner, Baldwin. The divisions in the Latin empire that would limit its reign to a mere fifty-seven years had already surfaced. Ultimately, they could not even agree on how to split the largest treasure in the world," Professor Abaz said, noting with relief that his time was up. He took his glasses off, rubbed the bridge of his nose, then looked out at the faces in the hall.

"I like to think," he said, "that we've progressed since the thirteenth century, but I fear that both our angels and our demons, having been with us from the beginning, will insist on being present at the end."

Applause filled the lecture hall, some polite, some heartfelt.

In the back rows, Ruya still stared ahead, watching Abaz pack his notes, as she directed her words to the being behind her.

"You murdered your best friend in a fit of jealousy because she loved something enough to try to change it. How is that different from any crime Sir Hugh committed?"

Others would have faced death for such an assertion, but Fatima recognized the question's honest ignorance, mixed with a deep need to know what her own future might hold. Nevertheless uncomfortable, Fatima shifted slightly as she allowed the echo of an old pain to surface.

"What I did that day, as a mortal, was a crime I will regret for the rest of my existence. Sir Hugh's slaughter of the family was the result of a conclusion he came to, an embrace of his base urges. Had he lived, he would have remained utterly animal, dragging along who knows how many into the deepest shadows of the world, irretrievable by any until the Day of Judgment. Who doesn't face a desire to bring harm? What I learned to battle, both in myself and in the world, what Haqim created us to fight, is what Hugh of Clairvaux finally learned he most wanted to become," Fatima said. "I offer you the chance to do the same, if you are willing to pay the price."

"As the wife of an important man," Ruya said, "I can fight for the rights of women all across the nations of Islam."

She could feel Fatima shaking her head. "But what of Bira, the aged crone who bruised your face just this past night? Andret found it in his heart to change, but your husband has no such will or desire. I think of him as more like Sir Hugh."

"Lamia magic drove Hugh insane," Ruya protested.

"Bira is Deren's mother. There is no greater magic than that. Supposed Bira's influence is one day removed? Do you think he'll then become what you want, or something else entirely? Even after she is dead, she will be in his bones, forbidding you, blocking you from your reflected power," Fatima said.

Ruya lowered her head and sobbed. "Tell me what should I should do, then. Tell me what I am to be."

Feeling her sadness, Fatima leaned forward until they were almost touching. As the centuries-old warrior whispered, her breath separated the black strands of hair on the back of Ruya's head. Her words were from the Persian poet Omar Khayyam:

> We are no other than a moving row
> Of magic shadow-shapes that come and go
> Round with Sun-illumined lantern held
> In Midnight by the Master of the Show.

As Ruya dwelled on the new world the whispered voice had opened for her, her mind ticked off all the familiar worlds she now inhabited—worlds of hypocrisy, worlds of defeat, worlds of surfaces, worlds of pain, worlds of denial and, at best, the shallow world of reflected being.

Assamite

But now there was this world of blood, with all its bold extremes that seemed to caricature all mortal shades of meaning. With its death, with its feeding, with all the frenzied rapture of a drug addict's dream—it seemed to push possibility to the edge of what her mind could now imagine, and perhaps laid out the road for what lay beyond.

Would she be cattle, then, or one who rode the herd? Mankind had always seemed so child-like. It was a sick comfort to know it might yet have something akin to a parent—abusive, yes, cruel, no doubt, but containing order nonetheless.

Blood, Ruya reasoned, if nothing else, is the very stuff of what we are.

With that thought, the lattice-work of carefully crafted rationalizations that held aloft her puppet-plans collapsed. She felt the madness of life swirl above her, while she sat below, staring up, wondering why she'd ever bothered with the pretty whirlpool in the first place.

She felt, perhaps for the first time since she was a child, a call from deep inside her, that pulled her very bones, connecting her back through time, not by mere biological parenthood, but by the heart-unity of inherited ideas, thoughts and loves, that tied her to all women, to all men, back to the very first, be it Lilith, Eve or the disenfranchised goddess Herself. Here was the war, here the peace, here the path—the heavenly chorus of the ages, the song of Haqim calling loudest to her soul.

She realized that this was why Fatima had been so forthcoming—she'd known all along what Ruya's answer would be.

A slight smile, meant for the unseen teacher that had conjured it, made its way to Ruya's lips, but it vanished as the mortal woman turned and saw that the seat behind her was empty. Scanning the crowd would be a pointless effort, she knew. Fatima was gone.

***

With the decision made, time went faster than she'd imagined, as if the burden of consciousness had been removed from her soul. The papers listing the contributors to Deren's campaign were easy to procure, her fiancé not bothering to conceal them. As she left his home for the last time, the precious files held in the folds of her jacket, she imagined Bira smiling, somehow knowing her rival would be gone forever now. For Bira, the loss of millions would be a small price to pay for having her son back in her sole command again.

Ruya drove for hours in a rented car to the city of Bursa, where she spent the night in the appointed hotel room. Sleeping alone for the first time in ages, she realized she was also sleeping comfortably for the first time in just as long.

In the morning, the package she'd left on the cheap hotel bureau was gone. In its place, on the worn acrylic surface, with its faux design and pressboard wood, a pale imitation of an imitation of an imitation replicated *ad infinitum* with the senseless abandon of fornicating insects, lay a singular, ancient, handmade doll.

At first, its black eyes seemed on the verge of weeping, but on closer examination, anyone could tell it was only a trick of the light.

About the Author

Stefan Petrucha is the writer of Topp's acclaimed X-Files comic. His work on that series has been republished in six trade paperbacks in the United States and abroad. He also writes the adventures of Mickey Mouse & Co. for Egmont Publishing in Denmark. He is also the author of "The Treatment of Dr. Eberhardt" in White Wolf's **Inherit the Earth** anthology and of **Tribe Novel: Uktena**. His first novel, *Making God*, was published in 1997.

Sometimes a novelist, sometimes a video director, sometimes a shared illusion, he has a gaggle of eclectic, top-notch writing assignments, in comics, prose and other fields, under his belt and slightly to the right of his loose change. He currently works for Westchester-based PBI Media Inc., the publisher of such notable periodicals as *Film & Video* and *AV Video Multimedia Producer*, as a feature writer, associate editor and web guru.

Dark Ages
Cappadocian

ANDREW BATES

Dark Ages
Vampire

ISBN 1-58846-819-4
WW 11207

Enjoy the following preview of **Dark Ages: Cappadocian™**, the third Dark Ages Clan Novel, available in November, 2002.

Constantinople, April 14, 1204

Markus Musa Giovanni roused his considerable bulk from slumber even as the sunset stained the western sky. He was not normally such an early riser, but this was far from a normal time. His rest during the past two days had been disrupted by the terror and pillage that swept the city above.

He was at the center of a storm of change, but he had yet to get a clear view of which way the winds blew. There were too many variables at work to gain a keen insight into his best course of action. Markus had spent the previous night weighing options. While this had at least narrowed his choices, none of the alternatives that remained were without risk.

Markus could return home, to Venice and his family. Safe from the ravages Constantinople suffered this night, he could relate all that he had learned during his years in the Queen of Cities. Alas, Markus had precious little worth telling. He had yet to succeed at what he had once thought was a laughably simple task. To stand before the great Augustus Giovanni with nothing more than excuses in hand… well. Markus could claim that the unforeseen challenges were greater than anyone had expected, but it would be nothing more than pathetic whining. Markus would be as much as saying he was not worthy of the dark gift he had been given. At the very least, he would be an embarrassment to the family, his name a joke among his peers, spurned even by the shades who whispered in the deep chambers where the Giovanni performed their necromantic studies.

Or Markus could remain in Constantinople. He could see what opportunities for discovery presented themselves in the wake of the massacre still raging throughout the great city's streets. The secrets he had been charged to find might more easily be gleaned under cover of violence. Yet to stay would expose Markus to mortal—and immortal—danger. His blood was more potent than many who bore the mark of Caine, but Markus was still young as vampires considered such things. Despite his power, he was not invulnerable. He might find that which he had sought for years, only to suffer ultimate destruction at the point of his triumph.

A third option—to flee, spending his nights far from familial responsibility and physical danger—never made it beyond the stage of a passing, barely acknowledged thought. Markus was many things, but a coward was not one of them.

Sandwiched between the twin specters of admitting failure and chancing final death, Markus Musa Giovanni was not eager to commit to either course. Still, continuing to lurk in the safety of his lair would accomplish nothing. The time for planning was done. Now was the moment to act.

A grimace of resignation stretched across Markus's broad features. He was born a Giovanni and made a Cappadocian. In the search for the ultimate secrets of life and death, failure was unacceptable.

***

"Look, Falsinar! A handful of Greeks approach. Ready the stone."

"You are certain they are Greeks?"

"Eyes like a hawk, my friend. You can tell by their armor; see?"

"You misremember your features, Beltramose. You have a nose like a hawk's beak, but your eyes are no sharper than a wooden spoon."

"I forgive you such a hurtful jibe, Falsinar. Your words are formed from the envy you hold for my unmatched beauty and intellect."

"Aye, unmatched indeed. I have never met a man as hideous and ignorant as yourself."

"Poor Falsinar. Count yourself lucky that I am such a kind-hearted soul as to accept you as my friend."

"Indeed, Beltramose. God is surely punishing me for some great sin."

"Ah, look now. We have missed our chance. They have decided not to try our door."

"Do not despair. See there, just turning yonder corner?"

"What? Ah, but they look to be Venetian. Would God forgive us for striking at our fellow men?"

"I do not see why He would start now. Besides, look how they come unerringly for the lone stout door that remains standing on this street. Only the suicidal would dare try to gain entry to our humble tower."

"Truly, I can find no fault with your logic, my friend. On the count of three, then?"

"I am at your command, good Beltramose."

***

Markus Giovanni heard pounding from the heavy banded door two floors above his hidden lair. Even as he reached the landing, shouts of surprise erupted outside, followed by a thunderous crash. Markus felt the ground shake at some impact, but lock and hinges remained firm.

Certain no one would come through the door for the moment, Markus spared a glance at the opposite wall of the squat tower that comprised the remainder of his home. Those who wished to gain entry from the street could not know that a significant portion of the tower's other side had tumbled in. That hole overlooked a series of ruined buildings to which the tower had once been attached, part of a Venetian merchant's warehouse complex. They still gave off a thick billow of smoke from the conflagration that had claimed them the previous day. Markus suppressed a shudder. He had been safe from the deadly flames, his lair being buried deep beneath the city. Still, the bones of the blackened structures were grim reminder of how easily all things might fall no matter the care taken in their construction.

His thoughts went from the metaphorical to the actual. The cries of pain and panic left little doubt as to what had happened. Markus slipped the rest of the way up the stone steps and entered the tower's top room. Peering out the jagged hole on the street-side wall, two men sniggered at one another as they levered another stone block into position.

"The city is in flames," Markus observed, "and all you fools can think to do is drop stones on looters?"

The man on the right jerked upon hearing Markus's basso rumble. The other fellow lacked the strength to hold the stone in place and barked in surprise as it fell three stories. Ignoring the renewed screams of outrage from below, the man on the left looked over at Markus.

"Ah, *Signore* awakens at last. You have a decision, then?"

"I have."

***

Falsinar and Beltramose huffed up the last few steps to the tower roof. Markus had sated himself with the victims of their rock-dropping stunt. It had fallen to the pair to remove the bodies and lessen the chances that other looters would take an interest in their abode. Markus stood at the tower's far side, backlit by the fires encroaching on the Great Bazaar. The men moved opposite their master and took a post over the tower's front entrance, leaving their lord to his privacy.

"That is something I never have grown used to," Beltramose confided. He nodded to Markus, who murmured at the air.

Falsinar looked over. "Aye, well. What is it he says? 'Different states of being?' "

"It makes them no less disquieting to be around."

"Hmm. And yet," Falsinar said, tapping a contemplative finger against his lips, "our gracious lord and master appears to have no problems trafficking with their ilk."

Beltramose frowned. "What a revelation! Truly, my friend, your insight is without limit."

"I must say that your compliment seems less than genuine."

"You know that I hold you in regard equal to that which you show me, good Falsinar."

"Indeed?" Falsinar quirked a bushy eyebrow at the taller man. "Perhaps we should each consider ourselves insulted, then."

Beltramose opened his mouth to reply but a surprised gasp emerged instead. He leaped to one side and shook himself, eyes darting about in a mix of panic and outrage.

Falsinar cut off his chuckle in the face of Beltramose's murderous glare. "Apologies, my friend, but you looked like a distressed stork, flapping about like that. One of his pets having fun at your expense again?"

"Went right through me. Like being doused with ice water." Beltramose shuddered. "Why do they not bother you?"

"Perhaps because I am resigned to the inevitable, while you retain a sliver of hope."

"It is true that, compared to yourself, I am an incurable optimist. Yet I would never be mistaken for hopeful."

Falsinar shrugged. "So you think that your fate will be other than that shared by our unseen friends? That our fine liege will not some day add you to his collection? It is the price men such as ourselves must pay."

***

His preparations complete, Markus waved off his intangible servants. He approached Falsinar and Beltramose with purpose, moving quietly for all his bulk. "Infantino claims that the Obertus monastery was sacked last night, not long after the crusaders breached the walls. He spied some activity within tonight, however. It is likely that some of the monks have returned to see what they may recover, now that the crusaders have moved on to the city proper."

Markus looked to the west. The Monastery of St. John Studius lay within the outer walls of Theodosius, nine miles distant. It would not have been visible from the tower, even without the thick billows of acrid smoke and clouds of ash that fell like black snow around them. Although he didn't see the glance that Falsinar and Beltramose exchanged, Markus knew his men well. "You need not worry yourselves, gentlemen. Remain here and guard the tower. Infantino and the others will offer me sufficient protection."

"You are certain?" Falsinar's voice was strong, but Markus saw the bright flicker of relief in the man's aura.

"Get some rest. I expect that there will be more than enough tasks to keep you both busy upon my return." Markus smiled. "If you get bored, perhaps more looters will oblige you with some sport."

***

Markus had to stoop to fit within the low underground passage. Thanks to Infantino's silent warning, he was not surprised when two figures emerged from dark cracks in the tunnel walls. The oil lamp in Markus's thick fist revealed two men in the simple robes of monks. One stood two yards before him, the other a similar distance behind. A sharpening of focus and Markus could spy the pulse of life in them, manifest as auras of shifting light. They were mortal—ghouls, servants of the Obertus Tzimisce.

"*Isxe; ektopizai pan sudie!*" one said.

Among Markus's many scholarly talents was an affinity for language. He translated the Greek words without effort:

Halt; take yourself away from here with all speed. Markus replied in kind, speaking like a native Byzantine: "My apologies, brother. I do not mean to trespass. I come merely to offer assistance in these times of danger."

"Danger indeed," the other sneered. "It appears you are the one in need of aid."

Monks they might be, but also acolytes of the vampire Gesu of the Obertus Tzimisce sect. Scholars of a sort, not unlike Markus's own clan, the Cappadocians. However, these Tzimisce pursued a misguided hope of finding transcendence within flesh and bone. Their so-called "studies" being often degenerate and cruel, Markus normally had little interest in dealing with their kind. *Pentaxa pamoneros*—depraved in the extreme, as the Greeks would say. Despite this, the Obertus sect had gathered a most impressive collection of scholarly works. Their not-quite-secret Library of the Forgotten was well protected, but there was no guarantee of safety in these nights. In the current confusion, Markus hoped he might gather some of the tomes for his family.

Whatever the ravages the monastery had suffered, the presence of this welcoming committee suggested that things of interest lingered in the remains. But wasting time with mortals was getting Markus no closer to meaningful discovery—the perennial problem he had faced since arriving in Constantinople years before.

Markus forced down the sudden, violent surge of frustration. Giving vent to the Beast would accomplish nothing. "Please, brother, quarrels enough exist elsewhere in the city. Inform Gesu of my presence—"

The monks cried out in sudden anger. Plumes of silver roiled amidst their auras, signifying intense grief. "You are not worthy to speak that name," the rearward ghoul spat.

Some tragedy had befallen the powerful Gesu. Curiosity blossomed within Markus. "I am known to him; trust that my interests—"

"Your interests are plain enough." A figure stepped into the outermost edge of the lamp's light. A lady of power and influence, clad in fine damask and with a stately demeanor that made the meager tunnel look even more dingy. Her appearance was one of advancing years that yet retained the ghost of youthful beauty.

Her deathly pallor revealed her as one of the undead—indeed, as one who shared the same lineage as Markus. Lady Alexia Theusa, mistress of death, elder of Clan Cappadocian.

She was the primary reason Markus had come to Constantinople. And she had become the main impediment to his success.

Markus should not have been surprised at her presence here. Like most Cappadocians, Alexia had no great love for the Tzimisce's cruel practices. But she held a vast thirst for knowledge. With her standing in Constantinople—she'd fed on the herd here ever since the great city first rose, it seemed—Alexia had long ago become involved in the compilation and care of the Library of the Forgotten. Along with other scholars of Constantinople's vampiric elite, she must be helping to relocate contents that had survived the sack.

Beyond that, she was Cappadocian. Members of the clan were well known for visions and insights from the depths. Markus had not cultivated the talent beyond a kind of faint intuition. Indeed, he was not alone among the Giovanni family in this. He suspected their traffic with spirits conflicted with the oracular nature otherwise common among the Cappadocian—which, in turn, might explain why those not of Giovanni lineage showed little aptitude in the nigrimantic arts.

Now was not the time for such ponderings, though. It took no great mind to understand that one as ancient and skilled as the Lady Alexia could easily have glimpsed a portent of Markus's arrival this night.

Markus did not need to see the pale green streaks of her aura to know that Alexia Theusa held no care for him. They might share an immortal blood lineage, but Alexia had long ago made it clear that she did not trust the motives of Markus's family, the Giovanni. Still, Markus was not one to admit failure while he retained thought and purpose.

"Lady Alexia," Markus replied. Shadows flickered along the walls as the lamp moved with his bow. "I appreciate that you harbor suspicions toward my family. As I have said in the past, the Giovanni bear you no ill will. Indeed, we share—"

"We share nothing, sir." Her voice remained gentle, but held an edge that cut through his words like an executioner's blade. "As with every other offer you have made, my response is the same. Your assistance is neither requested nor desired."

Frustration grew despite Markus's efforts at self-control. He might have had a chance to persuade Gesu or one of the other vampires protecting the Library of the Forgotten, but once again Alexia Theusa blocked him before he could make any headway. Everywhere he turned in this city, the elder Cappadocian was there to restrict his efforts. Markus could not even lay the blame upon Infantino or the other shades. Alexia defeated his spirits' investigative efforts as easily as she deflected Markus's diplomatic attempts.

His lips curled in his neatly clipped beard, barely restraining a snarl. It was an effort to hold the rage of the Beast in check, but Markus prevailed at last. Pushing the issue here would accomplish nothing. Indeed, having regained his equilibrium, Markus could sense an undercurrent of danger lacking in previous encounters with Alexia. She was not known to be violent or confrontational, but there was no disputing her power and influence. In these nights of chaos, it was possible that Alexia Theusa might decide it was time to remove this thorn from her side. "You have made yourself very clear, Lady Alexia. I regret that we could not come to terms."

Markus backtracked after another bow, forcing the rearmost monk into his hiding hole to give sufficient room for Markus's massive form. He saw the triumphant glint in Alexia's eyes as she slipped into the shadows cast by his retreating light. Just as he could sense her surface emotions, Markus knew Alexia had read his own irritation… and his spark of fear.